Blue Christmas Bones

ALSO BY CAROLYN HAINES

SARAH BOOTH DELANEY MYSTERIES

Lights, Camera, Bones
Tell-Tale Bones
Bones of Holly
Lady of Bones
Independent Bones
A Garland of Bones
The Devil's Bones
Game of Bones
A Gift of Bones
Charmed Bones
Sticks and Bones
Rock-a-Bye Bones
Bone to Be Wild
Booty Bones
Smarty Bones
Bonefire of the Vanities
Bones of a Feather
Bone Appétit
Greedy Bones
Wishbones
Ham Bones
Bones to Pick
Hallowed Bones
Crossed Bones
Splintered Bones
Buried Bones
Them Bones

NOVELS

A Visitation of Angels
The Specter of Seduction
The House of Memory
The Book of Beloved
Trouble Restored
Bone-a-fied Trouble
Familiar Trouble
Revenant
Fever Moon
Penumbra
Judas Burning
Touched
Summer of the Redeemers
Summer of Fear

NONFICTION

My Mother's Witness: The Peggy Morgan Story

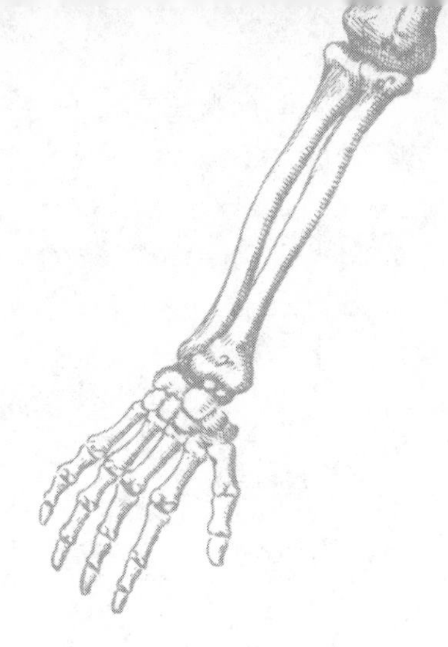

Blue Christmas Bones

A Sarah Booth Delaney Mystery

CAROLYN HAINES

MINOTAUR BOOKS
NEW YORK

This is a work of fiction. All of the characters, organizations, and events portrayed in this novel are either products of the author's imagination or are used fictitiously.

For information, address St. Martin's Publishing Group, 120 Broadway, New York, NY 10271.

www.minotaurbooks.com

The Library of Congress Cataloging-in-Publication Data is available upon request.

ISBN 978-1-250-88596-8 (hardcover)
ISBN 978-1-250-88597-5 (ebook)

Our books may be purchased in bulk for promotional, educational, or business use. Please contact your local bookseller or the Macmillan Corporate and Premium Sales Department at 1-800-221-7945, extension 5442, or by email at MacmillanSpecialMarkets@macmillan.com.

First Edition: 2024

1 3 5 7 9 10 8 6 4 2

For Lucille Deas Armstrong,
a woman who really loves books

Blue Christmas Bones

1

The vast, flat landscape of the Mississippi Delta has given way to the rolling hills and timbered verges of the northeast region of my home state. As the limo rolls through this intriguing terrain, I listen to the happy chatter of my best friends and think how Robin Hood would thrive in these forests. The girls and I are on vacation for the Christmas holidays, and set for adventure: drinking, eating, singing, and having fun. We have left our cares back in Sunflower County. Behind us is the rich alluvial soil of the Delta. We are now in the land of the black prairie, the Appalachian foothills, the impressive Tennessee-Tombigbee Waterway, and a rhythm of life different and exciting from our norm.

Tinkie's rented limo deposits us in front of the Hound Dog Hotel in the heart of Tupelo, Mississippi. The December morning is crystal clear and brisk, and I step into the sunshine and take a deep breath. We are here at last. My partner in the Delaney Detective Agency, Tinkie Bellcase Richmond, has arranged another Christmas adventure with our best friends.

I'm followed out of the limo by Cece Dee Falcon, journalist extraordinaire; Tinkie, a force of fashion and nature at only five foot two; and Millie Roberts, owner of Millie's Café and mother hen of our group. The boys—my lover, Coleman Peters; Tinkie's husband, Oscar; Cece's main squeeze, Jaytee; and the dazzling Harold Erkwell—will join us on Thursday night for an amateur Elvis competition. We are here to compete—and partake of the fabulous Elvis impersonators who have flooded the small city.

"Sarah Booth, you act like you've never been out of Zinnia," Tinkie teases me as I look around, drinking in the setting.

The Hound Dog Hotel is decorated to the teeth with strings of colorful Christmas lights—all fashioned as Elvis doing his famous swivel. A giant neon Elvis in the doorway beckons us inside. It is Christmas, but it is also Elvis. The town is abuzz with excitement.

"Let's head to town to grab some lunch," I suggest. Truthfully, I am eager for my first encounter with an Elvis impersonator; they are roaming the streets of Tupelo, performing on street corners, in bars, and wherever they can gain an audience. I know Cece wants some footage for the newspaper website that she and Millie contribute to with their column, "The Truth Is Out There." It's a genius mash-up of outlandish theories, gossip, and scandalous revelations. Sometimes true and sometimes not.

Millie, who adores reading tabloid stories of Elvis and Princess Di sightings, along with two-headed calves, crazy diets, and hysterical "revelations" of celebrity scandals, is certain she'll really see the ghost of Elvis. I am one thousand percent in on this belief. I, too, want to see the ghost of the legendary singer.

I love Elvis. I inherited my addiction to Tupelo's native son from my mama, who basically had an altar to the Mississippi icon. One of my best memories is sitting on the blue velvet sofa in the music room watching my parents dance to Elvis classics. I'd never heard anything more romantic than his love ballads. His appearance on TV shows—my mother had purchased the entire collection—reeked of wholesome sexuality. He was a man ahead of his time and completely unprepared to deal with the fame that dropped on him like an anvil. Generous to a fault, he was easy pickings for some of the unethical people drawn to his life.

"Look!" Millie squeals as she points out a handsome Elvis in a white jumpsuit arriving at the hotel. As bellhops load our luggage onto a cart, we rush to the Elvis. He sings a few bars of "Love Me Tender" and Millie all but swoons on the spot. The Elvis impersonator has a great voice, and he's clearly studied the poses and postures of the real Elvis. He pulls it off flawlessly.

"I'll be at the Copa Bar tonight," he tells us. "Come watch the show. It's always a good time."

"Are you from Tupelo?" Cece asks him, making notes for her story. She'd filmed everything, and she is loving it.

"I am." He sticks out a hand. "Tommy Beech, at your service."

"You make a fine hunk of Elvis," Tinkie tells him. "We'll see you later tonight."

"You girls have some fun." He gives a few pelvis thrusts and heads on his way.

"My heart won't be able to take more of that," Millie tells us. "Whew! It's like a dream come true. Is it possible to overdose on sexy Elvises?"

"Let's find out," Cece says, putting an arm around Millie. "If you fall over, smote by too much Elvis, I'll catch you."

"Let's get some food," Tinkie says, amused at all the Elvis worship. Before this vacay is over, she'll be wearing rhinestone jumpsuits and dyeing her hair black. No one is impervious to Elvis worship.

We head down the street, drinking in the delicious atmosphere of celebration and love. Elvis may be dead, but he isn't gone from Tupelo.

When we pass a shop filled with riding tack and fun equestrian items, I send them on their way, saying I'll catch up. I have a gift to buy for Coleman, Sunflower County sheriff and love of my life.

I found exactly what I needed in the Rough Riders shop—a rope for Coleman to practice lassoing. Always a prankster, I'd added a werewolf head to a sawhorse for my lover to rope. While standing at the counter of the shop, I watched the street traffic race by. I counted four Elvises in the short time it took me to pay and leave. The mayor and city council had been very smart to add the Christmas Elvis festival. Normally held in June, the Elvis impersonator events proved so popular the city decided to create a Christmas-themed Elvis festival. I had to admit this weather was also much better than the blasting hot June sun. This event was going to be a financial bonanza for Tupelo. It would also be my debut as a backup singer for Cece when we performed "Blue Christmas" in the amateur division.

My friends had walked down to Cadillac Café, where the decor was centered around a pink Cadillac. I knew from my mother's memorabilia that Elvis bought the pink Cadillac Fleetwood in 1955 and then gave it to his mother. Elvis and I shared a great love of our mothers, which was another reason I adored him.

I had suggested the Cadillac Café for lunch because of Tinkie's fondness for all Cadillacs and also because it was likely to be a buzzing hive of impersonators! This was what we'd come to Tupelo to experience.

I caught a glimpse of an Elvis in a classic outfit cutting down a narrow alley, and I stepped off the busy street and followed. The Elvis was lost from sight, but I knew which way he'd turned. I picked up my pace, hoping for a photo, when I heard someone singing "Danke Schoen," a song that was the calling card of the iconic Las Vegas performer Wayne Newton.

I whipped around to see Wayne—a very young version of Wayne—only five feet behind me. He wore a beautifully tailored tux and bow tie, his dark hair coiffed and his body moving to the sound of a big band as he sang. Only this was no Vegas showman—this was my nemesis.

Jitty! My haint had followed me to Tupelo. There was no escaping Jitty.

"Why Wayne Newton?" I asked her as I kept walking, hoping I could outdistance her. Of course I couldn't. She was a ghost, so she didn't even have to walk. She kind of glided along behind me. I could only be relieved that no one else was in the alley listening to me talk to myself. No one could see Jitty but me. When I was beset by her in a public space, I often appeared eccentric, if not downright loony, talking to myself and carrying on.

"I love Wayne," Jitty said, still in his body and voice. "That man was smooth when he came out of the womb."

Wayne Newton had been a child when he started his Las Vegas act. He'd been a staple there for decades. I admired him, though not with the fervor I had for Elvis.

"Point taken," I said. "Go home."

"And miss this fun? Not on your life. I know your mama, Libby, loved Elvis, but I actually went to some of his first shows."

"You were just free, roaming Elvis performances at fairs? A ghost on the loose?"

"You bet. He was something in those younger days." She was genuinely wistful. "That young man took gospel, the blues, rock and roll, and hillbilly swing and turned it into something that made your feet tap and your hips want to jiggle."

To have seen the King of Rock and Roll perform in the 1950s must have been something else. I couldn't help it. I was jealous of Jitty's non-corporeal status where she could just float around, visiting—and tormenting—whomever she chose. "What's your favorite Elvis song?" I asked Jitty.

"Oh, that's easy. 'Love Me Tender.' That song just says it all."

"It does." I couldn't disagree. "So many great songs. What a career he could have had if he hadn't gotten taken for a ride by that manager of his."

"A lot of people share that sentiment," Jitty said. She'd slowly begun to morph back into her normal self. She now wore a pretty red sweater and black slacks. Her clear, mocha skin and natural hair reinforced that she didn't need makeup or time-consuming hairstyles to showcase her beauty. Wayne Newton had completely disappeared.

"What was the real deal on Colonel Parker, Elvis's manager?" I asked.

"When I see Elvis, I'll ask him. But no matter what really happened, I firmly believe Elvis holds no grudges. He wasn't a man who held on to blame or judgment."

"Being a nice person only got him hurt in the end." Elvis might not have bitterness toward Colonel Parker, but I did. And I believed my mother would agree, though we'd never discussed it. She'd died when I was twelve, so the ins and outs of Colonel Parker's influence in Elvis's life hadn't been a subject we'd broached. "Elvis died so young. It makes me angry."

"I know," Jitty said. "The price of fame can be really high, especially for a person who is truly tender. Elvis had a big heart and a good soul."

The same could be said of my parents. And they had also died young. I needed to get this train of thought onto another track. The past was gone. It was "accept it" or drive myself mad. That was the price of love and loss.

"Jitty, you should go home and haunt DeWayne. He and his girlfriend are staying at Dahlia House. He needs some tormenting. Just think, you could scare them silly and then they'd have hot sex. That would make you happy. Maybe she'd even get bred."

Jitty snorted. "You can't talk about DeWayne's girl like she's a brood mare."

"That's how you talk about me," I sputtered. "You say all the time that I should be wed and bred, in that order."

"You are mine to tease," Jitty countered with a huff.

"Get over it. Now, I have work to do." And with that, she swiveled her hips and disappeared on the sound of the whooo-ah background of "Blue Christmas."

"She is going to be the death of me," I said to no one as I exited the alley and found myself in front of the Cadillac Café. My friends were seated at the window table and waved me in. No time like the present to jump into the middle of Elvis mania!

2

We finished lunch and walked over to the Cadence Bank Arena, where the competitions and festivities would be centered. Tupelo's downtown was blocked off to cars, and folks were milling about. Elvises—some the spitting image of the King, and some so far from the svelte Elvis of my dreams that it took a moment for their posture and pose to convey the essence of the singer—performed wherever they could drum up an audience. Some signed autographs as if they were really the King. It was all about believing in oneself and the power of the Elvis transformation.

At the Arena Center, we went inside to view the incredible bejeweled belt that a local woman had allowed the festival to display. It was a perfect replica of Elvis's Las

Vegas belt and was worth a fortune. We gathered around the glass case and inspected the work of art.

"Who owns this?" Cece asked as she walked around the display with her camera on. She was filming for a newspaper story. I knew how her brain worked.

"Someone local," Tinkie said. "I read it somewhere, but I don't remember the name. We can find out at the hotel. They had brochures on the festival and who was participating. Allan Malone, from *Who's Singing Barbra,* is in town to emcee some of the events. He's a native of Tupelo, but he has a mansion out in Hollywood, too." She looked around to see if anyone in the center would have useful information. The only thing we saw were two security guards who were positioned to watch the belt. I noticed there were also several cameras in the ceiling aimed at the valuable bejeweled belt.

Tinkie walked to one of the guards. "Who owns the belt?" she asked.

"Grace Land," he said.

"I didn't ask where Elvis's home was. I asked who owns the belt?" She pointed at it.

He frowned. "And I told you. Grace Land." He separated the words, making a distinction between the name and the famous Memphis home of the singer.

Tinkie recovered quickly. "I apologize. I didn't understand what you were saying. Who is this Grace Land?"

"Local lady." He grinned and turned away. "You should check her out. She's a trip."

"Is that really her name?" I asked.

"It is. Her mother was a giant Elvis fan, and she named her daughter after Presley's Memphis estate. Not a nickname. The mom *legally* changed Grace's last name to Land.

I went to school with Grace, and her life is all tied to Elvis. She hired us to guard this belt. It's her most prized possession, and she has loads of possessions."

"How much is it worth?" Cece asked. She was getting down to the brass tacks.

The guard shrugged. "I don't have a clue. All I know is that the jewels are real, and the gold was crafted by a master artist, Sippi Salem. His work is known internationally."

"I've heard of him," Cece said. "He makes jewelry that's as valuable for the craftsmanship as the content. He created one of the crowns for Queen Elizabeth's Ruby Jubilee in 1992. It was a gift to her and is now a valued part of her heritage as a monarch."

I was wowed. Cece and Millie really knew their stuff when it came to celebrities. No surprise since Millie had been obsessed with Princess Diana and the whole tragedy of her life with the royals. Currently Millie was trying to decide whether she supported Harry and Meghan or William and Kate. It was a rocky ride for her to believe the royal family had done anything wrong, but the youngest prince had captured her heart when his mother died. Her loyalty was torn.

"Who is this guy? This artist?" I asked. I knew a lot about my state, but I'd never heard of him.

"He's a recluse, really almost a hermit," Tinkie said. "Very antisocial, except when he's on the prowl for a good-looking woman. He has a lot of notches on his bedpost, if you get my meaning."

I did get it. Loud and clear. "Were Grace and Sippi involved?" I asked the guard.

He shook his head. "Ask Grace. She'll tell you what she wants you to know, and I honestly don't know anything. Rumors fly in a small town. Grace is a hot-looking female, no doubt about it. Sippi has a reputation." He shrugged again. "Who knows. Who cares."

I was still chewing on the fact that a mother had named her infant daughter Grace Land. "Is Land a family name or something? Surely she didn't just name her daughter after the Elvis estate."

"You should ask Grace. I'm sure she'll tell you all about it."

And that was good advice. I respected the fact that the guard didn't want to gossip about his employer—much.

Cece had put her cell phone away. Obviously she had enough photos of the belt, the display, the heavy foot traffic in the Arena Center as folks oohed and aahed over the Elvis belt. Now she wanted the details that could only come from Grace Land. "The arena is closing," she said. "Let's head back to the hotel. The bonfire is tonight, and I want to change into a sweatshirt and some jeans."

It was a good idea. The December day was ending, and as dusk began to fall, so did the temperatures. A sweatshirt sounded lovely. We were already the last people in the Arena Center, so we walked out together and one of the guards locked the door behind us. Booths and kiosks had been set up on the apron of the center and merchandising was going strong. We stopped to examine handmade jewelry and pottery at one vendor tent. The artist was talented, and I picked up several items for Christmas presents. We'd been there for about twenty minutes when the nerve-racking sound of an alarm went off. I looked all around, as did everyone else, but no one seemed to know what was happening.

In a moment the doors of the Arena Center burst open and a beautiful woman in a vibrant caftan and glossy black hair rushed out of the door. "Everyone, stop! Someone has stolen my belt!"

"Holy Christmas," Tinkie said. She was trying to stop cursing, mostly without success. "That must be Grace Land."

"Let's get out of here." I grabbed Tinkie's arm and tried to direct her away from Grace, who was coming toward us like a great white after a swimmer. Due to my last case, sharks were heavy on my mind.

"Are you Sarah Booth Delaney and Tinkie Richmond?" she asked.

"Maybe."

Tinkie kicked me on the shin. "Don't be an ass, Sarah Booth. Yes, we are," Tinkie said, holding out her hand. "I'm Tinkie." It was like she was mesmerized by Grace's nest of curls. I could only think of Medusa. This woman was going to be trouble in my life.

"One of the guards told me you were asking a lot of questions about the belt." Her voice broke. "You're private investigators. I want to hire you to find my belt."

The one thing I didn't want was another case at Christmas. Sure, I needed the money. Dahlia House was noble and had a grand history, but it was also a money pit for maintenance. But I also wanted a Christmas holiday where I didn't have to work. Every single time we tried for a few days off, we caught a case.

"We're only here on vacation," Tinkie told her. "I'm sorry. I'm sure there are some local PIs who can do this job. And of course the local law will be looking, too. You're better off going with a local who lives here and knows the ropes."

"I want you." She pinned Tinkie with her green gaze. "And I always get what I want."

That was the best reason I knew to skip this whole mess. "Thanks, but we're not taking any cases right now. We're on vacation."

"I'll double your fee."

Now she was talking a language I couldn't ignore. "You don't even know what our fee is," I pointed out.

"Doesn't matter. I'll pay double. That belt is valuable monetarily, but the sentimental value is everything to me."

It had been a beautiful creation. "Is Sippi Salem highly collectible?" I asked.

"He is, and the belt is unique and also part of a much bigger history that's important to this state."

Elvis was, indeed, one of the most successful exports Mississippi had ever created. "The arena had cameras and trained security guards. How did this happen?" I asked.

"That's what you need to find out. The guards are highly trusted. Whatever role they played in this, it wasn't intentional to help with the theft."

It was a peculiar defense of the people most responsible for allowing the theft to occur, but I didn't press it. Not then and there.

"Do you have any suspects?" Tinkie asked.

Grace shook her head. "That belt is beloved. Sippi is a treasure and is very respected. Elvis is virtually worshipped. Folks might not like me, but they would never mess with Elvis or Sippi."

"Who might not like you?" I asked her.

Before she could answer, we were beset by two barking pugs. The little dogs, with their smashed-in faces and big personalities, were all over us—except for Grace. The dogs backed up from her and growled.

"Little damn ankle biters," Grace said, dodging behind Tinkie. "If they try to bite me, I'll kick them," she warned the owner.

"Kick them and I'll break your leg." The man who spoke

was tall and handsome. His baritone voice left no doubt he meant every word he said. "Avery Wynette! Lovely Katherine Malone! Come here this instant."

The pugs scurried to him and when he held out his arms, they leaped into them. He gave them smooches and praise. When he looked up, he gave Grace a baleful glare. "You were asking who might want to do Grace a bad turn. Only everyone in town! She's about as popular as syphilis."

Oh, goodness. The fur was about to fly!

"This is Allan Malone, host of the soon to be canceled TV show *Who's Singing Barbra*. He's one of the hosting emcees of the festival." Grace grinned. "He has no talent as a singer or a judge, yet here he is, licking his wounds in his hometown." She tried to sound tough, but I could see tears in her eyes.

"My ratings are sky-high. Your jealousy, Grace, is green and putrid," Allan said. He looked at Tinkie. "She's only jealous because she wanted to sing on my show, but her voice wasn't up to the high standards."

"Adorable dogs," Tinkie said, trying to turn the conversation. "I love their names."

"They are stars in their own right. Surely you've seen them on my show. They are there every week as part of the judging panel. Avery Wynette is truly an excellent judge of voice, and Lovely Katherine has impeccable taste for performance, costuming, and choreography. So many people have some of the necessary talent but not the whole package. Avery and Katherine are invaluable to me." He leaned over to whisper to Tinkie, "And Grace has none of the talent. Hence the reason my babies would like to chew her feet off."

The dogs squirmed to be put down, and Allan obliged. It

was then I noticed that both pugs wore little pink-sequined Peter Pan collars and pink feathered angel wings.

"They're Daddy's little angels," he said. "I think Grace should get a dog so at least one living creature likes her."

Why these two sparred with each other was something I'd have to find out later. I looked at Tinkie and she gave a subtle nod, saying she'd be okay taking the case. I nodded, too.

"We'll take the case," Tinkie told Grace. "Now we need the names of the security guards and the company they work for." Tinkie looked at Cece. "Can you look into Sippi Salem? If he made the belt, he'll be well aware of the value. Millie, would you contact the mayor and see about getting the video footage from the Arena Center so we can see who was paying close attention to the belt? It'll be a starting place."

Allan drank it all in with amusement. "Let me know when you find the thief. You might check under Grace's bed. But wear a hazmat suit," Allan said as he picked up the two pugs and walked away, back straight and shoulders squared.

Though I was still reluctant to take the case, it appeared to be a done deal. And if we got the video footage, it should be a simple case of identifying the thieves and getting the local law to arrest them. It was a lot of money to make for what looked like a minimal amount of work. In my heart, I could hear Aunt Loulane: *If it looks too good to be true, it probably is.*

Aunt Loulane had a lot of wisdom I ignored at my own peril.

3

We gathered at the site of the bonfire beside the lake in Veterans Park. We weren't far from the modest cottage that was Elvis's birthplace. I was impressed with the turnout for the bonfire, despite the fact the temperatures had dipped. We were only about two degrees above freezing, but the fans of Elvis were hardy folk.

The vendors had followed the populace out to the bonfire, and I bought a terrific Elvis sweatshirt for Coleman—just another little Christmas present. I'd racked my brain trying to come up with the perfect gift for the man I loved, but I wasn't satisfied with my choices. I'd picked up half a dozen presents I knew he'd enjoy, but the one big gift had evaded me. Cece, Millie, and Tinkie were no help at all. If I didn't come up with a really good idea in the next day or so, I'd have to ask Jitty. She wouldn't tell me, of course, but I'd at least ask.

Cece showed up with some bad news. "I checked in with the security guards at the Arena Center. The cameras focused on the belt display malfunctioned." She blew air out. "I can't believe it. What kind of screwed-up security is that? And the two guards? They said they were relieved at five o'clock by two more guards wearing the uniforms of the same security company, yet when I went to question them, they were long gone. I hate to say it, but I believe they're telling the truth. They left their post because they thought the belt was covered."

"How convenient." I meant to sound snarky. How did the guards and the cameras both malfunction? "What about the lasers that were supposed to trip an alarm?"

Cece looked as incredulous as I felt. "They'd been turned off. Again, conveniently."

"This is an inside job." It was the first conclusion anyone would jump to.

"Possibly, but inside meaning who?" Millie asked. "Who would have the cojones to take that belt and try to fence it or resell it?"

She had a point. A good one. "I don't know but it's a good idea to contact all the local fences and also any that do international business. My guess is that the belt will either be broken apart and sold as pieces or it will go to a big broker. Someone who can get it out of the country and into a place where a lot of scrutiny won't be applied."

That would be the end of Grace Land's prized belt. "We have to find it before that can happen. Tomorrow I'll check the local pawnshops and try to get some leads on a business that could handle this big of a prize."

Tinkie nodded, then pointed to the bonfire. A line of twenty Elvis impersonators were backlit by the flames as they danced to "Jailhouse Rock." The night was off to a rocking start, despite the theft that had brought all the county and city law enforcement officers to the Arena Center. But as with all good events, the show had to go on. I would just be glad when Coleman arrived.

So far, Cece had garnered all the information we had. She had to find the facts for the story she was posting, so why duplicate efforts? But tomorrow, Tinkie and I would step up our game. The others could eat, drink, and frolic, but Tinkie and I now had work to do. We needed to find that belt as soon as possible, before someone melted it down. That was my biggest worry, and I knew Grace Land must also be thinking about it, too, though she hadn't voiced that concern.

I focused my thoughts on the gyrating Elvises, determined to have a few hours of vacation. There was nothing else I could do at that moment. The local police chief had dusted for fingerprints and other forensic evidence. I'd get that report in the morning. I had to find local pawnshops where I might get some leads on fences for stolen items. The Elvis belt would be a problem for a thief to pawn. It was easily recognizable, required a buyer with a deep, deep pocket, and had a public hue and cry attached to it already. Unless it was melted down and broken apart. Then selling the jewels and gold individually would simply be a lucrative deal.

"Hey!" Tinkie nudged my shoulder. "Where are you off gathering wool?"

"Thinking about our case."

"Tomorrow morning every place we need to go will be

open. We can work a few hours while Millie and Cece shop."

"They'll be working on this for the newspaper," I reminded her.

"Right."

Like it or not, this was going to be another working holiday. For all of us.

The group of Elvises were all singing a rousing rendition of "A Little Less Conversation." Everyone was clapping and we joined in, keeping the beat. Tomorrow we would work. Tonight, the bonfire was beautiful. The Elvises were sincere. My friends were with me, and life was good.

The next morning, I was up at the crack of dawn. To be honest, I hadn't slept well. I'd gotten used to sharing my bed with Coleman, with reaching out when I almost woke up, feeling his warm body, and spooning myself against him and falling back to sleep. I missed him.

I got up and stretched. I missed the critters, too. Sweetie Pie often got in the bed with us, as did Pluto. Poe, the raven who'd taken up with us, was not a big snuggler, but he often tapped the bedroom window to be let into the warm house. He didn't stay inside long, but he knew he was welcome to come in, warm up, and eat.

I thought of Allan Malone and his pugs and got out of bed grinning. He was a character, and he took no prisoners. I hadn't watched his TV show, but I was going to look it up and catch a few episodes. I loved Barbra Streisand's voice, but I couldn't imagine anyone who could sing like her. Still, trying might be fun. Maybe I could convince Cece to enter the show's competition. She had a great set of pipes.

When I thought of Allan, it made me think of Grace—a subject I truly wanted *not* to think about. We'd had difficult clients in the past, but somehow I figured she would take the cake. She was beautiful, rich, spoiled, and entitled. I'd also seen a more tender side—or maybe it was just wishful thinking. At any rate, Grace was our client. We had nothing good to report, but still we had to tell her something. And we also had to get busy. I checked my watch. It was just after six. Time to wake Tinkie. I dialed her room.

"What?" She sounded sleepy and grumpy. I'd forgotten that she no longer got to sleep in. Since she'd had the fantabulous Maylin, Tinkie's time was no longer her own.

"Sorry. I just thought maybe we should try to track down Sippi or talk to the pawnshops in town." I was itching to get busy.

"They aren't open, Sarah Booth."

She had a point. "Okay, then we can plan our day. Meet me downstairs for coffee."

"I'm going to meet you with the iron from the room and hit you with it. Can I sleep another hour?"

"Okay." I had to relent. Tinkie was usually the Energizer Bunny, but caring for an infant had drained her charge. I was on my own.

After a fast shower, I dressed warmly and headed out. The city was waking, but the sidewalks were still empty. Walking around Tupelo before anyone else was up made me think of an old Johnny Cash song, "Sunday Morning Coming Down." It was one of the best songs I'd ever heard about loneliness. It wasn't a Sunday morning, but the town had the feel of that song as the sun began to creep up in the sky.

I walked over to the Arena Center and examined the doors. There were other exits, but I wondered how the thief had gained access to the interior. Had he or she been hiding in the building when the doors were locked? How had the thief avoided the two security guards? I had a lot of questions and no answers.

When Tinkie got up we'd start with the local police chief, Yuma Johnson. His mama and daddy must have loved the TV show *The Rebel*. Johnny Yuma was the main character, and Johnny Cash sang the theme song. My aunt Loulane had given me a great education in classic early television, and she would have married Johnny Cash in a heartbeat. I hadn't met Yuma yet, but when I'd talked to Coleman the previous night, he'd said Yuma was an unknown factor. He was relatively new to the police chief position.

Just on the off chance, I tried the doors of the Arena Center. Locked, as they should be. Too late. Kind of like locking the barn after the horses had run away. But at least I knew the locks worked. I looked inside and saw only emptiness. Had I been hoping the belt would magically reappear? I'd once believed in fairy-tale endings, but not any longer.

I found a bench and sat down to think. If we had a clear plan of action to find the culprit who'd taken the belt, we'd work more efficiently. Tinkie was the master planner. I was the "fly by the seat of my pants" investigator. This case, we didn't have a lot of options. Chief Johnson would handle the forensics. That left only the leads we could find via talking to people. The slow but true legwork of the PI.

We needed to talk to Grace again. I'd forgotten to ask her if the belt was insured. That would be another angle. Chief Johnson might know of other jewel thefts in the region. To that end, I could call Coleman and get him to do a regional check on jewelry and art heists. Eyewitnesses were also important. Surely someone had seen something when the belt was taken. We'd have to canvass the festival attendees. It was a very long shot, but we might get lucky.

The wind roused, rattling the few dead leaves still clinging to some sycamore trees. A chill hit me. It was time to go back to the hotel and wake up my friends. We had work to do.

As I started back, I saw a young woman walking to the door of the Arena Center. I'd seen her the day before. On the off chance, I hurried over to her and introduced myself. I explained we'd been hired to find the missing belt.

"It's just awful," she said. She was a young woman, maybe twenty-one.

"Were you here yesterday?" I asked. I was positive I'd seen her, but I liked a softball opening question that I absolutely knew the answer to.

"Yes. I was in the center. I saw you and your friends admiring the belt."

"Did you see anyone else near it?"

She sighed. "You won't believe me. In fact, I don't really believe it myself."

"Believe what?" I tried to keep it light. She was young and easily spooked. Intensity wouldn't work.

"I saw a man in a suit with a hat. He had a big double chin and was smoking a cigar. Oh, yeah, a pair of aces fell out of his shirtsleeve."

The person she'd described, especially the tucked-away cards, sounded a lot like the man who'd managed Elvis, Colonel Tom Parker. Parker was known to have a terrible gambling addiction.

"He looked like Colonel Parker?" I asked, still trying to keep it light even though that was impossible. Parker had died in 1997.

"I know it sounds crazy. I know that man is dead. Good riddance." She turned and spit over her left shoulder. "But I swear he was there, looking at the belt. Lusting after it. I thought he was going to reach through the glass enclosure and grab it."

I didn't know what she'd seen, but I doubted it was Parker. I had a terrible thought. Was it Jitty? Was Jitty still screwing around in Tupelo? That would be a terrible situation for me, especially if others could see her.

"This man with the hat and cigar was the only person you saw around the belt display?"

"Sure, folks were looking at it, but not like this guy. I'm telling you. He's the thief."

I gave her a business card with my phone number on it. "If you happen to see this character around town, would you give me a call, please?"

"Sure thing," she said. "I work here. There's some fresh coffee already made. Would you like a cup? It's cold out here."

Coffee sounded like the best thing I'd ever heard. I was chilled to the bone, as Aunt Loulane would say. "I'd love a cup." And a chance to talk to some other employees of the center. They would have had more opportunities to notice things. It was a fortuitous turn of events.

4

The employee lounge in the Arena Center had coffeepots, stacks of fresh pastries, tables, and chairs. My new friend, Laurie, showed me the cups, coffee, and condiments. The center employed an impressive staff. There were at least twenty people there, all working to make the Elvis festival a success. Most of the workers were at least ten years younger than me, and I thought what a perfect job this was for a young adult. A little glamour and a lot of hard work, but it would be a fun holiday or summer job for high schoolers or kids home from college.

The coffee was good, and I sipped a cup while watching the clusters of employees mingling and shifting. Everyone knew everyone else. That was the joy—and horror—of a small town. I picked out a few people I thought I'd seen the evening before in the display area. Laurie was in a corner talking to a handsome young man, so I introduced myself and began the tedious job of canvassing.

Luck stuck close to me, and several women gave me detailed descriptions of folks they felt had shown too much of an interest in the belt. "I told Grace not to put it on display," one of the ticket takers, Darcy, told me. "She'd kept the belt pretty much a secret for years, but she had to show off. By the end of the first day, everyone in five surrounding states knew Grace owned that belt, knew that it was valuable, and knew the exact procedures in place to protect it. It didn't take a rocket scientist to disable the lasers and lure the guards away."

I noticed she hadn't mentioned anything about the cameras supposedly focused on the belt to provide a digital record of any unseemly interest—or actions. Was that a fact that had eluded most Tupeloans?

Darcy waved me to a table. "If Grace gets that belt back, she's going to have to lock it up in a vault. Everyone knows she owns it now. They'll break into her house. In fact, whether she finds the belt or not she is going to be a target for all kinds of criminal behavior." She rolled her eyes. "She has all the looks and none of the brains." She sighed. "I shouldn't say that. Grace is plenty smart but she doesn't always think."

If Darcy and Allan were examples, people in Tupelo spoke their minds.

"Did you notice anyone else around the belt?" I asked her. She was a pretty redhead who waved another young woman over. I inhaled sharply. Darcy's friend could have easily passed as a young Priscilla Presley. And she was dressed for the part. Her dark hair was in a bouffant, and she wore thick black eyeliner that set off her lovely eyes. Folks in Tupelo pulled out all the stops.

"I didn't," she said, clearly ready to be on her way.

When a tall, slender, very handsome Elvis walked up to the dark beauty, it was almost as if the King and his young bride were alive and well. Millie would have a conniption! I took several photos as surreptitiously as I could.

Chill bumps danced up my arms and neck. I loved a good ghost story, but between Jitty, Colonel Parker, and Elvis, I was hearing about—and seeing—a lot of haints. Too many. William Faulkner had nailed it: The past is never dead. It's not even past. Living with Jitty, I always had one foot in the past. It was part of a certain melancholy Southern perspective on life. Relatives, or those considered family, were never abandoned—not even dead and/or crazy ones. Elvis was still a part of most Southern families of a certain era.

Since Darcy wasn't going to introduce me, I stepped in front of the beautiful young woman and made my own introduction. Her name was Sonja Rivera, and she looked upon the handsome Elvis with great fondness, if not love. She didn't even take notice of the awful leopard-print jumpsuit and black cape that he wore. The stretch material hugged his lean and muscular body, but the print made me dizzy. Couple that with thick sideburns, greased-back black hair, and a pair of gold-framed sunglasses. Bad Taste Elvis.

"Darcy, did you see anyone paying undue attention to the belt in the display case?"

"Rufus was fascinated by it." She nodded in the direction of the Elvis. "Rufus Trilby."

"Are you local, Rufus?" I asked.

"Native of Tupelo," he said in a passable Elvis voice.

"Rufus and I grew up together," Sonja said, brushing a stray curl off her forehead. She really did favor Priscilla.

"Do you know anything about the artist who created the belt?" I asked.

"Sippi Salem," they said in unison and then high-fived each other.

"He's something of a local legend," Rufus said. "Like a bedroom legend."

"I've heard he's something of a ladies' man."

"Those women are *not* necessarily ladies," Sonja scoffed. "Take Grace Land, for instance. She is really smart and I do believe she loves Elvis. She's just . . . damaged. Tragic past and all of that."

They were about to drag me off the road and down a rabbit hole of gossip about my client. I had to put a stop to it. "So, where does Sippi live?" I asked.

"He's got a place on the edge of the forest. He's very reclusive. The place is fenced off with locked gates. You can only get in if he wants you to."

"Can you give me an address?" I asked.

They exchanged a glance. "Grace can tell you, and it would be better coming from her. She can call Sippi and set it up for him to talk to you. If anyone can make him see you, it's Grace."

"Because they were lovers?"

"Partly. And because Grace hired him to create that Elvis belt." She leaned in closer. "Rumor has it that Grace actually stole some of the jewels from the real Elvis belt. There's never been any proof of that, and you know how some people have only negative things to say. Don't believe it, but check it out, maybe."

Too late. I couldn't unhear it. I didn't look forward to working for someone I couldn't trust. "Thanks. I'll ask Grace."

"Sippi travels a lot, too," Rufus said. "I don't know if Grace keeps tabs on him, but if anyone can, it's her."

Grace had a lot of magical powers, or so it would seem. "Thanks, guys. Rufus, will you be competing in the Elvis show?"

"Oh, yes he will," Sonja said. "He's going to sing to me. It will bring the house down. I hope you'll be there."

"Wouldn't miss it for the world," I assured her. I meant it.

I asked a few more questions, then moved on to a cluster of high school graduates. None of them reported seeing Colonel Parker's ghost, but they were all over an Elvis in a leopard-print jumpsuit who was salivating at the display case. I glanced across the room at Rufus, who was waving goodbye to Priscilla. I wanted to follow him, but I also wanted to stick close to Priscilla. And I wanted to go back to the hotel and wake up my partners in crime. As it turned out, both Elvis and Priscilla eluded me. When a surge of workers came into the break room, I lost sight of the King and Queen. They disappeared like smoke. I searched for them, but they'd vanished.

I left the break room after a few more futile interviews and stepped outside. The sun was up and while it wasn't exactly warming the city, it gave me hope. I loved daybreak. There was nothing better than a sunrise with the thought of a productive day ahead. Tinkie and I had to get on the stick because Coleman and Oscar would be joining us soon. Oscar would bring Maylin and her nanny, Pauline, who was now pretty much an official part of the Richmond family. Tinkie's days of freedom were thinning. We had to make hay while the sun shone.

My brisk walk back to the hotel left me eager for breakfast, and I made up a tray of coffees for my friends and headed up to the eighth floor where all of our rooms were. I knocked and delivered a hot brew to each gal pal. "Let's meet in the dining room at eight," I told them all.

I sipped my coffee as the water in the shower ran hot. Twenty minutes later I was warmly dressed and on the phone with Coleman.

"All the critters are fine," he told me. "We had an accident on Highway 55. No one you knew. It was an active night. A couple of kids stole a car off the Ford lot. DeWayne found it abandoned out by the old Jimison plantation. It wasn't harmed and has been returned. We know who the kids are. DeWayne and Budgie are picking them up."

Kids today. We'd enjoyed our mischief, but grand theft auto had never been on the table. "I miss you," I told him.

"Only a few more days and I'll be there. Don't get arrested before my arrival," he teased.

"I'll try not to let that happen." There was something in his voice. Some hint of withholding. "What's wrong, Coleman?"

"Nothing is wrong. I just found out that Hugo Bradford is going to run against me in the next election."

Hugo was a big, loud, lying liar and moron. But he had a lot of money and no ethics. Coleman was respected in Sunflower County—by the law-abiding citizens. The crooks would be funding Hugo's campaign.

"That's a good laugh. He doesn't stand a chance. Folks in Sunflower County value integrity and truth. Hugo has lied about everything from his family to his construction business."

"I hope you're right. I just can't match him dollar for dollar in spending."

"You have your record to run on and his record as a contractor is filled with lying, cheating, and shoddy work."

"It's a bit more serious than whether I win or not. Hugo belongs to several organizations with white supremacist notions. It could be a really bad thing for Sunflower County residents who don't have a lot of money or political power."

He was right about that. Hugo could undo the years of hard work Coleman, DeWayne, and Budgie had put into making sure that the law was applied equally to all citizens. Six months of Hugo's reign as sheriff and a lot of county residents would feel the lash of prejudicial enforcement of the law.

"That won't happen, Coleman. You have the best campaign team on the planet. Hugo can bring it! We'll beat him fair and square at the polls." But even as I spoke with such confidence, I knew how dirty politics could be. Coleman had never faced a challenge like Hugo—a man with big pockets and no ethics. Luckily there were still a few months before the real campaigning would begin. After that, my friends and I would have to focus full-time on turning out the vote for Coleman.

"I can always count on you, Sarah Booth, to make me feel better."

"Don't borrow trouble. You're on the winning ticket!"

"Because I have you in my life. Now let me get off the phone, I have a job to do."

It was good to hear his voice, even if he had to leave for work and I had my own work to do. I hadn't told him about the case, not that Delaney Detective Agency had officially been hired. Still, I'd need him to help me by checking the region for other art thefts. I'd ask later on, when I was sure we'd officially taken the case. Until then, he had enough on his brain. With any luck at all we'd be able to find the belt and the thieves before he and Oscar arrived.

5

Everyone was up and dressed by the time I returned to the hotel lobby. We'd planned on spending the day shopping, drinking, and having a relaxed holiday. Such ambitions were scuttled to make way for working on the case.

Cece and Millie volunteered to find Sippi Salem for me and see if he'd consent to an interview about the belt. They rejected asking Grace for an introduction—and I understood why. If Grace had stolen jewels for the belt and Sippi knew about it, he likely wouldn't want to talk to us.

While Cece and Millie would help me and Tinkie, they would also get information for their newspaper column. That left Tinkie and me to follow up with Grace, Chief Johnson, and the security guards and to explore places where a multimillion-dollar piece of jewelry might be fenced. I doubted any local dealers could handle the belt, but they might give me some leads.

"I'd rather go find the artist," Tinkie groused as we stepped out of the hotel into the winter sun.

"You can go with Millie and Cece." I felt bad that I hadn't suggested this before they left. "We can call them, and they'll come get you."

"No." Tinkie huffed. "I really didn't want to work today."

"Same here. But let's wrap this up. That belt is likely on its way to New York City or someplace else where it can be dismantled and sold in pieces."

"I hope not. It really is beautiful. And it is so perfect for the King."

I didn't point out that Elvis wouldn't be wearing it. At least not on this mortal plane. He had left the building.

Before we left the hotel parking lot, I called the police chief, only to learn that he had no new information. He'd cleared the security guards of any involvement in the theft, and he was checking the security equipment at the center. So far, he had no leads and nothing to offer us. Or if he did, he wasn't sharing.

We walked toward downtown. I'd seen a pawnshop there, and it was a place to begin.

"We should rehearse our song tonight," Tinkie was saying as we pulled open the pawnshop door. A bell jangled, and a young woman came from a back room to stand at the counter. Behind her was a wall of guns. Pistols, shotguns, assault rifles, you name it. She noticed that I was staring at the weapons.

"You need some protection?" she asked.

"No, thanks." Tinkie and I both had guns, but we hadn't packed them for a holiday.

"I'd like to see that Glock," Tinkie said.

I left her to talk to the clerk while I explored lawn equipment, power tools, and the like. I stayed close enough to listen in.

"This feels good in my hand," Tinkie said. "How much?"

The clerk named a price and Tinkie said she'd take the gun and a box of ammunition. It wasn't a bad idea to have a weapon with us, but it made me kind of sad that we even considered we should have one. Growing up in an agricultural community, I'd known farmers who kept a shotgun or rifle in the cab of their truck for farm emergencies. The guns had been a tool, not a badge of personality or personal power. Now it seemed everyone had a gun on their person and a lot more people were dying because of it.

"Did you hear about the jewelry heist of the Elvis belt?" Tinkie asked the young woman as she filled out the application to buy the gun.

"I did. That's terrible. Grace Land has plenty of money, but I don't know anyone who would steal from her."

"If the thieves wanted to get rid of the belt, who would they ask?" Tinkie just put it out there.

"An item that big—and that hot? I don't know," the clerk said. "I'm sure there are fences willing to take the risk for a cut of that, but I don't know any."

"Any leads would be helpful," Tinkie said.

"And if I knew, I'd say so. I know a lot of pawnshops take stolen goods, but I don't. By now, everyone will know that belt is stolen, so it's going to take a fence who already walks on the wrong side of the law."

She had an excellent point.

"Is there anyone you can think of who might be . . . helpful to the thief?" Tinkie asked.

"There's a shop north of town on 45. Just head out. You'll see it. It's by a sex shop and medicinal marijuana place."

Tinkie giggled. "I guess it's one stop for all your needs."

The clerk laughed, too, and I suppressed a giggle. "Yep. Anyway, Mavis works there. Be sure you only talk to her. The owner doesn't like cops or private investigators."

"You knew we're PIs?" Tinkie asked.

"Everyone knows," the clerk said. "Tupelo has a grapevine like nobody's business. And when you talk to Mavis, you might not want to be so forthright."

"Got it," Tinkie said. "Can I pick up my gun soon?"

"Day after tomorrow."

Good news for Tinkie. She'd have her gun by the time the big Elvis competition began—in case she had to escort any atrocious impersonators offstage at gunpoint.

I found an antique compass, which I bought for Harold for Christmas. He loved such things, and it was truly handsome.

"We can stop at the sex shop so you can get Oscar a Christmas present," I teased Tinkie as we walked out.

"Keep it up," she said. "Just keep it up."

We both laughed as we flagged down a taxi for the ride up the highway. Next time I would not let Tinkie bully me into the limo. Actually, she hadn't bullied me. She'd offered the limo and we'd all jumped on it. I loved the journey, yakking and drinking champagne with my buddies, but time had shown me we always needed a car. Because we always got a case at Christmas.

We found the pawnshop and took our time looking around while the clerk rang up a sale. When everyone had left, Tinkie and I approached the man behind the counter and asked for Mavis. When he made it clear she wouldn't be in for the rest of the day, we introduced ourselves, pretending to be tourists in town for the Elvis show.

"Pleased to meet you. I'm Sherman Manning, cousin to Archie, and one of the Elvis competitors. I heard about you two. Private detectives. Grace Land hired you."

So much for keeping a low profile. He had the basic facts correct. "We heard you could handle some large, expensive items if someone needed to pawn, say, a lot of jewels and gold."

"Chief Johnson has already been out here snooping around." Sherman didn't bother to hide his defensiveness. "Whenever anything goes amiss in this county, everyone wants to believe the evil pawnshop operators are behind it. Well, we're not. My brother Wilbur and I run a very clean business. We don't traffic in stolen goods, and we don't cheat people. So, take your questions and leave." He pointed toward the front door.

Tinkie and I turned to look at the door, but we didn't move. "Did anyone contact you and try to move that belt?"

"People know we're honest businessmen. So, no! No one has tried to get us to move the Elvis belt that was stolen. Although I have to point out that Grace Land, with her sniveling TV show, has more enemies than Hannibal Lecter. And she's twice as likely to eat her prey. Now get out of my store or I'll be the one calling the cops on you."

Tinkie held up a hand, palm facing Sherman. "Stop. What TV show?"

When he grinned he was a little bit handsome. "You didn't know that your client stars in the most disgusting TV show ever made?"

"What show?"

"*Boyfriend Boot Camp* is the name. She's like some demonic dominatrix who lures couples to her Malibu mansion and then proceeds to reduce the men to crying, dribbling toddlers."

"I've never heard of this," I said. "Is it online or something?"

"Cable. Reality TV. It's hideous. Grace goes for the weak underbelly of each male contestant and guts them in front of their fiancée. She cripples them so they'll be obedient little husbands."

Tinkie's eyes were big. "That sounds dreadful."

"It is. And you're working for the woman who engineered it and profits from it."

"Our case has nothing to do with her TV show." Even as I said it, I knew it was incorrect. "I mean, people with half a brain know most of those shows are scripted and the contestants handsomely paid. That doesn't sound like much of a case for revenge."

"Really? You don't think some of the men she castrated on television might want to strike back?"

I didn't have an answer for him. "Why is Grace here in Tupelo instead of filming her show?"

"Winter break. They'll finish filming the new shows for next year some time in February."

Sherman sure knew a lot about Grace's schedule.

"One of the Elvis competition emcees, Allan Malone, also has a television show," Tinkie said. "Do you know him?"

"I know that he and Grace dislike each other. They've been competitors since they were in diapers. Each one wants to outshine the other. Grace was supposed to be up for a role on *One Life for Erica*, the TV soap that everyone loves. It was a meaty role, from what I know, but she didn't get the part. Then Allan got his reality TV show, *Who's*

Singing Barbra, and Grace almost lost her mind with jealousy. That's when she pitched the boot camp idea. I heard she stole it from one of her friends."

Rumors were cheap, but Grace sounded lower than a snake's belly—stealing from friends. *If* that was true. Then again, my shit detector had been going off regularly with Sherman. I didn't for a minute believe he was related to the football-playing Mannings or that he was master of gossip in Tupelo. But I was still willing to let him talk.

"Who would a person take a very expensive belt like that if they needed a quick pawn?"

Sherman rolled his eyes. "The seller would take out the jewels and melt the gold down so it couldn't be identified. Don't be naïve, ladies. If Grace didn't steal the belt from herself just to be the center of a pother, then you should accept the belt is gone. Disassembled and sold in pieces."

I didn't like to admit it, but he was likely right about that. The first thing I'd do would be to remove the jewels and contact European buyers. Although the belt itself was a work of art, for the thief it was too distinctive to keep intact. I suspected this news would hit Grace like a Mack Truck if she hadn't thought of it already herself. The belt was a beloved work of art to her, not just something of monetary value.

And while Sherman hadn't given us any great leads for finding the belt, he had given us several great motives for someone wanting to hurt Grace. Now all we had to do was track down the contestants from the show—and it sounded like there could be dozens of them who might want revenge. Time to head back to the hotel and a computer.

We left a business card with Sherman, but I knew better than to anticipate he'd be helpful. As soon as we cleared the door, Tinkie grabbed my arm and tugged me toward another shop in the strip mall. The sex shop.

"Time to buy some stocking stuffers for the girls," she said.

I couldn't help but laugh. For all of her proper Daddy's Girl upbringing, Tinkie loved a joke.

I gave her space to shop without me hanging over her shoulder, and I picked up a cute item for her—a little Christmas surprise that I looked forward to her opening at Harold's Christmas Eve shindig. I had no doubt she'd pay me back with interest, but I couldn't resist the outrageous little bit of peekaboo fluff that was sold as a teddy. After so many sleepless nights with the baby, she and Oscar would enjoy the gift.

We called an Uber and headed back to the hotel. I was eager to see what Millie and Cece had unearthed in their search for the reclusive artist Sippi Salem.

On the drive, I called Coleman. I confessed Tinkie and I had taken another Christmas case, and he took it with more grace than I expected. I shared the basic details and asked if he could check law enforcement sites for any big jewel heists in recent months. If this was a professional job, it would be good to know and enlist the proper authorities. Tinkie and I were solid private investigators, but we didn't have the reach or resources for an international jewel theft ring or anything of that nature.

The Uber pulled up to the hotel and we got out. We'd missed the regular lunchtime, but once we found Cece and Millie, we'd find something wonderful to eat.

6

My cell phone buzzed and it was Cece telling us to walk a few blocks to where she and Millie were at a local restaurant that specialized in Elvis food and drink. I didn't need urging. I'd worked up an appetite, and I couldn't wait to check out Elvis cuisine.

The girls were perched at a tall table, looking for all the world like happy tourists. Cece was snapping photos and Millie was taking notes. She had a stack of postcards she'd bought.

"By the time you mail them we'll be home," I told her.

"Doesn't matter. People like to know you were thinking of them while having a good time."

I couldn't argue with that. They both had tall, yellow-colored drinks that intrigued me. "What's that?"

"It's a Fat Elvis and it is delicious." Millie took a long sip through her straw.

"That's a terrible name for a drink," Tinkie said. She hated it when people mocked Elvis for any reason. And I was a little shocked that Millie would do so. She was an ardent supporter of all things Elvis. Whether it was the lean Elvis of the 1950s or the "more mature" Elvis of the 1970s, Millie adored everything about him.

I took Millie's glass and sniffed. Banana wafted up to me. "What's in it?"

"Blue Chair Bay banana cream rum, Skrewball peanut butter whiskey, banana puree, bacon garnish." She listed the ingredients like she'd been making the drink her entire life.

"It sounds . . . wicked." I was at a loss for words.

"It's really good." Millie waved the waitress over, pointed at her drink and then at me and Tinkie, and held up two fingers. We were going to get acquainted with Fat Elvis whether we wanted to or not.

"We're having BLTs, in honor of Elvis," Cece said. "Should pair well with the banana drink."

I had no clue how Cece's brain worked sometimes, but I was happy to take her menu suggestions. "What did you find out about Sippi?" I asked.

The excitement on their faces made me hopeful.

"That man has slept with half the women in Mississippi," Cece said. "He's very charming, and also very reclusive—except for his habits with the ladies."

"Did you see him?" Tinkie asked.

"Well, kind of," Millie said. "We talked to him, but he didn't invite us to his home or studio. We kind of talked through the intercom on his fence."

"What did he say about the belt?"

"He was upset. It's his work of art. He said he'd help us find it."

That was a bit of good news. "Did he mention Grace?"

Cece and Millie exchanged glances.

"Spill it," Tinkie said. "Sarah Booth and I need to know if there's something hinky going on with Grace."

Millie sighed. "He basically said that Grace was a liar and a thief—even though he insisted she had reasons to be the way she is. He said she'd bamboozled him out of the belt. She paid for the jewels and gold, but never for his design work and in fact took the belt from his studio."

Oh, no! A person who couldn't be trusted was not worth a paycheck. I'd come to accept that almost every client we had would have his or her own agenda. I still didn't like it, though. "Do you believe him?"

Cece sipped her drink, thinking. "I don't know. We couldn't see him. Just a disembodied voice over an intercom. Heck, it may not have even been Sippi. It could have been anyone."

"Confront Grace," Millie suggested. "That's the smart thing. Just ask her. If you don't get satisfaction, then walk away."

"But do it after lunch," Cece said. "I'm sure you're dying of starvation."

I flagged a waitress down and ordered BLTs for me and Tinkie. I was hungry, too.

Tonight we had the Elvis trivia games. Every restaurant/bar in the area offered the contest. It would be fun. I had actually studied up on Elvis facts before I left Zinnia. Plus, Coleman and the men would join us soon. Anticipation tingled through me. I missed Coleman. I wasn't one of those ooey-gooey people who melted at the thought of love. I was perfectly fine alone. But I couldn't deny that Coleman brought a lot of joy to my life. I did miss him.

The drinks arrived and then the food. The Fat Elvis drinks were delicious. Banana rum, peanut butter whiskey. It didn't make any sense, but they were tasty. It didn't take us long to eat and then hit the bricks. I was going to see Grace, and Tinkie wanted to go, too. We left Cece and Millie preparing for a shopping spree. I was about to die to tease them about the interesting things Tinkie had found at the sex shop, but I held my tongue. In a few days I could watch them open them in front of everyone, and that would be the best!

Tinkie and I took an Uber to Grace's address. When we got out on the sidewalk, I whistled. It was the kind of house often described as a McMansion. It had to be at least six thousand square feet, with a high sloping roof, bay windows, a beautiful front porch, and even a swing. Looking at the layout of the flower beds, I could only imagine how beautiful it would be in spring.

A maid answered the door and showed us into a modern parlor that led onto a screened back porch.

"Ms. Grace will be here shortly," the maid said. "Would you like some coffee or tea?"

"We're fine," Tinkie said, thanking her. My partner wasn't anxious. She was annoyed. If Grace had been trying to pull the wool over our eyes, Tinkie was going to make her pay.

Grace appeared in a flowing paisley caftan. She was a beautiful woman, and even with the negative comments we'd heard, I detected a hidden vulnerability. "I hope you have good news to report. I've been in a funk all day. I haven't left my bed."

Bacon could have sizzled on the top of my head, but I kept my composure. Tinkie just grinned. "Did you try to stiff Sippi Salem on his fee for creating the Elvis belt?"

Tinkie wasn't holding back. And Grace looked like she'd been slapped in the face.

"What do you mean?" Grace spluttered.

"Sippi told our friends you hadn't paid him for his work designing the belt."

"He would say that!" Grace had recovered and anger flushed her cheeks.

"Is it true?" Tinkie wasn't going to relent.

"I didn't pay him the exorbitant fee he wanted—wanted at the last minute, let me add. Our agreement was that he would design the belt and then I would use the beautiful piece he created to advertise his skills. I did everything I agreed to. I took out ads, sent flyers to art brokers, and all of that. I paid him as we agreed. Money was never part of it. If he said differently, he's lying."

"He said differently," Tinkie said, but her tone was less aggressive. "He told our friends you refused to pay him for his work and that you stole the belt from his studio."

Grace snorted. "That man has lied so much he doesn't even know when he's doing it."

I'd met compulsive liars before. They did lie when the truth would be so much easier. We didn't know Sippi or Grace. Either or both could be lying. "Did Sippi file any charges against you?" I asked.

"No," she answered. "And there is the truth. If he'd had a legal leg to stand on, he would have sued me."

She did have a point. "Why would he say such things?" I asked.

"Because he's a man and I got the better of him," Grace said. She gave a big grin and mischief sparked in her eyes. "He thought he was such a hound dog, chasing women, charming them, leading them on, then dumping them for someone new. I got hold of him and twisted him into a knot before I kicked him to the curb. He couldn't forgive me for that. I did to him what he does to other women." She laughed. "He was upset about that."

Neither Tinkie nor I said it, but looking at her I could tell we were thinking the same thing. Sometimes Karma rode a fast horse. That would really torque some men. Especially ones who had begun to believe their own press.

"I'm a little insulted you would believe Sippi," Grace finally said. Again, there was something in her eyes that led me to believe she'd been deceived in the past.

"We didn't believe him. We came here to ask," Tinkie pointed out. "Grace, we need some photographs of the belt, if you have some good ones. We can go online and post the photos to websites of businesses where the thief might take the belt."

"We all know that the belt will likely be melted down," Grace said with resignation. "As an object of art, it's very valuable. But the jewels and gold on their own are worth a lot."

"How much?" I asked.

"The last appraisal was three million dollars." Grace didn't stutter. "I'll add a one percent finder's fee, too."

I swallowed hard. That was a lot, and Grace had offered a one percent finder's fee on top of what she was paying us. We were talking big money.

"The belt is insured, isn't it?" Tinkie asked.

"Of course. Do you think I'm an idiot?" Grace asked. "But it isn't the money I want. It's the belt. It's mine and I love it and I want it back undamaged."

"We'll do our best. Would you mind if we talked to your insurance carrier?" Tinkie asked.

"Not at all. Her name is Krystal Bond, and she has an office by the courthouse."

"Have you notified her of the theft?" Tinkie pressed.

"I'm waiting on Chief Johnson to give me a copy of his report. Then I'll file it."

I wasn't going to give Grace advice on how to manage her business, but if it were me, I'd be at the insurance carrier's office this red-hot minute. Some things you didn't want to delay on.

"We'll stop by and talk with Ms. Bond," I said, edging toward the door. Tinkie was right beside me. "Thanks, Grace. We'll let you know if we find out anything useful."

"If you talk to Sippi again, tell him to kiss my grits." But there seemed to be more hurt than anger in her tone.

I could tell she wanted to say something a lot stronger, but she was checking herself. Which gave us the perfect opportunity for an exit.

When we were outside, I glanced at my partner. "We didn't quit," Tinkie said.

"No. I don't know if I believe Grace, but I think *she* believes what she's saying."

"I'm not certain that makes me feel more secure," Tinkie said. "I don't mind solving crimes and even risking life and limb, but damn, I don't want to work for a manipulative liar."

"I second that." I gave it a beat. "Do you want to quit?

We can, Tinkie. Coleman isn't all that thrilled we have another vacation case."

"I haven't even told Oscar," Tinkie admitted. "We love Maylin like the breath in our lungs, but we could really use some alone, adult time. I've neglected him."

"I don't believe that, but I'm sure he misses not being the focus of one hundred percent of your affections."

"And I miss it, too."

Tinkie and Oscar had been going through a rough patch back when I first returned home. Since that time, they'd strengthened their marriage, and Tinkie had even conceived little Maylin despite all the doctors who'd told her she could never get pregnant. Tinkie credited the Harrington sisters, a trio of witches who were running a very successful boarding school focused on honoring nature and the natural world. They'd given her a potion to conceive. I thought Miracle Maylin was the manifestation of the power of Tinkie and Oscar's love.

"Let's just solve this thing. I mean, that belt is not exactly going to be easy to sell locally."

"And we have no clue if it's still even in the area. It could be in Tasmania by now."

"I don't think so."

She touched my arm and turned me to look into her eyes. "Why do you say that?"

"Call it a hunch," I said. "I don't think this is about money. I think it's about personal revenge on Grace. Someone wants to make her suffer."

"I agree," Tinkie said. "But having the belt stolen is pretty good punishment, don't you think?"

"Yes, but it would be so much richer if the thief was

right here, watching his or her handiwork. Taunting Grace."

"So you think there will be a ransom request?"

"I do. Likely insincere and designed to make Grace jump through a number of hoops."

"That makes perfect sense." Tinkie linked her arm through mine. "Let's walk back to the Arena Center. That Fat Elvis has settled in my stomach and makes me feel like I need to burn some calories."

"Let's do it."

7

It was a beautiful December afternoon. We had plans for dinner, and later that evening was the trivia contest. Millie, who had read every *Sun, Globe,* and *National Conspiracy* article about Elvis (and Princess Di) sightings, was determined to win the competition. And Cece, who'd been spending a lot of time with Millie writing their newspaper column, was no slacker in the Elvis department. Tinkie and I hoped to make a respectable showing, but we had no illusions about winning. Our friends would go for the gold.

Tinkie and I both had hoped to get some shopping done, but instead we decided to check with the insurance agent on Grace's policy. Krystal Bond operated Top Notch Insurance. She specialized in expensive jewels, and from what Tinkie had dug up on the internet, she had a good reputation and insured a lot of the valuable jewels in Mississippi.

Google gave us her business address, and we found it with ease. The office was small but beautifully appointed with art and expensive antiques. If her digs said anything, it was that she ran a successful business.

When we went in the front door, we stopped. A pretty blonde sat at her desk and Allan Malone was perched on the corner. They were sharing a joke when we walked in. I recognized Allan from our first encounter and his TV show—I'd looked it up on my phone—and I knew he was an emcee of the competition, along with Grace. He was a local who had made good, even better than Grace, actually, as far as his TV show went. He had created the number one reality competition show on its network.

"Look what the cat dragged in," Allan said. I couldn't determine if his remark was caustic or just Hollywood bitchy.

"Holy crap!" I yelped as I jumped forward. I looked behind me and saw a grinning pug. The dog had bitten me. "That ankle biter is dangerous," I said to Allan. His other dog was lounging on the best chair in the office.

"Avery Wynette, apologize to this woman," Allan said as he picked up the pug. "That's very unlike my baby girl. She's having a temper tantrum because she wanted to wear her Elvis cape today and I wouldn't let her. Are you okay, Ms. Delaney?"

The dogs were dressed in matching red and green velvet collars. They had jingle bells on their collars. No wonder they were in a foul mood. The little dog had such a terrible underbite she hadn't been able to get a good grip on my ankle, and I did like dogs a lot better than most humans. "I'm fine. Dogs usually like me, though."

"To be honest, Avery has impeccable taste in humans. She must have viewed you as a danger to me."

Allan was six foot three. I was no danger to him. But Krystal was tall and slender. No bigger than my blue-eyed partner. And judging by her composure, she was equally as skilled as Tinkie at manipulating men.

"If you're intending to sue about the dog bite, just know that the dogs belong to Allan." Krystal Bond stood up and held out her hand. "What can I do for you ladies?"

"We need to talk to you about a client," Tinkie said.

"Grace Land, no doubt." Krystal sat on the edge of her desk beside Allan. "Did she send you?"

"Yes," Tinkie answered before I could prevaricate.

"Okay, I've been expecting her to call. She's not going to be happy."

Dread tingled in the pit of my stomach. This was going to be bad news.

"What's going on?" Tinkie asked.

"Grace didn't pay her premium on the Elvis belt."

It took a full minute for the implications of what she was saying to sink in. "What?"

Krystal drilled me with a look that clearly said she thought I was a moron. "The belt isn't insured."

I swallowed. This was not acceptable. "Surely she has a policy?"

"She did," Krystal said. "She had a three-million-dollar policy on the belt. But it lapsed. We no longer carry any policy on the Elvis belt."

"Grace didn't pay her premium?" Tinkie was stunned.

"No, she didn't."

"Why not?" Tinkie asked.

Krystal shrugged. "I don't know. I didn't even realize she hadn't paid until I checked the policy this morning."

Grace didn't strike me as the kind of person who didn't keep up with her important paperwork. Insurance was pretty dang important on a multimillion-dollar bejeweled gold belt, especially one on display in a public building with hundreds of tourists going in and out every hour.

"Did you send her a notice the bill was due?" Tinkie asked. Clearly she felt Krystal had fallen down on her duties.

"She gets an email notice and one in the mail." She shrugged. "It isn't my job to babysit clients. Most people know to the day when their insurance is due. Grace has so much money, she never thinks about anything. Seems like she just assumed someone would look out for her best interest. That's a luxury in a world where no one looks out for anyone else."

"Now, now, now," Allan said. He picked up Avery Wynette and gave her a kiss, then gave Lovely Katherine a cuddle. "Avery, Katherine, and I will always look out for you, Krystal, darling." He turned to us. "We've known each other since preschool." He looked back at Krystal. "Why are you being such a hard-ass about Grace?"

Krystal's lips set in a thin, hard line. "I'm tired of entitled people who believe my only job is to cater to their whims and make sure their expensive homes, cars, and jewels are all protected. It's not my stuff, it's theirs."

"And you are providing a service to *them*." Tinkie's eyes sparked blue jolts of anger. "If you don't like providing insurance to rich people, no one is stopping you from developing the clientele you want."

"No one else has the money to afford the policies," Krystal said, without any awareness.

"Maybe you should sell something else," Tinkie said. "Shampoo, or jewelry."

"Now, now, now!" Allan got between Tinkie and Krystal. "Enough of this foolishness. What we should focus on is checking Grace's policy to be sure she didn't pay. Krystal, please do that. Maybe the payment went in, and you didn't notice."

Krystal threw a glare at him but went to her computer and opened it. "Nope. The policy is canceled for nonpayment. It was due October first, and notices were sent. She didn't respond. Nothing I can do."

There was plenty she could have done—she'd just chosen not to. She knew Grace personally, and I was sure she'd had some kind of computer notification that Grace's premium was due. She'd ignored it. And this would have terrible financial consequences for Grace.

"If it makes you feel any better," Krystal said, looking to Allan for support, "the policy wouldn't have paid out anyway. The security at the center was too lax. There weren't proper protocols in place. It's all stated in her policy."

It was clear Krystal took a grim satisfaction in Grace's predicament. Not the person I'd want for my insurance agent.

"Can we get a copy of the policy?" Tinkie asked.

"No, you can't. You have no authority to even ask for—"

"Give it to her, Krystal, so we can get out of here and find a drink."

"It's against protocol."

"What could it hurt?" Allan winked at me. "She just needs a little sweet talk, don't you think?"

"I think she needs a kick in the tush," Tinkie said.

Allan's laugh was heartfelt and contagious. I laughed, too. Only Krystal was not amused, but she printed out the policy and handed it to Tinkie. "Since you're working for Grace, you can have it. I'm sure she's probably lost her copy anyway. Share it with her."

Allan walked us to the door and opened it for us to leave. "Don't mind Krystal. She takes good care of her clients, but she's got a problem with Grace right now." He leaned forward and whispered in my ear, "Grace broke up Krystal and Sippi. It's all about a man." He chuckled. "Girls will be girls."

"Thanks, Mr. Malone," I said. "I'm looking forward to watching you emcee the Elvis competition. I've heard good things about your TV show, too. Barbra Streisand, what a voice."

"There are two American musical prodigies. Elvis and Barbra. I'm so glad you appreciate both of them." He turned back to Krystal. "Come along, Krystal. Avery and Katherine need sustenance. I hear the Brick Oven has magnificent ribs. I can't wait another minute."

Krystal locked the door and they sailed off, chattering and laughing as the little dogs led the way.

8

Tinkie and I walked back to the hotel. I wanted a minute to read over the policy and to think about the case. We had the trivia contest later in the day, and Coleman and the men would arrive soon. There was much to get done before they pulled into town.

I entered my hotel room and stopped. A beautiful white plumed feather drifted to the floor in front of me. Someone was in my hotel room.

"Who's here?" I asked, wishing the gun Tinkie had put money down on was in my coat pocket instead of waiting at the pawnshop for her application to go through.

A low, sultry voice sang out, "I was born in the wagon of a traveling show."

Cher! Cher was in my room.

I rushed forward to see the actress in a skimpy costume that mostly consisted of white feathery plumes. Vegas Cher was in my room.

"I can't take this right now, Jitty." I loved my haint's creativity, but sometimes she just pushed a little too hard.

"What are you whanging on about?" she asked in that distinctive Cher voice.

"Sing 'That's Amore' from *Moonstruck*," I suggested. "That was my favorite movie role you did. And I'd much rather hear you sing than devil me."

"I prefer live performances, mostly in Vegas," she said.

"I'm very much alive and you're in my hotel room, not Vegas." The banter was quick, but I had things to do. "Why are you here as Cher?"

"When I signed the three-year Caesars Palace contract, I made sixty million," Jitty/Cher said. "Top that."

"I can't." I wasn't about to get into a pissing match with Cher about money. Or singing. Or Vegas. But I did have a question. "Did you ever want to date Elvis?"

That stopped her in her tracks. "I should have dated him. He was such a talent. Do you think I might have made a difference?"

That was an even more interesting question. "Maybe." I felt an overwhelming sadness. Could anyone have made a difference in the outcome of Elvis's short life? If his mother had lived, Gladys would have done her best.

"Elvis was a good-hearted boy who got pushed into things he didn't believe in. That last year he was so sick, and no one cared enough to check it out." Cher sat down on the edge of my bed. The mattress didn't even dent. Jitty not only could adopt the beauty and form of Cher, she was also weightless.

"What's your favorite Elvis song?" I asked.

"'Walking in Memphis.'" Jitty didn't hesitate.

"Did you ever meet him?"

Jitty/Cher sighed. "He asked me to Vegas, but I was nervous about meeting him face-to-face. I should have gone. You know you only regret the things you're too scared to do."

Jitty might be a devil and a thorn in my flesh, but she was right about that. Regret was a deadly emotion, but it most often came from fear of and failure to meet a challenge. "I may regret this later, but get out!" I pointed at the door. "I have work to do, and you are sucking up valuable time."

"You could learn some useful things from me."

"Not true. You never tell me anything. It's against the rules of the Great Beyond."

"There is that," she said, rising. She did that creepy ghost thing toward the door where she didn't walk but floated. It always got under my skin and she knew it.

"Goodbye, Jitty."

"See you later, alligator."

And she was gone. Just like that. I picked up the insurance policy and sat down at the desk to read over it. Before long, I was due to join my friends for Elvis trivia. We'd booked a booth at the Heartbreak Hotel Café. It was going to be a fun evening—but only if I made some progress on the case.

An hour later, I'd studied the policy. Grace had been an idiot to ever sign this. It offered little protection, and the premium was way too high. I texted Tinkie to join me if she had time. Three minutes later I answered her knock on the door.

"This policy is a rip-off." I handed it to her and she read over the parts I'd underlined.

"It is. Why on earth would Grace pay for this? She's a businesswoman. It doesn't make any sense."

"Perhaps that's a question we should ask her."

"Today might not be the day to do that," Tinkie said. "If she just found out the belt wasn't covered, she's going to be livid. I feel no obligation to take the spleen of her poor decisions or failure to pay her premiums."

Tinkie, as usual, had an excellent point. I was about to say just that when my phone rang. Caller ID showed it was Grace.

"What's up, Grace?" I asked after I put the call on speaker.

"I'm in the hospital. Can you come here now?"

"What happened?" I was concerned. She sounded kind of pitiful and lost.

"I was on my way to find Krystal Bond and beg her to tell me why my insurance payment didn't go through when I was run off the road. I went into a ditch and hit a culvert. The airbag busted my nose and the seat belt bruised my ribs. I'm okay, just beat up."

"Who ran you off the road?" Tinkie asked.

"I didn't recognize the car," she said.

"Have you talked to the police chief? He's going to want details."

"I have. The best I could give him was a white SUV, one of the most common cars around."

"Was it deliberate?" Tinkie asked.

"Yes. I'm sure. The car cut right into my lane at a high speed. I aimed for the ditch to avoid a head-on. The SUV just kept going."

It did sound deliberate. The case had just gotten a lot more serious than a stolen art piece.

"What did Chief Yuma Johnson say?" I asked.

"He's setting up roadblocks. They're looking for the car, but I didn't give them much to go on."

That was true. She hadn't seen enough to be of any help at all. They could spend the next five weeks stopping white SUVs. Since Grace's car and the other vehicle didn't make contact, there was no body damage on the car in question. "Where's your car?" I asked.

"The wrecker took it to Paulie's shop. He's a friend."

"I'll check there. Do you need anything? Toothpaste, brush, clothes?" I didn't know if Grace had someone who took care of these needs for her, but it wouldn't hurt to ask.

"No, a friend brought all of that."

"A friend?"

I had wanted to ask that, but Tinkie beat me to the punch. Grace didn't seem to have a lot of close friends.

"Yes, as hard as it is to believe, I do have friends," Grace said. "Now the nurse is here. I have to go."

I'd intended to rush over to check on her, but with her current prissy attitude, maybe it was better if I didn't. "We'll check back," I told her. "We need to speak to you about your insurance policy on the belt when you feel up to it."

"I talked to Krystal on the phone. She was positively gloating, I must add. I've never seen her so happy to deliver bad news. She's envied me for years."

"Why did you buy insurance from her if she dislikes you?"

"When I know the answer to that, I'll tell you. Laziness, I suppose. And just so you know, I'm positive I paid that policy."

For that moment, I felt sorry for Grace. She sounded sad and defeated.

"Talk later," Tinkie and I said in unison. When we hung up, we both just sank onto the bed. If the theft of the belt was the goal of the culprit, why were they still going after Grace? To tamper with her insurance policy—if that was what someone actually did—was way more than a heist for profit. This was bigger than a simple theft, and it was up to me and Tinkie to find out why.

9

We had a couple of hours to work before we were due at the bar for sustenance and games. Grace's car had been towed to Paulie's Automotive, a mechanic shop and local junkyard, and Grace was waiting on the insurance representative to declare it totaled. We took an Uber there and talked our way into examining the car. I didn't expect to find anything, but it never hurt to cross all the T's in an investigation.

"Did Ms. Land imply that there was a mechanical issue with the car?" the junkyard owner asked. He was on red alert.

"No, she didn't. It's just that she could have been seriously injured," I told him. He was a handsome man with twinkling blue eyes and an easy grin filled with perfect teeth.

"That's the truth. Folks in Tupelo don't want anything to happen to Grace. She's the best ambassador this town has had since Elvis himself." He led us out to the yard where the car was still hooked to the tow truck. He offered to free it from the wrecker, but I wanted a chance to look around and it would be easier if it was hoisted up. He tossed me the keys. "For the trunk," he said. "Motor is ruined."

I didn't know a lot about cars, just enough to check the brakes and a few little things. When we were talking to the junkyard owner, whose name was Jacko Jones, he helped us by pointing out a few things. "She could have had a blowout," Jacko said. "You can tell by the tires. Now, in this instance, she hit a culvert so hard it blew both front tires out. Impossible to tell if something was tampered with, if that's what you're thinking."

"Brakes?" I asked.

He got a high-beam flashlight. "You'd have to know . . ."

He clicked off the light. "I was told this was an accident. That Grace had swerved to avoid another car."

"That's what she said happened. What's wrong?"

"These brake lines have been damaged." He clicked the light back on and crouched so he could show me. "See. They were barely sliced. Just enough for a slow leak. There's no brake fluid left. It's probably been oozing out since I picked up the car."

So it wasn't just an accident. Whoever forced Grace to swerve had also made sure she wouldn't be able to stop her car.

"Can you tell what implement was used to do this?" I asked.

"I'm not a forensic mechanic, and you aren't going to find one in this part of the state. Jackson would be the closest place. I can tell you it was a sharp blade. One cut. The person who did it knew just how much to cut so it wouldn't be detectable right away. Driving the car and using the brakes would have increased the loss of fluid. That's all I can tell you."

"Thanks, Jacko. Would there be any evidence of a leak at Grace's house?" I asked.

He shrugged. "Maybe. Probably not enough for her to notice, but it depends on when it happened. Ms. Grace doesn't pay a lot of attention to things like fluid deposits around her. She's more focused on art and beauty. Stuff like that."

He sounded like a fan. "You seem to know her pretty well," I said.

"I've worked on her cars for the past ten years. Whenever she's in Tupelo. She has a big, fancy mechanic out in Los Angeles when she's there to do her show, but when she's in Tupelo, I do all the work for her. She's treated me very well, too. Too bad I can't fix this Lexus for her. She really loved it."

Oh, I had plenty of questions for Jacko now that he'd started talking. "Are you a fan of Grace's TV show?" I asked.

He looked beyond me for a moment. "If she asks, please tell her that I love the show. Truthfully, though, it just seems to be an excuse for women to be mean to the men they say they want to marry. The guys on the show have to cook, clean, buy groceries, take care of Halloween costumes for kids, or plan a party with food and drink. It's a lot to ask of a man."

"I haven't seen the show." I had a grudge against reality

TV shows and, to be honest, this show sounded even more unpleasant than most of the others.

"My wife loves it. She records it and watches it when I'm home wanting to watch something relaxing, like *Ancient Aliens* or such. *Boyfriend Boot Camp* isn't relaxing. It's like a confrontation. But Grace always looks real pretty on the show. And she has a wicked sense of humor. I have to give her that. She can make those men laugh even when they're on their knees scrubbing a floor."

I suppose that could be considered a talent. "Jacko, do you know anyone who would want to harm Grace?"

While I was talking, Tinkie was creeping around the car and taking dozens of photographs. She was a smart cookie.

Jacko stood up tall and cleared his throat. "I hear talk around town. Folks think Grace is pushy and has a superiority complex. They don't care for the way she puts people down. I don't think she means to, but it looks cold and mean. She has a lot of money, and people resent that, too. I tell them she's worked hard to get it. Hollywood ain't no Sunday picnic, if you know what I mean."

I nodded. "What people don't like her?"

He threw a suspicious look at me. "Just folks. You can ask around at the beauty parlors. I think that's where Grace does herself a lot of damage. She goes in acting like no one in town can compare to the stylists out in Los Angeles. I think it's because Grace isn't confident in her abilities. It's defensive, you know. Whatever, it pisses folks off."

"I can see where that would. But pissed off enough to try to kill her?"

"Now, whoa there! I didn't say that at all. I just said

she could get under a person's skin like a burr on a pair of undies."

"But you like her."

He shrugged. "I don't have nothing she wants and vice versa. We get along fine."

"Who might want what she has?" Tinkie asked. She'd suddenly rejoined the conversation. "Look, Jacko, if someone is out to kill her, we need to stop it before it goes bad."

Jacko blew out a breath. "I heard Grace giving Kent Madison what for at the last symphony in the park gathering. She was brutal. I tried to step in, and she lit into me, too."

"Over what?" I asked.

"She said the seats had been set up crooked. It was stupid. But that's Grace. She has to make a mountain out of a molehill if you're on her bad side."

"And this Kent was on her bad side?"

"He's assistant mayor and I heard he and Grace were planning on going into business together. He might be worth looking at. He had access to the Arena Center. From what I remember Grace saying, he was also supposed to put the security procedures in place to protect that belt." He waved us to follow him back to the office. "That belt should never have been left out in public like that. Never. It was a fool's decision. But that's Grace. She likes to show off and this time it's gonna cost her a pretty penny."

"Did you ever date Grace?" Tinkie asked.

Jacko laughed long and full. "Lord, no. That woman is not interested in me. I have pretty good self-esteem, but she's a man killer. Not literally a killer," he said quickly. "But she doesn't always remember that men need support and tenderness, too. She can be relentless when she wants something."

"And yet you still have a soft spot for her?" I was puzzled.

"I went to school with Grace. You have no idea how she was teased about her name. About her mama being cuckoo for Elvis. And it was the same in every class, every roll call, the other kids would mock her. It wasn't a great childhood."

"Why did her mama do that to her?" Tinkie asked.

"Rumor was that Elvis might have been her father. That's likely just cruel school gossip. But days after Grace was born, her mother submitted paperwork to change her last name from Jenkins to Land. No father was given on the birth certificate."

"And Grace's mother?"

"Alana Jenkins died when Grace was fifteen. Or at least that's one of the stories. By that point Grace was forged in steel. She was making her own way, working and going to high school. She stayed with an aunt, who died when Grace was a senior. Grace was tough and she was going to shove it down the throats of everyone who tormented her. When she graduated, she moved out to Hollywood and worked as a script reader for Paramount. She told me all about how exciting it was to read scripts and have input on movies. She made powerful friends, did a few bit parts in bad movies, realized she didn't have what it took to be a great star, so she changed directions and started producing reality TV."

"And then she created her own show." Tinkie put the icing on the cake.

"Exactly. And she got to stick it to the type of people she felt held her back in Hollywood."

Well, there was something to be said for that. "What's the story on Kent Madison?" I asked.

"They were close. Like, business close. From what I heard, Grace got him the job in the mayor's office as assistant mayor. He was supposed to help her with some rezoning issues. Grace wants to build a permanent stage devoted to Elvis impersonators. She had a plan for a theme park, a movie studio, lots of things. It was a big, big vision."

"Is it going to happen?"

"No. The city thinks twice a year is enough time devoted to Elvis."

I didn't see a whole lot of other big draws for the region, but I kept my lips zipped.

"It could be very good for tourism," Tinkie said. "I mean, the June celebration is terrific, but you have to admit it is hot as Hell in Tupelo in June. This time of year, at Christmas, is much better. What if they did an Elvis festival every month or two? Different themes, different age groups. Like baby Elvis."

I could see it. Little babies with sideburns. Adorable!

"Kent thinks it might pollute the draw. You know, if it's available all the time, then why is it special? He didn't want to do this Christmas one, but Grace prevailed with the mayor. She twisted a few arms, but she got it done. Kent was pretty irate about the whole thing."

"You said that Kent had access to the Arena Center, and the belt, the security cameras, the codes, everything. Do you think he stole the belt?" Tinkie got us back on track.

Jacko waved us into his office out of the cold wind. "No. He could have done it, but I don't think he did. He's performing as Elvis in the competition. From what I've heard, he's pretty good. I think his plan is to win the competition and haul ass to Las Vegas to do a show as Elvis. That would be sticking it to Grace in the worst kind of way."

He had a point. "Why didn't Grace change her name back once her mother died?"

"She had become Grace Land. She truly grew into the name, and it wrapped around her and changed her. I look at it like a form of child abuse, but I don't have kids or any experience. I just remember a timid little girl in grammar school who fought every day against bullies and asshats who tormented her. By the time she could have changed that name, it was a badge of honor."

"Jacko, you need to tell Chief Johnson about this. Whoever cut that brake line was trying to kill or harm Grace."

"I'll give Johnson a call," he said. "Grace aggravates some people, but not enough to want her hurt or dead. There's a side of her most people don't know. A good side." He frowned. "This is more than just a jewel heist. Grace may be in real danger."

He wasn't wrong. We thanked him and headed over to the police department. Chief Johnson needed to know how so many coincidences were adding up.

10

We arrived at the police station only ten minutes later, but the chief had already dispatched a forensic unit to comb through Grace's car. Yuma, as he insisted we call him, was angry and concerned. "Stealing is one thing. Attempted murder is something else."

We nodded.

"Did you find any clues as to who is behind this?"

"We didn't," Tinkie said. "We were hoping you might have found out something about how the cameras at the Arena Center were disabled."

"Oh, we know what happened. We just don't know who did it."

"What happened?" Tinkie was a little peeved he'd made us ask.

"Someone turned the cameras off. No fingerprints. No witnesses."

"Where is the control switch?"

"In the arena office. We've questioned everyone who was there. It was a madhouse. They have interns from the local colleges and high schools to help show tourists around. The fact is, everyone and his brother had access to the cameras. No one working in the office paid any attention to the control panel for the cameras. All we could find out was that they were turned off at about two o'clock on the afternoon of the theft."

"Someone got in there and disarmed the cameras, knowing they would steal the belt at a later time."

"Looks that way," Yuma said. He rubbed his chin. "The thief appears to be someone we all know. Someone who wouldn't draw attention."

"Or it could have been one of the kids that someone paid to do it. They wouldn't know why they were asked."

Yuma nodded. "That's a possibility. I can have the tourism office pull the names of the volunteers. It'll take some legwork, but it has to be done."

"We can help," Tinkie offered.

"Has Grace talked to you about how her insurance policy was canceled?" I asked Yuma.

"Yes. And I spoke to Krystal. She has a real burn on for Grace. It's almost as if she enjoyed Grace's predicament."

"Can you check her out through the computer system? See if her name pops up with any other big insurance thefts or anything else?" Tinkie asked.

"Already have," Yuma said. "Her criminal record is clean, but her employment record is sketchy. Before she moved here, she was let go by a big Nashville firm. No reason given. We called and talked to the owner, but he wasn't forthcoming. My gut instinct is that she got involved with her boss, became a problem, and he solved it by letting her go."

"It's always the woman who pays the price," Tinkie said. "I mean, if she was fired for sleeping with her boss—if that was indeed the case—then her boss should have been fired, too."

"Totally agree," Yuma said. "But we don't make the rules. When is Sheriff Peters coming to town?" he asked.

"He'll be here for the amateur Elvis competition."

Yuma laughed. "Is he competing?"

"No, but we are," Tinkie said.

"This I have to see."

Yuma's amusement at the idea of us competing did nothing to bolster my confidence. But he hadn't heard Cece sing yet. That was our secret weapon.

"Have you had a chance to talk to Sippi Salem?" Tinkie asked him.

Yuma shook his head. "Not at home. I drove out to his place and there's a sign on the gate. Gone to China."

"Did he really just up and leave for China?" I was shocked.

"Hell no. It's one of his practical jokes. He doesn't want to be bothered."

"You would think he'd be concerned about his artwork."

Yuma motioned us over to the coffeepot. He poured us all a cup of coffee so thick and black it reminded me of the witch's brew that Doc Sawyer kept going in the ER in Zinnia.

"Rumor has it that Grace never paid Sippi for the work he did on the belt. She provided the raw materials, and he crafted the belt. She never paid him for his work." Yuma dropped the information like it was a golden nugget, but Tinkie and I had already heard it.

"He didn't sue her?" Tinkie asked, pretending we didn't already have this intel.

"Nope."

"Why not?"

Yuma shrugged one shoulder. "There was talk that Grace tried to pay him. In a fit of pique, Sippi tore up the check and then Grace wouldn't write another one. Lots of talk, but no legal action was taken by either party."

Grace had left a long trail of angry people behind her. "Do you think Sippi might have retaliated by stealing the belt?"

"He never comes into town," Yuma said. "He has everything delivered to his gate. But"—he paused dramatically—"a man fitting his description was seen at the Arena Center the afternoon the belt went missing. He had on a hat and shades, like a tourist. I have a deputy going through some cell phone footage to see if we can pinpoint that Sippi was there. I suspect this is a waste of time, but it has to be checked."

I thought about the man with a hat that another witness had seen. I'd assumed it was someone dressed as Colonel Tom Parker. I relayed the info to Yuma. He put it on his list.

"And what about the destruction of Grace's brake lines?" I asked.

"Sippi worked as a mechanic before he started selling his art; most of the men in Lee County know how to work on cars. The women, too. It could be anyone."

Yuma wasn't helping us narrow our suspect pool at all. As luck would have it, my phone rang. Coleman was on the horn. He'd had time to run a check on regional art and jewel thefts. A couple of jewelry shops had been robbed in Mobile, Alabama—a smash-and-grab scenario. But nothing on the order of a three-million-dollar heist. I gave Yuma the news and when he held out his hand for my phone, I surrendered it. Coleman might be able to offer some advice or at least weasel more information out of Yuma.

I couldn't tell what the men were talking about, so I took the opportunity to see if Tinkie had a suggestion for our next lead. We decided to check out the street scene near the Arena Center. As Tinkie brilliantly pointed out, someone in an Elvis costume wouldn't draw much attention scoping out the belt display. She was right about that. It was a good place to start.

"And we need to talk to Kent, the assistant mayor," I pointed out.

"We might as well start with him. Until we can find Sippi," Tinkie said. "He's looking more and more like the prime suspect. He got the belt he designed back, and he almost got rid of Grace altogether."

My partner was on a streak of drawing conclusions. "And he's conveniently unavailable." I had to wonder why Yuma wasn't more excited about Sippi's bizarre refusal to talk. That was one I'd ask Coleman to probe for me. I didn't want to alienate the Tupelo lawman, but I also didn't see his conduct as completely professional. He seemed perfectly willing to let Sippi waltz in and out of town when he appeared to be the number one suspect in a theft and attempted murder.

Yuma returned my phone, saying he was looking forward to meeting Coleman, and Tink and I left. As we walked toward the middle of town, she called home to check on Maylin. Tinkie almost never left her little girl, but the

Christmas trip was the exception—besides, Oscar had begged Tinkie to let him bring Maylin when he came up for our competition. She'd obliged, though she suffered not having her little girl with her. The baby was growing up, too! The precious years of baby to toddler were passing too fast. For Tinkie *and* me.

I called Coleman to see if I could pry any additional info out of him. Whatever he and Yuma had talked about, he was keeping it under his hat—until he arrived in person, and I could apply my own formula of persuasion.

We turned a corner onto a busy street. A cluster of Elvises were in a semicircle on the curb, vying for the attention of a gathering crowd. One wore a leopard-print jumpsuit. He was a long, lean Elvis with hooded eyes and major sideburns, and when he started singing "I Believe," he sounded just like the King. Tinkie and I stopped in our tracks. The man could put on a show.

When he was done, I walked up and asked his name.

"Wilbur Manning," he said, pleased as punch with his performance.

I did a double take. He looked exactly like another Tupelo resident, who was also a Manning. Sherman Manning. When I asked, he admitted they were identical twin brothers. "But I have the better voice," he said. "And I'm the nicer person."

"Sherman has the better hip action," a woman passing by called out.

"You wish!" Wilbur yelled after her. He grinned. "That's Sherman's girl. I don't need a woman to talk up my Elvis impersonation. And Friday night I'll show him when I win the contest!"

There was good-natured competition among the Elvises, who ranged in appearance from near look-alikes to more outlandish interpretations who'd come to show off their Elvis moves.

"Elvis has been dead nearly fifty years and he still has such a grip on so many people," Tinkie said. "He was a handsome man and a great singer, but I think it is his heart that people are drawn to."

Elvis's generosity was well known in his home state. "And his love for his mother. After Gladys died, there really wasn't anyone capable of protecting him from greedy and corrupt influences. That manager put that poor man on the road and worked him near to death." I'd heard my mother talking about this. She had zero use for Colonel Tom Parker, his manager. "Thinking of Colonel Parker, have you seen anyone around here wearing a hat and smoking a cigar? Big man with a giant double chin?"

"Nope. And I don't want to." Tinkie made the sign of the cross to ward off evil spirits. "Elvis doesn't need him tagging along on his memories. He did enough damage when the King was alive."

I'd told Tinkie about the witness who'd seen someone resembling Colonel Parker eyeballing the belt when it was in the display case. "We have to check it out," I told her.

"You do it. Anyone who'd show up here in that guise needs to be flogged."

It was clear she wasn't going to be helpful if I did find the person. "What if he's a ghost?" I still had time to devil her a little.

"There's no such thing as ghosts." She gave me a wary glance. "Is there?"

"You tell me. I think I'm haunted." I expected to see Jitty pop up behind her and give me the dickens.

"I think you're a bruise masher," she said. "Go find the

Colonel. I'll stay here and talk to the Elvises. They may know something."

Cooperation wasn't in her wheelhouse, so I hoofed it down the street, looking for anyone who might have the distinctly bad taste to show up as Colonel Parker. I didn't see the man—or the ghost—but I came across my witness, Darcy the ticket taker. She was sitting on a bench under an oak tree enjoying the crisp day and watching the antics of the impersonators.

11

"Ms. Delaney," Darcy said, waving. "What are you doing here?"

"Enjoying the Elvises," I said, taking a seat beside her. "Did you happen to see the Elvis from yesterday?" I asked.

"The one Sonja left with?"

"That's the one." I should have nabbed him then and there and asked him questions. I was fairly certain he wouldn't cop to stealing the belt even if he had done so.

"Not after he hooked up with Sonja. She pulls that Priscilla look every year. The Elvises fall all over themselves to talk to her." She made a face and laughed. "Sonja could do a lot better than these impersonators if she'd try. She's afraid to leave Tupelo."

"Sometimes it's hard to reach for the dream." I'd left

Mississippi as soon as I graduated from college and spent a while in New York City trying to engage my dream of a Broadway career. My stomach still churned with the anxiety of that bold decision. The years in NYC had been hard and difficult, and ultimately disappointing. But never a waste. I'd learned so much about myself and the bigger world. In a crazy way, acting had prepared me to be a private investigator, which I now felt was my true calling. Thanks to Tinkie.

"Look! Here comes Sonja."

I watched the raven-haired beauty approach. Her pile of dark hair was teased to a fare-thee-well, and I wondered if she could do that in the summer when the sticky humidity would turn it into a clump of gummy hair spray. I remembered the urban legends of girls with hair teased and sprayed so much that roaches were said to nest in their hair. The girls wouldn't know—until the roaches ate the hair off at the scalp and then suddenly in a brisk wind, their hair would fly away and cartwheel down the road. They'd be left totally bald! After I heard that, I'd sworn never to use hair spray, even after my mother laughed at the story and said it was all foolishness.

"Ms. Rivera." I stood and held out my hand.

"Are you going to the trivia games tonight?" Sonja asked. "Darcy and I could use another player on our team."

"I'm already obligated to be with my friends," I said. "I'm afraid I'm not going to be much help, but Millie and Cece are total Elvis authorities."

"It's all in fun," Sonja said. "Have you found the missing belt yet?"

I shook my head. "No. Have you heard any gossip?"

"The consensus of opinions from my group of friends

is that Sippi somehow stole the belt back, since Grace had stolen it from him. Reputedly," she quickly added.

Someone had chewed on Sonja's toes about slander. "Do you know Sippi?"

"Everyone in town knows Sippi. He's famous."

"I meant do you know him personally, as a friend?"

"We've shared a few drinks." Her look was sly and sexy. "He's a hard man to forget."

"Apparently quite the charmer."

She laughed. "I'd dare to say that if there's a woman he fancies, he can get her. He has that rare ability to make everyone he wants to charm feel like a princess." She shrugged. "It all disappears like a rainbow or unicorn fart the minute his interest flags, but while it's there, it's something special."

I had to laugh. Sonja was incorrigible. "Do you worry about roaches in your hair?" I teased her, much to Darcy's amusement.

"Not at all. My hair spray is loaded with DDT. The roaches go in, but they never come out."

"Ugh!" I couldn't help but laugh at her repurposing of an old commercial about roach motels, but I could also imagine Tinkie's reaction to that statement. She'd be appalled. I was made of coarser stuff.

"Have either of you seen the leopard-print Elvis?" I asked.

"He'll be at the trivia games tonight," Sonja said. "Or I should say, they'll be there. There is a group of them, as I understand it."

"Do you know which restaurant he's playing at?"

"I don't. Most of the Elvises will make the rounds of the bigger bars with playing consoles, so if you're on a team, you'll likely see him and a bunch of other impersonators."

"Sonja, does it ever strike you that Elvis would hate all of this?"

She thought for a long minute. "I don't believe he would. Elvis never took himself seriously in that way. I mean, he worked hard until he was so exhausted he started using pills to stay on the road. Even so, he always had a sense of humor about the mania that surrounded him."

She spoke with such sadness that for a moment I felt I was talking to the King's true bride. Melancholy permeated my heart. It was odd how visceral the loss of Elvis was for even women of my generation. His mark was indelibly printed on so many.

"What's your favorite Elvis song?" Sonja asked me. "I'll see if I can't get Sherman or Wilbur to perform it tonight at one of the bars."

"'Can't Help Falling in Love.'"

"I'll ask them," she promised. "Prepare to cry. That one will wring the salt water out of you."

I didn't doubt it for a minute. Watching my parents dance to this tune had given me the classic idea of romance and love. I'd been lucky that my parents had that, that I'd witnessed it, and that I'd also found it with Coleman. Elvis's ballads were the bedrock of how I rated love, and I felt as if my partnership with Coleman was absolutely inevitable. "Thanks. Tell me about Wilbur and Sherman, the twin Elvises."

"Wilbur is a good guy. Sherman is a little . . . competitive." Darcy was supplying the information.

"How so?"

"Sherman had a chance to leave Tupelo and play sessions in Nashville. He's a talented guitarist and has a good voice. The problem was that Wilbur was the one who wrote their songs, and he didn't want to go. So Sherman stayed, too. And then there's the whole claim to be related to the football Mannings. Sherman started all of that. He just needs to be special. It's total hogwash. They lost a lot of credibility in town with Sherman insisting it was true. He even pretended to be a high schooler to participate in the Lee County High School punt, pass, and kick competition last October. A grown man, trying to beat kids. It was shameful, and he couldn't even kick the football. He'd been drinking and when he tried, he missed entirely and flipped on his back. Knocked the breath out of himself so bad they thought he was having a heart attack. They put a portable defibrillator on him, but it was charged too high and they thought they'd electrocuted him. The ambulance had to be called, but on the way to the hospital—they left him unattended in the back—he jumped out and ran off into the woods. Took them two days to find him. He thought the US of A had been invaded by the Russkies and he took off to hide."

Judging by the fact Darcy had dropped into a real Southern twang the more she talked, I knew she was pulling my leg, but it was a damn good story.

My cell phone rang, and while I expected it to be Tinkie, it wasn't. Grace Land wanted me to stop by her place. I didn't want to go without Tinkie, but I wasn't far, and I wanted to get it over with so we could go eat and play trivia. "I'm on the way."

I loved that I could walk around town. It was the same in Zinnia, but since I had to drive to town from Dahlia House, I always ended up driving my car everywhere. I needed to change that. I was thinking about how much better walking was than driving when I knocked at Grace's door. Her maid let me in, but not before rolling her eyes. "She's in a mood," she warned.

Glad not to be her maid, I found Grace in the bedroom, among piles of pillows, trays of uneaten food, magazines, and at least five TV remotes. There was only one TV; I checked.

She saw me staring at them and frowned. "The maid insists on letting Ray Charles into the bedroom and he tries to hatch the remotes. When I move to get it, he bites me."

"Ray Charles?" I wondered how many ghosts Grace actually lived with.

She pointed across the room at a huge black cat draped on her dresser. He covered the whole top. One paw hung down, his intense green eyes watched me with insolence, and his tail flicked as if he knew he were the topic of discussion.

I made a move to pet him, and Grace said, "Beware. He is rabid."

"Does he play the piano?" I asked wittily.

"No. He has no talent other than biting and clawing."

Grace had met her match in feline form.

"He's a handsome kitty. I have a black cat named Pluto, but Ray Charles is at least twice his size."

"Ray Charles isn't really a cat," Grace said. "He's a demon of retribution sent by Elvis to hound me to my grave."

Grace was either smoking something or her meds had worn off. "Why would Elvis have it in for you, Grace?"

She only shook her head. "No one ever gets away with anything. The piper must be paid." She took a breath. "I heard you were at Paulie's Automotive asking Jacko about my car. Did you find anything or are you just seeing how many Elvises you can notch on your bedpost?"

Jessica the maid came to the door. When I cast an imploring gaze at her, she shrugged and walked away as quickly as she could. I was on my own with the temperamental millionaire.

"Grace, someone cut the brake lines on your car. The crash was deliberate. Someone intended to harm you, if not kill you." I just put it out there.

"Who?"

"We haven't been able to answer that yet."

"Then what good is that information? You want me to go all over town looking over my shoulder to see who wants to off me?"

I regretted telling her a damn thing. If an anvil fell on her head, I would not feel guilty. Grace had an unfortunate personality, where every kindness done for her was treated as if it were an insult inflicted upon her.

"I wanted to give you a heads-up so you could be more alert and watch for danger. But if that's too much trouble, just forget it."

Her jaw dropped. She wasn't used to anyone talking back to her. "How dare you!" She finally found her voice.

"Grace, I'm working on your case. I don't have to like you to do the work, but it sure does help. Now I wanted to give you a report about what we've found, but if you want to bicker and quarrel, I'll type up the report and email it to you."

Jessica appeared at the door with a tray of coffee and flaky pastries. I wasn't hungry until I saw them.

"What do you have to report?" Grace asked stiffly.

I gave her the full details on the car brakes, what the Manning twins had been up to, my conversation with Darcy and Sonja, and the fact that Sippi was apparently unavailable to speak with.

"He's not missing. He's hiding out," Grace said. "That man is a coward."

"Do you think Sippi had the motivation and the skill to steal the belt?"

She set her mouth in a tight line. "Yes. Is that what you want to hear? That I think he'd do this to me?"

Whew. She was the sun and everything orbited around her. "Because he felt you owed him money?"

"I told you I've never walked out on a bill in my—"

I held up a hand to stop her. "I didn't say you cheated him. I asked you if he might feel that you had. There's a big difference."

"Who knows what he feels. He's an artist. He's temperamental. All fire and ice." Her face softened and her voice got a little dreamy as she talked. She still had an itch for the man—that much was plain to see. "That was our problem. Sippi could be smart, funny, and entertaining one minute, then that temper would ignite. He was like a moccasin. Strike first and regret it down the road."

My opinion was that they were well-suited for each other, but there was no need to speak that aloud. "Did Sippi have the skills necessary to turn off the cameras and laser lights, then unlock the display case?"

"Sippi is slippery as an eel. He was a mechanic, so he certainly knows how things worked. He's good with his hands. Seems to me he has the necessary skills."

Though her words said yes, yes, yes, something in her eyes told me she didn't believe Sippi was guilty. She was mad at him and willing to throw him to the wolves, but it didn't make him the guilty party. The hard reality was that I'd sent my friends to talk to him. That was my job, and one I could no longer shirk.

"Where do you suppose I might find Sippi?" I asked.

Grace gave it some thought before she answered. "He travels to Europe and Latin America a lot. But I don't think that's where he is. His has a cabin not too far from Tupelo. He used to go there to paint in the winter. He said the light was better there than anywhere else. He's likely in the woods. Like I said, it's the light. Sippi is all about natural light when he works. Unless he's sculpting. Then the light is industrial anyway."

"If you called him, would he answer?"

"Oh, heavens no! If he thought I was looking for him he might leave the country. We didn't exactly part as friends."

"Is there anyone who might be able to arrange for him to talk with me?"

"Yuma might. They know each other. Or Krystal Bond, that . . ."

She didn't finish it, but I knew the word she'd left out. Krystal couldn't be counted on Grace's friend list. If I asked her to call Sippi, she might call him and tell him never to speak with me, just to thwart Grace. "Anyone else?"

"Kent Madison knows him."

"The assistant mayor?"

"Yes, Kent has sucked up to Sippi for years now. He's trying to get a federal grant for Sippi to create a bronze sculpture of the King. Kent wants to place the new sculpture beside Elvis's birthplace."

"Good to know."

"Kent's a snake."

"So I've heard."

"In fact, Kent had access to the Arena Center the day of the theft. You might ask him about that while you're talking to him."

"And I believe he's an Elvis impersonator?" I'd done a bit of homework.

"He is. He actually sings pretty good. He's almost got that golden baritone down. Not quite Elvis, but pretty darn good." A smile touched her lips. "When we were looking to start a business, he used to sing to me. I could close my eyes and it was almost as if it were real."

I didn't know Kent Madison, but I felt a spike of compassion for him, a man whose claim to fame was impersonating a dead man.

"I'll talk to Kent." I checked my phone. It was almost time to meet up for the trivia contest. As much as I hated to put off the interview another day, city hall would be closed. Kent Madison was likely already on his way to whatever bar or restaurant he intended to compete from. I had no doubt that a serious Elvis impersonator who was also a Tupelo city official would be in it to win it.

12

The name of the quaint dive we'd chosen as our home base for trivia escaped me. The name didn't matter anyway. They had excellent martinis, big fat green olives, and pistachio nuts.

The girls were already there when I walked in. My group was at a corner table with the game controller in the middle. The questions would pop up on the screen behind the bar and we would answer. As I understood the rules, all of the answers were being collected and tabulated at city hall. The winner of the contest would receive an all-expenses-paid trip for four to Las Vegas. I enjoyed games, but the title of winner was riding on Millie and Cece. They were the ones who knew their stuff about Elvis.

The bartender beat on the bar with a stick and got everyone's attention. "Round one will start in five minutes. There will be thirty minutes of questions. Answer each one, even if it's not correct. Then move on when the next question pops on the screen. Remember, this is for fun. Some of the questions are serious, some are silly. Grasp your inner child by the throat and enjoy."

I had to laugh. Cece and Millie were clutching the game controls like they were in a life-or-death scenario. Any other player would have to pry it from their cold, dead hands.

The first question dinged on the board. "What is Elvis's twin brother's name?"

Cece nailed that one in one second flat. Jesse Garon, the older brother who had been stillborn. I sipped my martini, swallowing a lump. I'd been told that twins had a special connection. Would that bond have held for Elvis and Jesse? Who could know.

The trivia continued and I offered suggestions when I had them, but Cece and Millie held the reins. We were on the board at number two in the citywide competition when the first round ended.

I got another round of drinks and some food for the table. We needed sustenance to continue. White bean chili warmed us up inside and out. The food was wonderful, though Millie's offerings at her Sunflower County café were still my favorite.

The game resumed, and Millie pushed our team to the top with the answer to the question of Elvis's favorite song—"Halfway to Paradise" by Tony Orlando. How she knew that, I would never know, but I asked.

"He told me in a dream," Millie said. "I dream about Elvis all the time. Last night, we were walking hand in hand along the streets of Tupelo in 1950. It was fantastic. He made me feel so special." She blinked back tears. She did seem to have a psychic connection with him and Princess Di.

"Did he have another favorite?" Tinkie asked.

"'Green, Green Grass of Home.' The Tom Jones version."

I understood that perfectly. Jones had some moves in his day, too. He and Elvis knew how to shake up an audience. This song was a beautiful ballad about things left behind and the final goodbye from a man in prison waiting to be executed and knowing he will go home—but only after he is dead.

"That song was covered by Porter Wagoner, Jerry Lee Lewis, and others. Jones heard the Jerry Lee Lewis version and decided he had to record it." Cece was no slouch on musical facts. "Then Elvis heard the Jones version and it hit him hard." She sighed. "I love songs that tell a story."

I hadn't given it a lot of thought, but most of my favorite songs were narrations of a story. Like books, songs could touch deep in a soul when they were done right. The combination of story and melody packed a mighty big punch.

Our group led the trivia match for most of the evening, but in the end, a team across town won the contest. I wondered if Cece and Millie let them win. It would be like them to do that.

It was only ten o'clock when we finished and walked out of the bar. Tupelo was alive with bright Christmas lights and fluttering decorations. The Elvis impersonators added another level of festivity. One Elvis sang "Silent Night" in a rich baritone that stopped us in our tracks as we listened to all the verses of the song. For just a moment, I wondered if the ghost of Elvis walked among us. But when the Elvis turned to face us, it wasn't the King. Just another man with black hair and sideburns who could sing.

I looked past the Elvis and clutched Tinkie's hand. A man who looked exactly like Colonel Tom Parker turned the corner by a drugstore and disappeared. "I have to talk to him. Someone saw him near the belt moments before it was stolen."

I didn't wait to explain further, and I heard Tinkie's short, fast steps running behind me. Luckily she was wearing boots with a reasonable heel instead of the stilettos she sometimes pranced around in.

When I made it to the corner, I slowed to see if I could catch sight of the Colonel. He was half a block ahead of me, and going into a pawnshop that was still open. I was hot on his trail, and Tinkie was hot on mine.

I burst through the front door and stopped. It was a small business with tall aisles that contained everything from lawn equipment to musical instruments. The jewelry was in the back near the cash register. I walked across the front of the store, checking each aisle, and failed to see a sign of Colonel Parker—or his doppelgänger.

Tinkie caught up with me and she went to the counter. "We're looking for a gentleman in a hat and suit. Did he come in here?"

The young man behind the counter flipped a hand, indicating the whole store. "Do you see him?"

I was about to tell him what a wiseass he was, but Tinkie stepped in. "We thought he came in here. Is there another exit?"

The clerk looked down and mumbled something. I went around the counter and pushed back a curtain that led to a large storage facility. The lighting was dim, and the space was filled with aisles of items. I didn't have a flashlight, but I looked for movement. A door in the back clicked into place. The Colonel had made a slick getaway with a little help from the clerk.

I returned to the front, where Tinkie was making it clear the clerk was in big trouble with us.

"Who was that man?" I asked him.

"I don't know."

Tinkie pulled out her phone. "That man is wanted in connection with the theft of a three-million-dollar piece of art. I'm calling Chief Johnson."

The young man reached across the counter to touch Tinkie's hand. "Please don't. I really don't know who he is. He came in here, asked if there was a back way out, and gave me two hundred dollars." He was almost shaking, his face ashen.

"And you helped someone you don't know?"

"A lot of people come in this shop. I was told to help the customers all I could. And he gave me two hundred bucks."

I believed he was telling the truth, and Tinkie did, too. She nodded slightly to let me know.

"Have you ever seen him in town before?" I asked.

"I haven't. I didn't get a good look at him, but a man wearing a hat like that hasn't been in here before. I'd remember the hat. Most folks here wear tractor hats. And we don't handle a lot of high-end jewelry. Mostly lawn equipment and tools. Those are the steady sellers. Maybe some of it is stolen. I can't say for sure, but we don't take it if we suspect it's stolen. I don't know anything about expensive art." He waved a hand around. "This isn't a place for expensive things. Guns, gold-plated wedding bands, cheap earrings, lawn mowers, chain saws, weed wackers—those are the things our customers want. When he came in here waving those hundred-dollar bills, I just focused on the money and pointed to the back. Most folks who come in here are desperate, not flush."

Looking at the display of handguns beside the jewelry, I was reminded that Tinkie had that awful pink, pearl-handled gun at the other pawnshop to pick up. Her waiting period was almost over. "Would you happen to know Krystal Bond or Sippi Salem?" It was a wild chance.

"Krystal, hell yeah!" He was clearly a fan.

"Is she a customer?"

"Back last month, she brought in some really nice stuff. She was having some financial issues." He leaned forward, flush with gossip. "I hear she lost a bit too much in Vegas back in the summer. She owed some people who didn't take excuses."

"Is her stuff still here?" Tinkie asked. She didn't say it but looking at what Krystal had pawned would be telling.

"Nope. She came in early this morning and redeemed all of it. Cash, with interest paid." He frowned. "She didn't want to chitchat, and usually Krystal always asks who's pawned what so she can keep up with the neighbors. She's always on the hunt for a bargain." His frown deepened. "She was either in a hurry or just not interested."

Tinkie and I shared a glance. Krystal was in financial trouble. A gambling addiction was as bad as drugs or alcohol, based on my experiences with Uncle Crabtree. He was pretty much confined to Dahlia House and penny poker games for several years before he got hold of himself. There weren't casinos to go to back in the day, but a gambling man can always find something to bet on. One saving grace was that he never bet on animals. Not horses or dogs. He thought racing was a wretched industry for the animals forced to perform.

"Thanks for your help." We left the pawnshop and strolled down the street while I called Cece. She and Millie had gone back to the hotel. They were relieved to hear from us. I almost called Grace, but it was moving on toward midnight and the town was beginning to look like it had fallen under the sleeping spell of a witch. Tomorrow morning was soon enough.

13

Sippi Salem was the first order of business for the new day. I put his address into GPS and also checked over his property from an aerial view. I found exactly what I was looking for. The property was gated and fenced with a wrought iron material that had spikes on the top. A little harsh for rural Mississippi, I thought. But then again, times had changed. The days of my childhood, where only screens were latched and often not even that, were far behind me. Coleman had given me a new awareness of the importance of taking basic steps for protection, and while he wasn't prone to overreacting, he did make me see how easily people could be hurt.

Tinkie and I rented a car and took off for the rural area where Sippi had his wilderness home and studio. I bypassed the road to the main gate and took a little pig trail through the dense woods. Just as Google Earth had shown, I found the place where the fence changed from wrought iron to field fencing. We lucked out that no barbed wire had been used. Field fencing was not a problem for a country girl to crawl over. Tinkie made it over safely, too.

We were giggling as we found a nice path that led in the direction of Sippi's abode. I didn't exactly view this as a covert operation. I intended to knock on his door.

Sippi's house reminded me a bit of the witch's place in *Hansel and Gretel*. The shake cedar shingles, the board-and-batten exterior painted in candy shades, each board different, and the magical colored lights and figurines tucked everywhere. Elves! It reminded me of my childhood fantasies, and I found it delightful—and a bit eccentric.

"He's an artist," Tinkie said. "I wish I had an imagination like that, where I could believe in fairy tales and fancies the way a child does. I'm already reading the classics to Maylin." The wistfulness in her voice told me yet again how much she missed her baby.

"Oscar and that bundle of joy will be here shortly. You'll bliss out, I'm sure. Just remember we're counting on you for the competition."

"Oh, I'll be ready. Wild horses couldn't drag me away."

No, but a fifteen-pound bouncing baby girl could! I knocked on Sippi's wooden door hard and long. I suspected he knew we were on his front porch and he would ignore us if he could.

To my surprise, the door swung open. Tinkie gasped. I swallowed whatever words I'd meant to say with a big gulp. No one had prepared us for Sippi. He wore a fake-fur loincloth that barely covered everything necessary. His chest was spectacular—sculpted and bronzed—and his long blond hair hung down to his shoulders. He was a sun-god. No wonder the ladies of Lee County and much farther afield couldn't get enough of him.

"Who are you and how did you get in here?" he asked.

"We're private investigators, and we're here to talk to you about the Elvis belt you created for Grace Land. It's been stolen, in case you haven't heard."

"Oh, I've heard. It has nothing to do with me. Maybe Grace's Karma just arrived."

"I would think you would care about something you made." Tinkie frowned.

"I care about things I'm paid to care about," he said, and when he stepped out onto the porch, I realized his eyes were a shade of emerald I'd never seen before.

"Do you have any idea who might want to steal Grace's belt?" I had to focus on my job.

"Have you met Grace?" he asked drolly.

"We have, and I realize she can be difficult, but no one has the right to steal from another." Tinkie had her hands on her hips.

Sippi laughed, and it was a genuine sound of mirth. "Well, aren't you cute."

Tinkie flushed. I'd never seen her at a loss. She was the master manipulator of men, the woman who could twist the brawniest of men around her little finger and get anything she wanted. Sippi had caught her flat-footed.

"How did you get your name?" I asked the artist. This information wasn't pertinent to my case, and I already knew the answer, but my train of thought had been derailed by his overwhelming physical presence. The man had unnerved me, too.

"I was named for my home state. I just shortened it. Too many i's and s's to write out the long way. Would you ladies like a drink?" he asked.

It wasn't even ten o'clock. "Coffee would be lovely," I said.

He grinned and waved us into the house. I wanted to walk behind him. The loincloth revealed a long length of thigh and hip whenever he walked. Tinkie kept looking back over her shoulder and I knew exactly what she was looking at.

"Would you like a caftan to wear?" Sippi asked. "You can change while I put the coffee on. It's a rare treat to have two such lovely women here. Perhaps I could photograph you for a painting?"

"A nude?" Tinkie asked, revealing exactly where her thoughts had gone.

"If you would like that." Sippi's smile was secretive and open all at once. He was a walking contradiction in so many ways.

"Oh, no! I didn't mean . . ." Tinkie turned even redder and stopped talking.

"We couldn't afford one of your paintings," I said, trying to get us both over the reaction we were having to Sippi.

"We might be able to work out a deal."

I'd heard the saying before that he undressed me with his eyes. I'd never understood how potent that could be. Sippi was sex on two legs. Everything about him screamed it. The man knew the way he affected women, and he was having a blast. I had to get this on a more professional level and fast.

"Who are your enemies?" I asked him, pulling a pad from my back pocket. Writing things down would help me focus on my work instead of the cut of his hip just above the loincloth.

"Number one on the list would likely be Grace."

"Why?"

"She cheated me, and I haven't taken it laying down. She said she was going to sue me for slander, but truth is my defense. Once upon a time I thought the truth mattered to Grace."

"But you were once close."

"Haven't you always heard that love and hate are just two sides of the same coin?" he asked.

I had. If there was a maxim written or spoken, I'd heard it from my aunt Loulane. "Who else?" I had to focus on my notebook. Looking at Sippi was very dangerous.

"Krystal Bond hates me. And so do those idiotic Manning twins."

"Sherman and Wilbur?"

"When I had an exhibition of my work at a local gallery, they attempted to deface one of my paintings."

"Wow. That's nuts." I nudged Tinkie with my toe. She was standing beside me in a daze.

"Yes, that's terrible." Tinkie startled back to reality. "Did they say why?"

"It was a nude of Sherman's wife. How was I to know she hadn't told him she was modeling for me? They divorced shortly thereafter."

Oh, I could see why that would stir fire in Sherman's heart. "Anyone else?"

He listed fifteen names in rapid succession: folks I'd never heard of.

"Is there anyone in town who likes you?" Tinkie asked.

"Allan Malone loves my work. And to be honest, the

local politicians love that I live here. Elvis is dead but I'm alive."

And I would bet he could put on a show if he wanted to. "Who do you think would want to hurt Grace by stealing that belt?"

"That woman is a train wreck in action. The easier question would be, who do I know who *wouldn't* want to screw her over."

He hurried into the kitchen to pour coffee for us, which he brought on a tray. I had a moment to take in his place. There were nude paintings and sculptures everywhere. A few were just weird, but most of them were beautiful. It was about form, not nudity. Even I could see that.

"Kent Madison has it in for her. I heard rumors back in the fall that he was trying to hire a hit man to take her out."

"Are you serious?" Tinkie asked.

"Yes."

Sippi's Apollo-esque features revealed nothing. I could only hope he was kidding.

"I heard that Grace had launched an all-out war on Kent and was determined to get him fired from the city," Sippi continued. "That assistant mayor's position is a cushy job. Go to meetings and be pleasant. That's about it. Kent didn't want to lose it, and Grace is like a woodpecker drilling into the back of your head. She just won't stop. Maybe he didn't hire a hit man, but he sure as hell wouldn't cry if Grace met a bitter fate."

That I did believe. Grace had a talent for making people want to have her knocked off. But I hadn't come to discuss Grace's popularity, or lack thereof. "What do you think happened to the belt?"

The little imp of malice left Sippi's eyes. "I don't know.

As much as I hate what Grace did to me, and so many others, I could never steal or destroy a work of art that I created. I don't know who took it."

I glanced at Tinkie and she nodded. We both believed him—up to a point. The truth was that if Sippi was behind the theft, he would have to be an accomplice in the destruction of the belt he created. The belt would have to be broken down, the gold melted, the jewels reset in other pieces. The Elvis belt that had garnered so much attention for Sippi would be no more. I felt Sippi's artistic ego would never allow him to participate in such a turn of events.

"Would Kent jeopardize his job by stealing an artistic display on city property? You know since Grace failed to have insurance on the belt, her next step will likely be to sue the city."

"She didn't have insurance?" For the first time Sippi looked concerned. "None?"

"Not one penny."

"That is bad for her. And for Tupelo."

"While we're here, would you mind if we looked around?" Tinkie asked. She was tired of dancing around the elephant in the room.

"Are you insinuating the belt is here? And that I would be so addlebrained as to leave it in plain sight if it were here? I'm offended. I'm neither a thief nor stupid."

"We're here. If you've nothing to hide, let us take a look-see."

He waved a hand. "Go for it. Open all the doors, look under the beds. Wear yourselves out."

I doubted the belt was here; Sippi also owned other properties. But it made sense to tick this one off the list if we could. I took the back bedrooms while Tinkie searched the kitchen. The house was amazingly clean. Not even a dust bunny under the bed. Either Sippi had professional cleaning help or he was OCD about dust.

Just as we made it back to the living room, the buzzer on the front gate sounded. It was wired right into Sippi's house. A little screen beside the front door clicked on and I realized there was a camera set to reveal whoever was at the gate. Big shocker—it was Kent Madison. He punched the gate button again and said, "Sippi, open this damn gate. We have to talk. Those private investigators are onto us."

Sippi hit the button. "Shut up and get up here." He pressed the button to open the gate. Less than ten minutes later, Kent was at the front door. Sippi opened it and ushered him in. When he saw us, his expression was priceless.

"What are they doing here?" he demanded. He whipped around to confront Sippi. "Did you set me up? What are you trying to do?"

"Shut up," Sippi said, rolling his eyes. "You are an imbecile."

"Interesting that you'd immediately jump to the fact that Sippi set you up," Tinkie said, walking around Kent and giving him a long once-over. "What do you have to hide?"

"Not a damn thing." Kent straightened his tie. He was all dressed up, meaning he probably should be at work. So why was he out here at Sippi's hurling accusations of a setup?

"I told you not to contact me," Sippi said. "You are your own worst enemy, Kent."

Kent flushed red, then white. "You did this on purpose, Sippi. You could have told me on the gate speaker that those two were here and listening to every word we said. Yet you let me talk and then come down here to spring all of this on me."

"You didn't give me a chance to tell you anything. You were jawboning and yapping like a terrier in heat. You do whatever you want whenever you want to do it. And now you're hoist with your own petard. And of course you want to blame someone other than yourself. Well, it won't work this time. If you took the Elvis belt, you need to come clean and give it back."

Tinkie and I were flabbergasted by the turn of events. I hadn't expected Sippi to champion the cause of finding and returning the belt. Or of throwing a local Tupeloan under the bus. But that was exactly what he'd done. Could he have warned Kent to shut up before he implicated himself in the theft? I couldn't say for certain. But Sippi hadn't even tried. It was something to ponder.

"I need to speak with you alone," Kent almost hissed to Sippi. He did look like an angry snake, and he was shaking his metaphorical rattles. It was time for Tinkie and me to press harder. We'd learned a lot—and it was delicious.

"We have some questions for you, Madison," I said.

Sippi grasped Tinkie's hand. "Help me in the kitchen, please." He was barely able to control his smile.

"Hold on, there," Kent said. "You can't just walk out and leave me holding the bag here."

"He can and he did," I said. Sippi pulled Tinkie into the kitchen and closed the door, effectively leaving Kent Madison there for me to exsanguinate. "If you return the belt, I'll speak with Grace Land about recommending leniency on your behalf."

"Screw you and Grace. I don't want her help or yours. I didn't steal the belt."

"Who did?"

He pointed at the closed kitchen door. "Ask the narcissist.

He tried to talk me into stealing it, but when I wouldn't, he did it himself. He said it was his creation and he deserved to have it."

This was very interesting. "Were you with him when he stole it?"

"Are you insane? If I were, do you think I'd admit it?"

"We've searched his house. The belt isn't here."

"Like he would have it here. Damn, you are not very bright, are you?"

Oh, I could see why Grace had grown to hate this guy. He was smug and loud. A bad combo. "I'm smart enough to know you've confessed to conspiracy to steal a three-million-dollar piece of art. I'm sure Chief Johnson will be eager to learn this."

"I didn't steal anything. Besides, Sippi and I weren't going to really steal it, we were just going to give Grace a bad day or two. We didn't get a chance to act, though. The belt was stolen before we had a chance to get it."

Sippi and Tinkie had returned to the room, and Sippi was glowering at Madison. "Can you shut your giant piehole, Kent?" he said. "You've just confessed to something that could get us both put in jail."

"Thinking of a crime is not the same as committing it." Kent looked to Tinkie for verification. "Right?"

"Not sure about that," Tinkie said. "You two would have stolen the belt just to torment Grace? You would have risked a ten-year stretch in Parchman prison just to mash a bruise on Grace? Are you morons?"

"I'm obviously a moron because I have friends like Kent." Sippi leaned against the doorframe. "We didn't steal the belt, though it would have been a grand prank. But we didn't do it. Now you ladies need to leave. Unless you want to do some modeling for me. I have to work. Kent, you go with them."

"Thanks, Sippi," I said as Tinkie and I moved to the door. "We know when we should take our leave." I grinned.

"Yeah, we got what we came for." Tinkie looked at Kent. "Mr. Madison, I'm sure Chief Johnson will want to talk to you. Sippi, I wouldn't leave town."

"You're misinterpreting what you heard," Kent said. "You can't do that."

"See you soon." I opened the front door, and we stepped out. No one had even asked us where our car was. Interesting. We cut around the house and stomped back through the woods to where we'd parked. In no time, we were over the fence and on our way back to Tupelo. I needed to check in with Yuma and talk to Grace. Again. Why did we always have clients who withheld things from us? Grace was holding some cards close to her chest, and we needed to see them.

14

"Why should I tell you about the men I slept with?" Grace asked. She'd finally left her bed and was floating around her kitchen in red silk pajamas.

"I'm not nearly as interested in your sex life as I am in the payment of your bills," I said. I was annoyed. "Did you pay Sippi for creating the belt or not?"

"Why do you care?" she asked.

"It goes to motive." I was weary of wrangling with her. "If he felt the belt was his because of lack of payment, he is a bigger suspect than if you've paid him and he has no claim."

She looked down at the floor, that vulnerable expression in her eyes. "Well, I didn't pay him, and he still has no claim. We were lovers. He crafted the belt for me as a gift.

Now he wants to go back on his word and make out like he's been cheated. I call bullshit."

Tinkie snorted. She sat in a chair at a small kitchen table and regally waved Grace to another chair. "Sit down. We need some answers. Pronto."

Grace threw us a wary look, but she sat.

"Tell us everyone in the area that you've wronged or cheated or done something to who might want revenge."

"Oh, dear." Grace put the back of her hand to her forehead like Nell about to be tied to the railroad tracks. "I couldn't possibly do that."

Tinkie stood up. "Okay, we'll keep half the retainer you paid us for the work we've finished, and we're done. We came for a holiday and only took your case because we felt bad for you. Enough already. We're finished."

I stood up, too, following Tinkie's lead.

"Wait!" Grace jumped to her feet and got a pad and pen out of a kitchen drawer. "I'll make a list. It's just . . . I don't want anyone hurt by gossip for being associated with me. Folks around here don't like me."

Tinkie grinned and gave me a thumbs-up. "We don't care who or what you've done, but we need to know the facts so we can investigate fully. If you hope to recover that belt, we have to determine if it was taken in an act of revenge, simple robbery, or by someone who really wants to hurt you."

"What difference does motive make?" Grace asked.

"It'll help us prioritize potential suspects and also figure out where the belt might be. Someone who just wants to hurt you might not be opposed to destroying the artistic value of the belt or even keeping it to gloat over." Tinkie explained the situation with more patience than I had. "Or if it's just for the money, that sets up another scenario for where the belt might be."

"So, if Sippi took the belt, you suspect he wouldn't harm it?" she asked.

"Something like that." I wasn't certain Sippi wouldn't melt it down just to spite Grace, but I didn't say that.

"If a professional thief took it, there's a chance it will be offered on the black market to a buyer. We can focus on all of the possibilities, but time is crucial and if we can prioritize, we will have better success."

"I hadn't thought of it that way." Grace clicked her pen on. "Let me get busy."

In a few minutes, she handed us a paper with a list of ten names. At the top was Kent Madison, followed by the Manning brothers, Allan Malone, Krystal Bond, three women I didn't know, Sippi, and another man I wasn't familiar with.

"The three women?" I asked.

"I slept with their husbands. They were torn up. Honestly, why were they mad at me? I wasn't the one cheating on them. And they were all separated at the time. I'm not a homewrecker."

I didn't think I could make Grace understand why she might be in the crosshairs of a jealous wife, so I didn't waste my breath. She told me the addresses and I jotted them down. Simple enough to stop by and ask a few questions, though I doubted a jealous wife would orchestrate a broad daylight grand theft jewelry heist. She'd be more likely to stage a public hair pulling with maybe a tar-and-feathering component added in. But what did I really know about the women Grace had named? Not much, but I would find out a lot more.

"Kent was at Sippi's," Tinkie said.

"What?" Grace was shocked and didn't bother to hide it. "Why was he there?"

"Exactly what we'd like to know. Do you think the two of them could be working together?" I asked. We knew they'd hatched a harebrained scheme together, but I was curious how Grace might read their relationship.

Grace gave it some thought. "I would never have thought they'd be friends. I mean, Sippi is . . . extraordinary. Kent is shallow and a boor. He wouldn't know art if it fell on his head. They have nothing in common."

"Except they both dislike you," Tinkie said.

"Well, there is that, but that's hardly a bond between two men who live in different worlds. Kent is Mr. Chamber of Commerce, and he wants to be a mover and shaker. Sippi is a man who lives through sensual experience. His stature as a beloved artist affords him a lifestyle of great pleasure. They may hate me, but Sippi would hate Kent just as much because of his . . . values. Kent would sell his soul for political power. And then he would abuse it."

She seemed to have a good handle on who and what Kent was. Was she as clear about who Sippi was? I couldn't judge her reaction. "Grace, when do you have to go back to Hollywood for your reality TV show?" I asked.

"I should have gone back this week, but I pushed it until after the New Year. I wanted to be home in Tupelo for Christmas this time." She bit her lower lip in concentration. "The truth is, I'm bored with the show. You probably think I'm shallow, but the contestants on my show are dumber than a box of rocks. I show those women how to twist their boyfriends into knots—and they love doing it. No matter how cruel or ridiculous it is. It's shameful what someone will do to be on TV."

How she manipulated people was not my business. "Would any of the contestants want to hurt you?"

She nodded. "Probably. The thing is, I doubt they'd be able to find Tupelo. They can't find their butt with both hands."

I wondered if her contempt was as clear on the show. Yikes! "Make a list, please. At least we can call around to make sure they're not in this area. And, Grace, keep in mind that each hour that passes makes it more likely that the belt is gone forever." The list would create more legwork, but it was always good to check out any possibility.

"Is all of this really necessary?" Grace had mastered the pout.

"Someone tried to harm you—probably kill you—by messing with your car. Someone is here, in Tupelo, and they mean you real harm. This isn't a game. It isn't even about a valuable piece of art. It's about your life." I didn't believe Grace was taking her situation seriously.

"People have hated me my whole life," Grace said. "Some days I think even my mama hated me, giving me this name. From the first day of kindergarten, I was viewed as an entitled little princess who believed she was special. Believe me, I didn't feel special at all."

Grace had plenty of annoying habits and behaviors, but I felt sorry for her. "I'm sure she thought it was a glamorous name you'd love."

"Yeah, you should have to live with the name Tinkie," my partner spoke up.

She had a point. But because Tinkie was kind, mostly,

folks hadn't turned on her. Grace had a talent for setting people's teeth on edge. "Look, we all live with things we can't control. Let's focus on who might want to take action against you."

Grace handed over another sheet of paper with another dozen names on it. "The names of contestants on the show who might have a grudge against me."

"Because?" Tinkie asked.

"Their engagements ended. Either the men got fed up with being bullied or the women realized the future held only work." She shrugged. "If you ask me, I saved some of them a world of grief, but they don't always feel that way, you know?"

I didn't know, but I could easily imagine. New love could be tender. Stomping on it and digging it up could lead to the death of romance, and Grace Land seemed to be a pro at clogging on top of other people's feelings.

"We'll check out these names." I held up both lists. "Stay home if you can," I warned Grace.

"I'm coming to the dance moves competition tonight. I'm responsible for this whole Christmas event. The city would have passed on it had I not agreed to oversee and orchestrate."

"They won't be able to thank you if you're dead," Tinkie pointed out. She was losing patience with Grace fast.

"I will not be frightened—"

Her doorbell rang and she flitted out of the kitchen, her red pajamas making a bold statement as she rushed to open the door.

"What!" She stepped back quickly from the door. Just before a whirl of energy grabbed for her ankles with a deep-throated bark.

15

"Avery Wynette, stop that!" Allan Malone stood in the doorway with the other pug in his arms. Avery ignored him. She was in hot pursuit of Grace, who ran into the parlor and jumped up on a chair. The little dog whirled and turned around the chair, making threatening jumps at Grace's feet.

Allan Malone rushed into the house and attempted to soothe the pug in his arms and catch the one creating mayhem. He looked at me. "Avery just adores everyone she meets. I've never seen her behave this way before. She wants to tear Grace's toes off."

In truth, Avery Wynette had such a severe underbite I didn't believe she could do any damage to anyone. But she sure made it look like she was in a murderous rage. I picked up the dog and Tinkie gave Grace a hand down off the chair.

"Put those little monsters on leashes," Grace demanded. "Or better yet, take them out of my home and you go, too!"

"I need a word with you, Grace." He took in her pajamas with a sneer. "If you're ever going to get out of bed and do your job here."

I thought the top of Grace's head would explode. She rounded on Allan. "Get out of my house, you impostor. You aren't a real Tupeloan. You're really from Amory! I know all about you coming here pretending, saying all kinds of untrue things on your reality show. And let me just add, who gives a hot damn about who is singing Barbra Streisand these days?"

Allan drew himself up and stared at her. "Blasphemy! Barbra is beloved by millions. Those with taste and an understanding of true talent. No wonder you don't care for her."

Before any of us could react, Allan stooped to put both dogs on the floor. "Get 'er!" he commanded.

Avery Wynette and Lovely Katherine were on Grace like white on rice. She leaped back on top of the chair and pointed at me and Tinkie. "Save me. Get those four-legged monsters out of my house. And put Allan out, while you're at it."

I felt no compulsion to obey Grace, but I couldn't ask Allan any questions while the dogs were in a frenzy of barking. One of them had a bark pitched at an intensity that felt like an ice pick in my ear.

I took Allan's arm and gently urged him toward the door. As soon as he stepped outside, the dogs and I followed, and I shut the door so Tinkie could calm Grace. She'd likely take to her bed again just to play the drama queen.

"What are you doing here?" I asked him.

"It's none of your business."

"You made it my business. Now tell me or I'll call Chief

Johnson and tell him those dogs are vicious and a danger. I hope they're up to date on their rabies shots." I had no intention of doing any such thing, but he didn't know that.

"I have information about who stole the Elvis belt." Allan drew himself up to his full six-foot-three height. "And I wanted to invite that friend of yours, Cece, to sing on my show. Someone said she was probably here with you. I've heard Cece can really belt out a tune. She was singing with one of the Elvises in front of a café this morning. They said she was stupendous."

I was thrilled for Cece, who would totally love the idea of being on Allan Malone's TV show. Plus, it would give her some leverage with her boss, Ed Oakes, to ask for a raise. "Cece isn't here at Grace's, but I'll tell her you're looking for her. But who took the belt?"

"Why should I tell you?" Allan asked.

I wanted to punch him in the nose. "Allan, spill the beans. Now. Don't make me any more irritated than I am."

"It was Sonja Rivera. She stole it."

"What? The Priscilla look-alike?" That seemed to come out of left field. "Why do you say that?"

Allan picked up his two pugs and snuggled them against his chest. The dogs sighed with pleasure. "I know because I heard her confess it."

"She just blurted it out?" My inner skeptic was screaming.

"She was talking on the phone with one of her friends. She didn't realize I was right behind her." He didn't meet my gaze.

I watched his face. "Tell me exactly what she said."

"Well, I didn't record it, but I'll do my best."

"Good enough."

"She was sitting on the bench outside of the Arena Center

this morning, smoking a cigarette." He made a face. "Anyway, I was walking my girls and I heard her talking."

And he no doubt listened because he was a nosy parker. Which was good for me! The problem with Allan and his information was that it was just a tad too convenient. "Go ahead, what did she say?"

"She was saying how Grace had never paid Sippi for the work he did creating the belt, and you have to admit that the design is what makes the belt so spectacular, right?"

The belt was patterned on the one Elvis wore in Vegas, but Sippi had added his own unique design touches; the dozens of jewels and 14 karat gold went a long way to making the belt special. "Keep talking," I prompted.

"You know the belt was created so that it could expand and contract—or at least appear to do so."

I didn't know anything of the sort, but I wasn't there to discuss jewelry design. "What else did Sonja say?"

"She was saying that a lot of people thought Sippi had taken the belt but that it wasn't true, and she knew that for a fact because she knew who had the belt."

Now I paid strict attention.

"Sonja said that she disarmed the video cameras, the lasers, and the alarms and took it. She said that Kent Madison had given her all the codes and told her how to do it. She gave the belt to him, and he was going to cash it in, and they would split the money."

"She said all of that?"

"Well, not exactly in those words."

Oh, boy. Just as I had suspected. Allan was making his story up out of whole cloth. "What exactly did she say?"

"She said Grace deserved everything that happened to her and that she hoped whoever had the belt sold it for a fortune."

I wanted to wring his neck. "You are a blowhard. You never heard any of this. You are just making up tall tales."

"I am not. I'm just good at telling people what they want to hear."

"You didn't overhear Sonja say anything, did you?" I wondered if he could see the lust for mayhem in my eyes. He was too tall and strong for me to kill him, but I could probably break a few fingers. "What did Sonja actually say?"

"I don't know who she was talking to, but she said that a local Tupeloan had committed the robbery."

"How did she know?"

He shrugged. "Ask her."

That would be the only way to get to the truth of what had been said. I would indeed ask her. Allan was just bluffing. Did he need to be the center of attention, like Grace did? Or was he trying to obstruct the investigation? I couldn't determine. "Why did you pretend to know more than you know?" I asked. I didn't expect an answer, but when he spoke, I listened.

"I want to help. I don't like Grace. I really don't. But I love the whole Elvis thing and I love my hometown of Tupelo. I want this stain on the town's reputation to be over, the belt found and returned, and the focus back on the Elvis impersonators and the remarkable legacy Elvis Aaron Presley left behind. This whole belt incident has tarnished Elvis's legacy. It must be stopped."

I didn't doubt Allan's devotion to Elvis—and Barbra. But he wasn't helping by trying to fudge the truth and put the blame on a possibly innocent person. "Tell me one more time. What did you really overhear?"

He made a face. "Nothing of any real importance." He kissed the dogs and put them on the ground. "Avery and

Katherine like Sonja. They have impeccable instincts about people. I shouldn't have maligned her."

At least Allan knew how to apologize. Sort of. "It's okay. Do you know anything that can help us find the belt—or the culprit?"

"I really don't. I'd help you if I could."

"If you had to name one suspect, who would it be?" I asked.

"Have you ever considered that maybe Grace stole the belt from herself?"

"But it isn't even insured. If there had been a big payout, I might have believed that was a possibility. As it is, she's out millions."

"There's another way to look at it."

I arched my eyebrows.

"If Grace stole the belt from herself, she could wait as long as necessary, cut the belt into pieces, sell the jewels and gold for market value, a little at a time. She'd have the rest of her life to feather her own nest."

"Still, without insurance—"

"She can't be charged with fraud. There's really no crime in stealing from yourself, is there? It's the perfect Grace scenario. She gets the money from selling the belt and she gets to be a victim."

I'd have to ask Coleman about this angle. "She'd be liable for the resources expended in searching for the thief and the belt."

"I don't see Chief Johnson tearing up the county trying to find the thief, do you? So far, the only money going out is to you and your partner. And let me say that whatever your retainer is, it can't compare to three million dollars in gold and jewels, and likely more if it's broken into smaller parcels and sold over the span of several years."

The man had a point. One I didn't like to hear, but one I had to now consider. "I'll take this up with Yuma," I said.

"Don't!" Allan held up both hands. "If he's in this with Grace, you'll only put him on notice."

"You have reason to believe Yuma is in on this with Grace?" Well, damn. He had a point that I couldn't argue against. Yuma certainly hadn't hustled to help find the belt or the thief. He'd been mighty laid back, not even bothering to search Sippi's property or bring him in for questioning. In fact, he hadn't brought anyone in for an interview. Was he part of the theft?

"You're smart." Allan's blue gaze was laser sharp. "You know what I'm saying is true."

"I know it *could* be true. And that's enough not to tip Yuma off. Yet." Coleman needed to get up here and fast. I needed his law enforcement expertise before I believed Yuma was corrupt.

Allan patted my shoulder. "I knew you'd see reason." He looked back at the front door of Grace Land's home. "Let's go back inside."

"I don't think so." At least Allan still had his jacket on. I was shivering. "Grace hates those dogs. She's afraid of them." I knelt and called them over to me. They were adorable little terrorists—my favorite kind of dog. I had a keen longing for Sweetie Pie, Pluto, and that crazy bird, Poe, not to mention Tinkie's little dust mop Chablis. I knew they were well cared for, but I missed their antics. Add the horses on top of that—I missed them, too. But I would be home soon enough.

"Grace hates everything that isn't Grace."

He'd made some good points for his theory, but like every other theory I'd come up with, there was no evidence to support it. And the lack of insurance on the belt made the whole explanation implausible. Grace owned the belt—she could see it whenever she wanted. "What do you know about Kent Madison?" I asked.

He made a face and shrugged. "Kent's obsessed with money and power. He'd sell his kid for medical research if he could make a dime from it."

"That's harsh."

"But true." He grinned. "Ask Grace. She has an . . . opinion about Kent."

"She's shared that with me," I said. "Did you see Kent around the belt the day it was taken?"

"Everyone was there looking at it. Few people had ever seen it. Grace had brains enough to keep it out of the public eye, until now. She just couldn't resist showing off. Grace perpetually underestimates the people who would delight in ruining her if they could."

"Is Krystal Bond one of those people?" She was still blipping on my radar of prime suspects.

"Oh, Krystal is a wicked piece of work," Allan said. "She's as bad as Grace."

I was freezing to death without a jacket and I'd learned all Allan would tell me. "I'll tell Grace you left," I said tactfully as I headed toward the front door.

"Tell her I said to kiss my grits," Allan responded. He whistled up his dogs and walked down the block.

16

Tinkie came out of the house in such haste she almost bowled me over.

"What's wrong?"

"I have to leave before I throttle the life out of her."

I put my arm around Tinkie's shoulders and gave her a squeeze. "I have to get my jacket and we can go."

"Leave it. I'll buy you a new one. Nothing is worth going back into that den of narcissism. I feel bad for Grace, I do. She's delusional. She insists no one in Tupelo would steal her belt. Duh! It's already happened."

I only laughed and went inside, scooped up my jacket, and yelled a goodbye. Before Grace could respond, I slammed the front door behind me. "We're off." And we were high-stepping it away before she could come out to stop us.

"Allan thinks Grace may have arranged the theft herself." I gave my partner his reasoning.

"I hate to admit it, but there's some merit to what he's saying, except for the lack of insurance on it. Grace technically gets nothing for stealing from herself."

"I know."

"Grace could be a scoundrel," Tinkie said.

"I know."

"Do you want to drop the case?" Tinkie asked.

"Not for all the tea in China."

"That's what I love about you, Sarah Booth. You're mad as a hatter."

"And you're the Queen of Hearts."

"Off with their heads." Tinkie was all about *Alice in Wonderland* since Maylin had been born. The bookshelves in the nursery at Hilltop were jam-packed with the best of children's literature. Maylin would be exposed to the best literary classics, music, and movies. It was the educational experience that should be the birthright of every child.

"You look pensive," Tinkie said.

"I was thinking of how lucky Maylin is to have you and Oscar for parents. She'll grow up with every advantage."

"She will. But she will not be spoiled or prissy. I want her to be like you, Sarah Booth, independent and able to enjoy life. I want her to ride and dance and swim—to do all the activities that open doors to a healthy life."

Tinkie had been raised never to get dirty, never to risk a bruise or injury. I was proud of her for staking out a bigger terrain for Maylin. "You're the best mom. I don't say it enough, but I admire you, Tinkie. You put your heart at risk every day, and you do it without ever showing how scared you must be."

"Fear is contagious, Sarah Booth. I refuse to bequeath that to Maylin. She will be healthy and strong and able to fend for herself. Because I admire you, I want her to be like you."

Tears stung my eyes, and I blinked them away. "Thanks, partner. Now let's go round up some bad guys so we can play with Maylin when she gets here."

"It won't be long now before the baby delivery arrives. And just for you, Oscar is bringing Sweetie Pie, Pluto, and Chablis. Harold found a weekend rental that allows pets, and he's bringing Roscoe, too, and he's volunteered to take care of all the critters. Harold is going to bach it until Janet arrives."

I grinned, thinking how much fun Harold would have with his girlfriend, Janet, the hot, hot, hot romance writer. "We may not make it home for Christmas if Roscoe acts out. We'll all be in jail."

"I hadn't thought of that. It would be just like that terrible dog to pee on the Elvis impersonators."

We both laughed as we headed to the rental car Tinkie had arranged. Time was short and we had much to do.

This was our last opportunity to find some substantial leads before the men, dogs, and baby arrived. Sweetie Pie and Chablis were good as gold, but Roscoe could be awful. The good news was that it was up to Harold to keep the little scamp in line. And I did love a bad dog. Roscoe acted in a way that gave me wish fulfillment. He'd never peed on anyone who didn't deserve a lot worse. Often it was like the dogs knew when and how to create a diversion that would allow Tinkie and me to investigate. Pluto and Poe were no slouches in that department, either.

"Where to first?" Tinkie asked as I drove through town.

"Krystal Bond. We need to break her. She knows a lot more than she's been telling us."

"Any plans on how to do that? Krystal is tough, all the way down to her diamond-studded toenails."

I hadn't seen Krystal's toenails, but I never doubted Tinkie. When it came to accessorizing, she had an eagle eye. "I do have a plan."

"What?"

"We're going to lie."

Tinkie threw her hands up in mock horror. "Oh, why didn't I think of that perfect solution."

I had to laugh. She was right. We needed just the right lie to wedge a crack in Krystal's steel-jawed self-confidence. We had to lie about something she'd done but wasn't aware anyone knew about. Which meant it was going to have to be a guess, a gut instinct, a gift from the angels or however a person wanted to view it. And, most importantly, an accurate guess.

As we drove, we tossed around a few ideas about trying to settle on which direction to go in. Finally, we came up with what we thought was our best bet.

We parked at the strip mall where the insurance office was, and we went in the door.

I stepped back to the door and locked it. The bolt going into place made a loud sound.

"What do you think you're doing?" Krystal asked, haughty as ever.

"Making sure we aren't disturbed," I answered. "Your buddy Allan won't come to the rescue today and you have some answers to give me."

She picked up the phone on her desk. "I'm calling Yuma right now. You're trespassing."

"Call him," Tinkie said. "Please, call him."

Her challenge hung in the air as Krystal assessed us both. "What do you want?"

"You failed Grace as her insurer when you didn't notify her the payment was past due. Isn't that part of your job?"

"Not anymore. You haven't been paying attention, have you?" she sneered. "Insurance companies no longer want to write policies that don't make good profits. Grace had a bottom-line policy that I wrote for her when I was new in the business. As long as she renewed, we wouldn't cancel her. But since she missed a payment, it was in the best interest of my company to simply let it slide. If she still had the belt, we'd be happy to write her a new policy at a price that made it worth our time."

"And what about Grace's best interest?"

"I'm her insurance agent, not her freaking medical doctor. I look out for me, not her."

My fingers balled into fists, and I had a moment of intense pleasure as I imagined giving her a knuckle sandwich. Not because I wanted to take up for Grace, but just because Krystal epitomized the worst of the insurance business. Out for profit, with no regard for the people who paid premiums. Eventually, even the slowest citizen would catch on to this and demand better. Corporate profits should never trump service to the people who bought policies.

"Ethics conflict," Tinkie said softly. "You and your company could see some serious repercussions from this."

Tinkie was probably lying, but it was effective. Krystal paled.

"Especially if we can prove that you deliberately did this.

I have a forensic technology agent examining all of the information that Grace received prior to the belt being displayed and stolen. If she wasn't notified by email, text, or mail that her premium was due, I think you're going to be held accountable for this loss."

Was Tinkie blowing smoke? I couldn't tell. And neither could Krystal. She gripped the back of her chair and steadied herself.

"What do you want?" she demanded.

"Your alibi for the time the belt disappeared."

She sighed. "I was with Allan Malone. We were discussing what song he'd perform in the impersonator competition."

I had no doubt Allan would corroborate her alibi, whether it was a lie or not.

"Where did this occur?" Tinkie asked.

"We were at the . . ." Krystal looked flustered for a moment. "We were at the center when the belt disappeared, then we left. Look, this can't get out. Allan has a relationship and so do I. It's tricky."

Two cheaters hooking up only made me shake my head. They deserved each other if that was the case. But I wasn't the sex police, and I didn't want to be. "Can anyone verify this?"

She shook her head. "We went to a lot of trouble to make sure no one could verify it, if you get what I mean."

I just didn't see Allan and Krystal as a couple. They were polar opposites. But what did I know. I wouldn't have given anyone five dollars on a bet that Tinkie and Oscar would make it and would ultimately create the sweetest, smartest, most adorable baby on the planet.

"I'm going to be blunt, Krystal. I think what you did to

Grace borders on illegal. I don't like you. And I don't believe you. I think you know who took the belt and I want you to tell me before you get in even bigger trouble." I put it out there.

"I don't know any more than I told you." She eased toward the door, but Tinkie subtly blocked her escape. She was actually going to make a run for it. Like we were mafia thugs or something. The thought of that made me want to do something thuggish, but I didn't.

"You remind me of someone," Tinkie said, narrowing her eyes in thought. "I know. It's Grace. You and Grace Land are a lot alike."

That was too much for Krystal. She stood up tall. "How dare you? I am nothing like that witch."

Tinkie had had her fun. I had to calm things down if we were to learn anything from Krystal. Now, it was time for a swift change in direction. "I wonder how your other clients will react when they learn that you did nothing to protect Grace."

Krystal started to say something and snapped her jaw shut.

"That big, fancy lawyer from Memphis that Grace hired should be in town tomorrow," Tinkie said, proving to be a far better liar than even I was. "I heard she was going to hold a press conference just before the Elvis impersonation contest. That will get national coverage."

"She hired a lawyer?" Krystal looked green.

"Big name," Tinkie said. "I think he's with the Johnnie Cochran firm or some such."

I didn't know if there was such a thing, but it sounded formidable. Tinkie was a genius.

"The lawyer will be here tomorrow?" Krystal asked.

"I'm sure you'll hear from him later today or early tomorrow. I know he wants to talk with you about that canceled policy."

"I'm taking a vacation day. A few days. I won't be in the office."

"Oh, so you'll miss the big night of the Elvis competition?" I asked.

She looked around like a trapped rat. "I haven't decided if I'm staying home or leaving town."

"I'm sure that lawyer will be happy to accommodate you however he can." Tinkie smiled like a shark. "If you're leaving town, tell me where to find you, so I can tell him."

"I haven't decided."

"If you see Allan Malone, would you tell him the lawyer is also looking for him to take a deposition?"

Krystal inhaled, her nostrils flaring. "Sure, I'll do that."

More like she'd warn him to get out of town. "Do you think those pugs could pick up the scent of the thief?" I asked.

"Avery Wynette and Lovely Katherine are useless at dog tricks," Krystal said. "They're Allan's pampered children. They don't do dog."

"Good to know. My hound dog will be here tomorrow, along with Tinkie's pup. They're excellent at following a trail. Even a cold one. Keen noses. I'm sure you've heard how they help us solve cases. I'll bet they can pick up the scent of the thief at the display case. Then we'll just have to follow them back to the criminals."

"I see." Krystal edged even closer to the door.

"You seem to be in a hurry to get somewhere," I said, unlocking the door. "We'll be in touch."

I had a new plan. My intention was to follow Krystal when she left her office to see where she went. It was at least a lead.

17

It was hard to tail someone in Tupelo without a car—we shouldn't have turned the rental car back in. Coleman would soon be in Tupelo with my vehicle—and Sweetie Pie. But that didn't help me and Tinkie today. If Krystal decided to drive, we could never follow her. It was sheer luck that she flew out of her office, locked the door, and dashed down the street on foot.

We followed, darting into doorways and behind cars. Once Krystal stopped and looked behind her. Tinkie and I tucked into an alley by a dress shop. When the coast was clear, Tinkie fell prey to window shopping. I almost had to yank her down the street after Krystal.

"But that's the perfect red velvet dress for Christmas Eve dinner at Harold's," Tinkie protested as I hustled her away from the shop. "And, did you see, they had a matching dress for a baby. It would be perfect for me and Maylin!"

"Fashion can wait," I told her, heading off after Krystal at a brisk pace. The insurance agent was fast! Like she'd been training as a racewalker. Even though Tinkie took two strides to one of mine, she was fast, too. Once she started moving, I had to hustle to keep up with her.

"Where is she going?" Tinkie asked, huffing as she talked. Wherever it was, she was intent on getting there—and setting a land speed record.

"I don't know this town, so I can't even guess," I told her.

"Call Millie and ask her to meet us with an Uber. Then we're going straight to rent another car." Tinkie wasn't all that fond of working up a sweat in a footrace.

Renting a car was smart but unnecessary—which was why we'd returned the one we'd already rented. The men would be here soon, and Krystal was on foot. A vehicle wouldn't help, unless it was a golf cart or something of that nature. At this moment, disguises would be more helpful than a car. Maybe beards and slouch hats. I pushed that out of my head as I concentrated on pursuing our speed-walking suspect. Where in the world was Krystal going? We were going to run out of town soon. Thank goodness for all of the tourists milling about Tupelo. They gave us a little cover, but if she kept going, we'd lose that advantage.

At last Krystal ducked into a building. We slowed our roll and sauntered up to the door. It was an old-fashioned drugstore with a soda fountain. As we peeked through the window, we saw Krystal sitting on a red leather stool talking to a man behind the soda fountain. In a few moments, he gave her a tall glass of ice cream with a spoon and straw. An old-fashioned milkshake. Even though the wind cut around my body and snapped at my ears and nose, I suddenly craved ice cream.

"I'd kill for a Coke float or a chocolate malt," Tinkie said, voicing my sudden strong desire for a dairy treat. Or even nondairy, as long as I could cover it in chocolate syrup.

"After Krystal shows us what she's up to, we can get us something," I said. "I hope she leaves soon." I tugged my coat more snugly around me and Tinkie leaned into me to share some warmth.

"Why would she hustle down here like her tail was on fire only to sit alone at a soda fountain?"

I didn't have an answer—but a few minutes later I didn't need one. Kent Madison came from the back of the store to take a seat beside Krystal at the counter. She leaned over and kissed him long and hard on the mouth. It wasn't a friendly greeting. It was more of a mantis sucking the brain out of an insect or bird or snake. I'd seen a movie in high school science class that had scarred me for life. The praying mantis had grabbed a hummingbird with its strong front legs and was digging out the bird's brain. Any minute Kent's head might collapse.

"Hot damn, are *they* a couple?" Tinkie asked. "I thought she was sweet on Allan."

"Who knows, but if she doesn't quit sucking his face, they won't be a couple for long. She's going to inhale the marrow out of his bones if she keeps on. Nothing left but a husk. Like the cicada."

Tinkie snorted. "I doubt he'd object."

"Some men have no sense of self-preservation."

"Or some would rather go out in a blaze of sexual glory."

I tried not to laugh because my teeth were chattering. I

looked across the street at a gift shop. "Let's go in there. At least we'll be warmer."

"We'll miss what they're doing."

"There doesn't appear to be a lot of variety in their actions." They were still kissing. "But we'll see Krystal if she comes out." I was freezing. The temperature had dropped a good ten degrees since noon. It was going to be a brisk evening for the Elvis dance moves competition. Cece and Millie had come in second in the trivia contest, but they were determined to take first place in the dancing. I would put my money on them, too. They were highly motivated and had practiced for a month.

When I'd warmed up some, I left Tinkie buying some Christmas gifts while I ran across the street to check on Krystal. She'd never left the drugstore. When I looked in the window, the soda fountain area was empty. No Krystal. No Kent.

I went inside and took a seat. The soda jerk, wearing a white apron and hat just like in the 1950s, slid a menu to me. There were dozens of delicacies available, but my hankering for ice cream had disappeared along with Krystal.

"Did you happen to see where the blond woman who was in here went?"

He tossed his clean cloth over his shoulder and studied me. I pulled a twenty from my pocket and put it on the counter.

He arched his eyebrows.

I found another twenty and added it to the pot.

"She left with that guy she was kissing. I told them they needed to get a room. Man, that's just not proper public behavior. They went out the back. Where they went after that, I don't know."

"How long have they been gone?" I wanted to kick myself. I should have been more diligent.

"Maybe fifteen minutes. She finished her milkshake and they left."

"Did you happen to overhear anything they said?" I was stretching for this.

"Maybe."

I sighed and put a ten on the counter. "That's all the cash I have." I wasn't lying.

"They were talking about the jeweled Elvis belt that was stolen at the Arena Center."

"And?" I tapped the money. "I've paid up. Give me the details."

He shrugged. "She said she was a suspect and so was he. She said some private investigators had been bird-dogging her all over town. She said she was going to lead them on a merry chase tonight."

Krystal had caught on to Tinkie and me trailing her. We'd been careful, but not careful enough. But Krystal had also been careless in letting the soda jerk overhear her brags. Now, at least, we'd be prepared for a false flag operation this evening when we saw her.

"Did they say anything else?"

The clerk laughed out loud. "They barely came up for air. Talk wasn't their number one objective."

He had a point. "Anything else you recall?"

"Those two are up to something," he offered. "They didn't talk a lot, but they whispered and giggled like schoolkids." He shrugged. "Takes all kinds, right?"

"Right." I pushed the money to him and stood. "Thanks for your help."

I was at the door when he called out, "Oh, yeah, the woman said something about Sippi Salem."

"What did she say?"

"I didn't catch all of it, but that he'd be really glad when something was returned to him."

"Did she say what?"

"Nope."

"Thanks." I hurried out the door. Was it possible that Krystal knew where the Elvis belt was and planned to return it to Sippi? That would be one for the books.

Nothing would satisfy Tinkie except to stop at the dress shop on our walk back so she could purchase the red velvet for her and Maylin. They were beautiful dresses, and I didn't blame Tinkie one bit. We were supposed to be on vacation—not working a case. This Christmas client business was becoming a bad habit.

When she had her purchases, we walked back to the hotel and put them away.

I checked my watch. The dance moves contest, which would be held in the open area of the Arena Center, was on deck in under two hours. I called Cece and Millie and offered to lend a hand with makeup and hair. I popped over to the room they were sharing until Jaytee arrived. It looked like a bomb exploded, with clothes everywhere. I found shoes in the bathtub. "What the heck?" I asked.

"Costume change," Millie said. "We found some better clothes while we were shopping today."

I swallowed. I'd spent hours and hours with Cece putting together just the right look. All for naught, it would appear. "So, show me."

They disappeared into the bathroom, where shrieks and

giggles ensued. Whatever was going on, they were having a good time. I got a little bottle of Jack from the minibar and made a bourbon and water while I waited for the show.

When the bathroom door flew open, I was not disappointed. Millie and Cece, wearing summer skimmers, Cece red and Millie blue, and white go-go boots came prancing out of the bathroom. They'd styled their hair in bouffants reminiscent of my girlhood idol, Annette Funicello, except they were both blond.

Cece punched her phone to start the music, dropped it on the bed, and began a high-stepping pony dance. She and Millie played off each other, reminding me of John Travolta and Uma Thurman in *Pulp Fiction*. I couldn't take my eyes off them. They were totally compelling, and Jaytee's mastery of music was evident in the track he'd made them for dancing. It was a montage of Elvis hits with choreographed dance moves to go along with each one. Cece and Millie were the perfect dance team.

When they were done, I stood up and applauded. "Brava! Brava!"

They bowed and giggled.

"I'm putting money on you two winning tonight."

"What about you, Sarah Booth?" Millie said. "Coleman will be here in time. You two should cut a rug and have some fun."

I loved dancing, but I wasn't very good at it. And I knew my limits. "Looking at you two, I don't stand a chance. Besides, we want to watch you guys and cheer you on. I'm happy to be a spectator at this event."

"Chicken," Cece said.

I didn't deny it. I was happy to leave this competition

to the talented, and Cece and Millie had practiced their moves. It was going to be great.

There was a knock at the door and Tinkie arrived with bar service for the room. "Lynchburg Lemonade all around," she said. "I considered a hot drink, but—"

"This is perfect," I said. I wasn't a fan of hot alcoholic drinks. I grabbed a glass and passed it to Millie. Then I passed one to Cece. Finally, I took one as Tinkie claimed the last and settled onto the end of the bed.

"You look perfect," she said to the competitors, taking it all in. She ignored the clothes tossed everywhere. "The red and blue skimmer dresses with the go-go boots reflect the innocence of the time. Good job!" She raised her glass in a salute.

We each found a comfortable place to sit, and Millie asked us about the missing belt. "Any leads?"

We told them what we'd discovered so far, which was not a whole lot.

"Any luck with the police tracking down the person who ran Grace off the road?" Cece asked.

"No." I felt dejection hovering around the edges of my evening.

"But you managed to brace Sippi Salem," Millie said, trying to elevate our accomplishments.

"I wouldn't go that far," Tinkie said. "We talked to him. Briefly." She rolled her eyes and fanned her face with her hand. "He is one hot guy."

"Is he involved in the theft?" Millie asked.

"We can't be certain. He has motive. He says Grace never paid him for the work he did on the belt, though she provided the jewels and the gold."

Millie frowned. "Where would Grace find jewels like that? Maybe she has a line on Elon Musk."

"What?" Tinkie said.

"His family owns emerald mines," Millie said, laughing. "Sorry, it was a tenuous connection at best."

"Maybe. Maybe not." She'd opened a new door for us to walk through. "What if the person who provided Grace with the raw material for the belt is behind the theft? I mean, if she screwed Sippi for his work in creating it, who's to say she didn't cheat someone else?"

"Good point," Tinkie said. "And tomorrow, we will pursue that angle. Grace can tell us where she got the raw materials. But I think the attack on Grace is our best lead." She checked her watch. "In fact, Sarah Booth and I should check in with Chief Johnson before he leaves for the day to see if they uncovered any additional facts."

"Coleman will stand a better chance at getting info from Yuma." It was just the truth. The Tupelo police chief was all grins and good manners, but I suspected he viewed Tinkie and me as real thorns in his side. Like so many other law officers, he would respond better to "one of his own."

"Right. So we have some time. To do what?"

Tinkie was getting antsy. Oscar and Maylin, along with the other men and pets, were on the way. They were coming a day early, which was a wonderful Christmas surprise, but it would divert our attention from the case. Our focus would have to change to include their needs and desires. It was the balance of family and work. We were all familiar with it, but Tinkie had it much harder than me because Maylin needed her. I had to keep Tinkie's needs—and the baby's needs—in mind.

"Girls, who would you say is the prime suspect?" I asked the room.

"Grace Land," Cece and Millie said together. "It makes perfect sense. She'll have the belt in the end and all the notoriety and press from the theft. And since it wasn't insured, no one can charge her with anything."

They had an excellent point. "What's your guess, Tinkie?"

She frowned. "I'm torn between several suspects. We have the twin Elvises. And Kent. And Sippi. And Krystal. And Allan Malone. It could be any of them, as well as Grace, who is a good bet as it stands now."

She was correct. We had a lot of suspects. Weeding them out was the problem. And those were just the easy ones to point the finger at. I suspected there were more bad apples in the barrel if we dug down deep. While Chief Johnson had been cordial, he hadn't really shared information with us. I'd have to talk with Tinkie about the possibility of the chief being a suspect.

"Tell us about Sippi," Cece said. "We never saw him, but I hear he's sex on a stick."

Tinkie laughed. "He is a god. If I weren't happily married, I'd hit that!"

Cece let out a squeal and Millie laughed. Tinkie never talked like that. She had decorum.

"I'll warn Oscar that he must attend to your needs," Millie said, trying to look prim before she burst into laughter.

I stood up. "You girls are just being bad. We aren't nailing down our suspects with this foolishness. Time enough tonight for carousing. Now I'm going to get busy. Tinkie?"

She sighed. "Sarah Booth works me like an old mule in a rocky back forty."

Millie rolled her eyes. "You don't look overworked to me."

"Tinkie is as stubborn as an old mule." I grinned.

"Hee-haw," Cece said. "Now leave us so we can practice our moves in these great new outfits."

"Back in time for the competition. We are your cheering squad," Tinkie said as we left the room and headed back to the street. "What now?" Tinkie asked.

I didn't have a great answer, but I'd give it a try. "Let's find the Manning twins. If they didn't take part in this, I'll bet they have a good guess who did."

"You're on!" Tinkie linked her arm through mine, and we set off into the cold of a December day.

18

The magic of Christmas flooded downtown Tupelo as the festive holiday lights came on and groups of Elvis impersonators caroled on street corners. Christmas magic at its best. I inhaled the crisp, cold air. Tinkie was looking at an explosion of multicolored LED lights with childlike innocence.

"I love this time of year," she said. A wistful look crossed her face. "I love the food, the decorations, the sense that the world actually has a chance to accept that love is the only thing of value."

Tinkie had been given every material thing a child could want at Christmas. The only thing she'd ever wanted, though, was a connection with her mother, and that had been withheld for whatever reasons.

"Merry Christmas, Tinkie." I put my arm around her shoulders and gave her a hug.

"Do you think Maylin will remember this Christmas?"

I didn't know much about kids, but I knew a lot about my partner. This wasn't a request for factual information. This was a need for affirmation. "She may not remember the specifics, but she will always remember the love. From you and Oscar, but also from your friends who adore her."

Tinkie's arm squeezed me back. "You're the best, Sarah Booth. You understand."

"Sometimes." I wasn't ready to take the honor of sainthood yet. "I don't remember all the specifics of Christmas with my parents. But I do remember that the holiday season was always filled with love and joy. I was safe and loved. That's all that really matters."

Tinkie moved the conversation to a safer emotional plane. "It's going to be special for all of us when we win the competition for amateur impersonators. And of course, Millie and Cece will win the dance moves competition tonight. This means so much to Cece. And Millie. We'll win for them."

I could count on Tinkie being positive for whatever dreams we decided to pursue. Most of the time. The only thing that really got her down was her mother's seeming indifference to Maylin. That was a topic best left alone.

"The men will be here soon," I said, checking the time. "We should probably hustle."

"Right." She whipped out her phone and looked up a phone number for the Manning brothers. They weren't hard to find. She dialed Sherman, and he agreed to meet us for a drink in the hotel lobby. Apparently the Hound Dog Hotel had a famous drink called the Porch Dog, which was supposed to imply it was so potent—and a real inhibition loosener—that the imbiber was rendered unconscious on the porch. According to Sherman, at least.

We set up in the bar, glad to come in out of the cold, no matter how festive Tupelo was. Sherman joined us about fifteen minutes later. He wore a tux for the dance competition, and I wondered if he was going to perform, too. Elvis wasn't necessarily famous for waltzing tunes, but Sherman looked ready to sweep his partner around the floor in that old Tennessee standard.

"Any luck finding the fancy belt?" he asked as he sat down and lifted two fingers to the bartender.

"We have some leads, but so far not the belt."

"Grace has it." Sherman shifted his elbow so the bartender could deposit two drinks for him. "Aren't you girls drinking?" he asked.

I almost laughed. We'd waited for him, but our good manners were wasted. I held up two fingers and pointed to the drinks Sherman had. In a few moments, Tinkie and I each had one in front of us. She eyed it with suspicion but was too well brought up to comment.

We sipped our drinks, and I sighed. A little bit of the Hound Dog specialty drink, consisting mostly of tequila, would go a long way. It was my personal opinion that such potent alcohol could cure nail fungus, dandruff, and varicose veins. I knew to go slow with this drink.

Sherman had no such compunctions. He downed the first drink and started on the second. All Tinkie and I had to do was wait. The Hound Dog concoction would loosen Sherman's tongue far more effectively than any interrogation tactics I knew.

The hotel bar was very modern, except for an old jukebox

that someone kept feeding quarters into and playing "Are You Lonesome Tonight?" It was one of my favorites, and the deep timbre of Elvis's voice gave the words emotional impact. I'd been lonely in the past. I wasn't now, but life was treacherous. It could change and go either way at any moment. Loss had taught me that no one could guard against loneliness.

"I hate that sl—song," Sherman said, giving me the first indication that the alcohol was hitting him. "In fact, I'll be glad when this Elvis mania is over. It was bad enough to have it in June, but now at Christmas, too. I hope the mayor and city council decide never to do this again."

"I thought Kent Madison was all for the Christmas Elvis event."

"Kent is an idiot."

I couldn't disagree with that.

"Where's your brother?" Tinkie asked.

"Busy." Sherman was focused on his second drink. "Did you hear Chief Johnson found the car that ran Grace Land off the road?"

This was news to me and Tinkie. "Who does it belong to?"

"I don't remember. Or maybe the chief didn't say." He looked at his drink and I thought for a minute his eyes would cross. "Call Yuma. He knows. Or at least he told me he knew."

"Thanks, Sherman." I wasn't done with him yet, but Yuma seemed the more important lead to follow at the moment. I left Sherman at the table, talking to Tinkie—if he knew anything, she'd get it out of him. I stepped outside to call the chief. I was agitated by his lack of consideration toward us. He should have called to tell us about the car. It was the hottest lead we had.

"Chief," I said, fighting to keep my tone level, "I hear you've found the car that ran Grace off the road."

"That damn Sherman," he said. "He saw the wrecker hauling it in. He can't keep his mouth shut for any reason."

"Wrecker? Was the car involved in an accident?"

"No, it was abandoned on the side of the road in the middle of nowhere. We didn't have a key, so we just towed it to the junkyard."

"Whose car is it?"

"Hattie Scarborough's."

"Who?"

"Elderly lady who lives not too far from Grace. She hasn't driven in a couple of years, but she kept an old Cadillac in good shape just in case she needed it. She wasn't even aware that it had been stolen."

"Any fingerprints or evidence in the car?"

"Working on that now."

Was he intentionally withholding information or telling the truth? I couldn't tell over the phone. No matter. Coleman would wiggle it out of him this very evening. In fact, the men should be pulling up within the next half hour. Tinkie had gotten a text from Oscar saying they were on the way.

"Can you tell me anything that might help me find that belt?" I asked Yuma.

"I can't tell you what I don't know. Call me back tomorrow." He hung up.

I'd do better than that. I'd send Coleman to interrogate him. And I'd get the information I needed in the process.

I returned to the bar, where Sherman was tilting on his stool. He looked done in. Tinkie rolled her eyes at me. "A man who can't hold his liquor is so unattractive."

"Or a woman," I reminded her.

She laughed. "True. Now let's get out of here and check out that car. Where is it?"

"The same junkyard they towed Grace's car to." I paid the check, said goodbye to Sherman, who merely blinked at us, and we were on our way.

"You think he'll get to the show tonight okay?" Tinkie asked as we walked toward the junkyard. It wasn't that far, but the night was freezing.

"He can safely walk there, or the bartender will call him an Uber."

"He was pretty wasted. On two drinks." Tinkie didn't care for a cheap drunk. If you guzzled it down, you ought to be able to handle it. "He'll be fine." She didn't have time to waste worrying about Sherman Manning, wannabe Elvis.

"You're a hard woman, Tinkie Richmond."

She only laughed. "Maybe so."

We hoofed it past the dress shop, where Tinkie tried to linger but I grabbed her elbow and moved her along. There wasn't time for window shopping. Darkness had dropped over Tupelo, and while the holiday lights were beautiful and colorful, the shadows of the night lingered all around.

"Being out in the dead of a winter night on the streets of a town you don't know is not the most comfortable thing," Tinkie said.

"True." I saw the gate to the junkyard glinting silver in the moonlight. It was on a portion of the street where an old warehouse had been shuttered. As we approached the junkyard, it was clearly locked up with a chain around the gate. Not much of an impediment for lock-picker Tinkie.

In under three minutes she had the lock off and the chain unwrapped. The gate swung open on creaky hinges.

We were in luck. The Cadillac in question was parked in front of the office. To my astonishment, there wasn't a dent in the car. It was, in fact, pristine. The paint job was weathered a bit, but for the age of the car, a 1986 model, it was in great shape. Tinkie and I weren't in the habit of carrying evidence gloves, so we didn't touch the car. We walked around it, confirming that there was no indication of an accident. I took some photos. We'd have to wait for forensics from the chief.

"Let's show Grace the photos."

It was a good plan that Tinkie put forth. We locked the gate and hurried toward her place. I was all for jogging, it was so cold, but Tinkie pointed to her shoes. Since she'd had the baby, her feet had gotten bigger and her fancy shoes now pinched. It was a sore point with her.

"Want me to call an Uber?" I asked.

"No. Just don't jog."

We walked, and arrived at Grace's in under ten minutes. She answered the door when we knocked, and I stood back to take in the full scope of her outfit. She wore a black-and-white sequined gown that hugged her curves and was split down to her waist in the front and up to her thigh on the side. Grace had been given a bodacious set of ta-tas, and she knew how to use them to good effect.

"What are you two doing here? It's the evening of the dance competition. I have to leave soon."

At least Grace was out of her bed. "We know. We have a few questions."

She stood in the doorway, unmoving.

"Can we come in?" Tinkie asked with some shortness.

"I guess." Grace stepped back. "What is it that can't wait?"

"We're going home Saturday," Tinkie told her. "If this case isn't solved, it will have to wait until we have time to work on it and come back up here. So, yeah, we're pushing you a little because we want to recover your belt before we go home."

"Okay, okay. I'm sorry. What can I do for you?"

I showed her the photo of the Cadillac. "Do you know this car?"

"No, but it's in mint condition, isn't it? Why should I care about this car?"

"Because the chief thinks this is the vehicle that ran you into the ditch."

Grace took the phone from my hand. "I'm not certain, but it could be. I just caught a blur out of the corner of my eye. It could have been this car. Anyway, I hit my head hard and I don't have a clear memory of what all happened. Who does it belong to?"

"We were hoping you could tell us." Tinkie was testy.

I sighed. "Chief Johnson said Hattie Scarborough, an older woman in town, is the owner."

"Miss Hattie? I know her but she hasn't driven in years. I didn't even know she owned a car."

"Apparently, she hasn't driven in a while. She didn't even report the car stolen."

"Who stole it?"

"Yuma won't tell us—if he knows. Maybe you could ask him." I figured Grace had a lot more political pull in Tupelo than I did.

"Sure. I'll see him at the dance moves contest. He's

partnered up with Krystal Bond, I hear. They're both very good dancers."

Not as good as Cece and Millie, I wanted to say, but didn't. Of more importance was the fact that one of our prime suspects was dancing with the chief of police. It didn't bode well for justice.

19

We'd done what we could. Without Yuma cooperating and telling us details of what he'd found, the car wasn't a good lead for us. Coleman could hopefully remedy that, but it was frustrating to wait. We hustled back to the hotel and went up to our rooms to get ready for the evening. I'd just put on a pair of guitar earrings, the final touch to my outfit, when Coleman knocked on the door. He stood in the doorway, a grin lighting his features. "Elvis is in the building," he said.

I jumped on him and wrapped my legs around him, making him laugh.

"You're a handful tonight, aren't you?" he asked as he eased me to my feet. "I'm glad to see you, too." He sealed it with a kiss that left me wanting more. "Are you ready for the dance competition? We should hurry out of here so we have great seats." He was tormenting me.

I stepped back from him. "We have reservations, but you bet. No time to fool around here." Coleman always looked handsome, even in jeans and a flannel shirt. He was a good dancer, but I was glad we were only spectators this evening. "Since you're so eager to get to the dance hall, let's go. Obviously we don't have time to play smacky lips." Two could play this game. I walked past him into the hall and headed to the elevators.

I called Tinkie and the girls as we walked to the lobby. They met us there, along with Harold, who'd left the pooches and the cat at the cabin where he was staying. I was itching to see Sweetie Pie and Pluto, but they would have to wait a little longer. Even Jaytee had made it to Tupelo, which set Cece's heart all aflutter. We were chatting and laughing as we entered the Arena Center. For this one evening, we were going to put the stolen Elvis belt aside and simply have the vacation we'd planned for the past four months.

The elves and fairies had been hard at work, converting the arena auditorium space into a theater in the round with a slowly revolving stage so the dancers could be viewed from all angles. We'd booked early and had terrific seats not far from the stage. After the competition, we'd grab a bite.

Tinkie ordered libations for all of us, and we settled into chairs at our table with anticipation. My friends were talented, and I wanted them to win.

Single dancers, couples, and groups took the stage, one after the other. I tried to assess their skills compared to my friends. There was plenty of talent, but I hoped the judges would see the merits of Cece's and Millie's homage to Elvis, *Pulp Fiction,* and the dance scene that the nation had been talking about when the movie was released.

When their time arrived, they took the stage and Jaytee turned on the music he'd helped them select and record. I'd seen them practice, but dressed in their very classy outfits and dancing like they'd trained together for years, I couldn't help but jump to my feet and applaud. By the time it was over, the audience was roaring their approval.

I felt a little bad for the dancers who followed them. Cece and Millie had sucked all the oxygen from the room. When they were announced as the winners of the dance competition, I wasn't surprised. They were simply the best dancers.

We were a merry crowd as we went to a charming downtown restaurant. The food wasn't fancy, but it was delicious—a good ending to a perfect evening.

The whole gang drove over to the cabin where Harold had installed the pups and Pluto. When we parked outside, I heard Sweetie Pie's fine hound dog yodel. She could sniff me a mile away and she was happy to know I was on the way to her. Chablis's little bark was like a machine gun. She had a way of making her point, too. Pauline, the nanny, was right there with Maylin. The drowsy baby woke long enough to clutch Tinkie's hair in her fingers and give her a drooly smile.

Pluto was typically standoffish, as only a cat can be. Sweetie Pie almost knocked me over with her effusive greeting, and Chablis grabbed the hem of my jeans and tugged with her whole heart. I gave them all cuddles, but kept a wary eye on Harold's dog, Roscoe. The scruffy-faced little demon watched me with a grin on his goateed face. When I stood up, he launched himself across the room and leaped into my arms. Whatever else Roscoe had to deal with from a past of abuse, he didn't have any trust issues when it came to me. He totally believed I'd catch him. And I did.

Tinkie was torn between Chablis, her little dust mop dog, and the baby. I scooped Chablis up and gave her some belly tickles and kisses while Tinkie renewed her bond with little Maylin.

The men had driven up in a caravan, so tomorrow there would be plenty of cars to use. Harold's main squeeze, Janet, was driving up from the coast and should arrive at any moment. It was time for us to make a discreet withdrawal, with big thanks to Harold for taking care of the dogs and cat overnight. The hotel didn't allow pets. But Pauline and Maylin were headed to the hotel with Tinkie and Oscar.

Coleman and I bade everyone good night and slipped back to the hotel where we could have some privacy. After we had our own reunion, I sat cross-legged on the bed and laid out my case for him. No one was thrilled that we had another case at Christmas, but Coleman was intrigued by the set of circumstances regarding the theft of the Elvis belt.

I had photos on my phone, and when he saw the belt, he whistled. "How much is it worth?"

"Three million or higher." When I'd told him about this case, I'd skimped on some of the details so he wouldn't worry about me.

"That's some heist," he said.

I went over the security levels on the belt once again, telling Coleman how it was assumed that the laser and other security measures had been thwarted.

"Chief Johnson," Coleman said. "What does he say?"

"That's what you need to find out for me."

"Local law stonewalling you?" he asked with some amusement.

"Yes, but you are going to remedy that, right?"

"That's the only reason you keep me around, isn't it?"

I shifted so that I was lying beside him. "Not the only reason, darlin'." I flipped over and sat on his chest. "You are my willing servant. Look into my eyes. Look deep into my eyes. My every wish is your command. Obedience is your only focus." I gave him my best Svengali effect, but he only laughed.

Before I knew what was happening, he tossed me off him and flat on the bed, rolled over, and sat on top of me, careful not to let his full weight crush me. "Now who is doing whose bidding? You will obey me, woman."

Even teasing me, he could still see the fire that ignited in my eyes. He laughed, but he didn't let me go. He didn't dare.

"The day I am obedient will never come," I told him.

"And I'm very glad." He kissed me and set me free. "How about one more drink? There's a minibar with some Jack in it."

"I'll get the ice," I offered. I'd noticed that the ice and soft drink machines were on the floor below us by the elevators. "I'll be right back."

I slipped into my jeans and sneakers and headed out with the ice bucket. I passed Cece and Jaytee's room, and then Millie's. I was tempted to invite them over for a drink, but I figured after the exuberant dance episode, they were sound asleep. Well, Millie at least. Jaytee was a night owl and Cece seemed to function on little sleep.

I got in the elevator and went down to the lower floor. I found some money in my pocket for a Diet Coke—normally I was a Jack-and-water kind of girl, but I needed a little fizz. I bought four canned drinks, filled the ice bucket, and stopped. Suddenly I was on red alert, though I didn't know why. Something told me danger was near.

I checked my pocket, but I hadn't brought my phone. I had no way to contact Coleman and tell him something wasn't right. The only option was to head back to the room and stay alert along the way. If someone was in the hotel watching me, I'd be prepared if they made a move.

I put the sodas in my jacket pockets, grabbed the ice, and walked back toward the elevator. I felt eyes boring into my back, but when I turned around, the hallway was empty. In fact, the hotel was eerily quiet. Perhaps that was what had set me on edge. There wasn't another person in the hallways or in the elevator, not even the janitorial staff. It was as if everyone had vanished—even though Christmas Muzak was still being piped all around me. It was really creepy.

I punched the elevator and waited with my back to the elevator doors, keeping an eye out down the hallway. When the elevator opened, I turned around and screamed. A smashed-in, solid black face with a long pink tongue stared at me. The tongue, which was at least a foot long, lashed out and slurped my face!

I grabbed a soda from my pocket, shook it vigorously, and then popped the top. Soda spewed across the distance into the face of the man who held the black-faced devil!

"Stop it, you're scaring Avery!" Allan Malone came out of the elevator holding one of his pugs and wiping soda from his glasses. He backed me into the opposite wall. "Have you no heart? Have you no compassion? You've scared my baby almost to death!"

Avery the pug didn't seem the worse for wear, and she slurped the other side of my face with that impressively long tongue. I was so startled I couldn't even react.

"Some people have no understanding of the sensitivity of a pup like Avery. Or Lovely Katherine. They are so delicate. Look at her! Just look at her! She's mortally wounded by your behavior."

The dog looked fine to me. "Back up, Allan." He'd startled me and I wasn't willing to trust him.

"I knew you were a dog hater when I first met you."

"I love dogs." It was stupid to argue, but I couldn't accept his view of me. "I even like little pampered dogs with breathing issues."

"Avery is one of the few pugs without breathing issues. She has superior nasal openness, and the little grunting noises are because she is so filled with love! They are love grunts. You should be lucky enough to know this from experience."

Okay, then, he was a little wacky about the pugs. But it was nice to see a man who didn't mind showing his love for his companions. Whatever else Katherine and Avery were, they were Allan's beloved family. He'd even featured them on his show *Who's Singing Barbra*. I'd seen a YouTube clip of the dogs howling as Allan sang. It was actually one of my favorite clips from the show.

"Where are you going?" I asked Allan.

"Who wants to know?" He grinned in a smart-aleck way.

"I do. Sorry I sprayed you, but Avery's tongue startled me." I reached out to pet Avery, but she growled at me, picking up on Allan's mood.

"I don't have to answer your questions. I thought we clarified that earlier."

"You could really help me out if you'd try," I said. "Just think, we can find the Elvis belt, clear your name, and you can head back to Hollywood to do your show. I know you must be bored to tears here in Tupelo."

He leaned against the wall between the elevators. "I love being home. I do. Everyone here adores me."

He was popular with some of the residents. He had celebrity, money, suave good looks, a great voice, and two really cute dogs. What was there not to like?

He continued talking. "Congratulations to your friends on winning the dance competition. They were fabulous. I'm really looking forward to hearing Cece sing. She's going to be perfect for my television show."

"Cece has a fabulous voice and her partner is one of the finest harmonica players you'll ever meet. They would both be an asset."

"I'd love for them to come out to Los Angeles and do my show. Wouldn't that be fun?"

It would. I was sure Cece and Jaytee would love it. "I'll tell them. Maybe you can audition them while we're here."

"I'll set something up. Please ask them to give me a call."

"Will do. And I'm sorry I sprayed you with soda." I reached around him to hit the elevator button. Coleman would think I'd run off with a traveling tent show if I didn't get back to the room. I was in the elevator when I realized Allan had never given an accounting of why he was in the hotel. He owned a house in town. I knew that much. So why was he here, and with only one of the pugs? I'd never seen him without both dogs.

When the elevator opened on my floor, I punched the down button and went straight back to the floor where I'd seen Allan. Once I got there, though, the hallways and elevators were empty. Both man and dog had vanished, leaving me with unanswered questions.

20

The next morning dawned bright and cold. Ice crystals sparkled on the hotel window as I looked out into the parking lot. To my surprise, Sonja Rivera was walking down the line of parked cars, grabbing door handles and checking for an unlocked vehicle. What the heck was she up to?

I threw on a pair of jeans, warm socks, boots, and tucked my T-shirt into my jeans. I slid into a warm coat. Coleman was sound asleep, and I did my best to keep it that way. My intention was to find Sonja and interview her, then pick up some coffee to take back to the room. There was always a pot brewing in the hotel lobby.

I didn't have any concerns for my safety as I trotted out the front door of the hotel and caught my breath in the cold air. The sun was just cresting the horizon, but there was plenty of light to find Sonja; her beehive bouffant was taller than all the car tops. I hustled across the lot and came up behind her.

"Sonja, what are you doing?"

She screamed and turned around so fast, her scarf popped me in the face. "I should punch you out for scaring me like that," she said, backing away.

"Why are you breaking into cars?"

"I'm not. I'm looking for something."

"Like what?" I was skeptical, so sue me.

"None of your business."

Even before the crack of dawn she was perfectly made up with the heavy eyeliner, bright blue shadow, and red lips. She was a rare beauty, even wearing makeup that was popular fifty years earlier. "Sonja, what are you doing out here?" I didn't want to call hotel security on her, but I would. The fact that she looked like Priscilla wouldn't cut her any slack with Johnson. Or at least that's what I hoped.

"I got a text message."

That was interesting but not exactly revelatory. "And?"

"It said the Elvis belt was in an unlocked car in this parking lot. I thought if I found it there might be a reward for returning it, though I wonder if Grace Land has sense enough to offer—and honor—a reward."

She had a point. "Who sent the text?"

"Anonymous."

I rolled my eyes. "Really? Anonymous. And you're out here in full makeup looking for stolen artwork because you always act impulsively on anonymous tips?"

"Have you found the belt?" she asked pointedly.

"Let me see the text, please."

She opened her phone and gave it to me. Sure enough,

the text was right there. "Find the stolen Elvis belt. Check unlocked cars in the Hound Dog Hotel parking lot."

Basic and simple.

I fell in beside her as we started to check the remainder of the cars. The Hound Dog wasn't a huge hotel. Maybe three hundred rooms, and likely all of them full for this special Elvis week. It was one long parking lot, with cars parked in rows. Sonja had checked about half the lot. With my help we finished quickly. No belt. No clue about a belt.

"I feel like a fool," she said. "I should have known."

"But it didn't hurt to check. You should show that text to Chief Johnson."

"He'll just mock and make fun of me."

"Words won't hurt you." I knew that from long experience. I'd been mocked by the premier mockers.

"I know that. I'm not a fool. But I don't like it." She sighed. "I really wanted to find that belt and return it. I would have been the hero of this town."

She was right about that, and it was a harmless ask. "I'm sorry. But at least we looked."

"Yep." She straightened her hair and then her coat. "I'll be glad when this event is over, and Tupelo gets back to normal. I never thought I'd say that, but I'm tired of the drama and turmoil. We have the amateur impersonator contest tonight and the professional one tomorrow night. Then it will be done."

I didn't have the meanness to remind her it would happen again in June. Or that the furor over a grand art theft wouldn't subside when the Elvises left town.

The conclusion of the festivities wouldn't bring the missing Elvis belt back to Grace, but it might put an end to further theft opportunities. And maybe Yuma would get on the stick and do some real investigating. I was more than disappointed at his performance.

"Would you like a cup of coffee?" I asked her.

"Hotel coffee?" She almost sneered.

"Wherever." I could text Coleman my location so he could join me.

"Let's go to BeBop's doughnut shop. They have fabulous doughnuts and great coffee. You know Elvis loved doughnuts. BeBop's claims that they got the fried dough recipe from Gladys herself." She rolled her eyes. "I wouldn't bet on that, but the doughnuts are really good."

I was sold; I didn't need more convincing. In my opinion, all doughnuts were delicious. Some just more so.

The dew that had fallen overnight had frozen in the bare branches of the trees, giving the downtown area the illusion that everything was crusted with diamonds. The air was so cold, when I inhaled deeply, I wanted to cough. I didn't mind. The air was crisp and clean. It only took ten minutes to walk to BeBop's and I texted the location to Coleman and asked him to join us.

"Your beau?" she asked.

I had to smile. I guess he was my beau, but what an old-fashioned word. "Yes. I'm lucky." She nodded as we took a seat at one of the small tables with red-checked cloths. "Sonja, what do you know about Allan Malone?"

"Local man makes good out in Hollywood. Folks love him and he has done a lot for forcing local establishments to open up to dogs. Avery and Lovely Katherine go everywhere with Allan, and if they can't go, he doesn't participate. It really has made a difference for pets."

That was good to know. "What about his relationship with Krystal Bond?"

She shrugged. "Who knows. They're both peculiar in the sense that they don't care about developing friendships. Krystal is very distant and she seems to get under people's skin really easily. Allan isn't in town a lot since his show is out in Hollywood." She pushed the sugar and creamer toward me when the waitress brought our coffees and a box of assorted doughnuts. "Dig in, Sarah Booth. They will melt in your mouth."

She wasn't lying. The doughnuts were light, crispy, and glazed. I ate three before I was even aware of what I was doing. "Sonja, who truly hates Grace Land?"

"Oh, that could be a long list. Grace is . . . pretentious. And folks feel that she shafted Sippi Salem over the belt. He created a masterpiece, but the word around town was that she never paid him for his work. Most folks had never seen the belt—it was only a rumor until she put it on display. That hasn't helped her out with the locals."

"And Sippi is well liked?"

She laughed. "I wouldn't go that far. He's eccentric and can be a total jackass. But he is an artist, so folks cut him more slack. Grace is just wealthy. That doesn't earn her any free passes for crappy behavior. She's snubbed pretty much everyone in town." Her eyebrows rose. "She's another one who has no real friends in Tupelo. I guess with all that money she can buy a friend when she has need of one." She cleared her throat. "That was really mean and I don't know her well. I have a sense she's timid and has had it tougher than she lets on."

Dang. The snark was getting waist deep, but Sonja had caught a glimpse of Grace's tender side. "What about the Manning twins?"

She sighed. "Harmless fools. Why do you ask? Do you think they were involved in stealing the belt?"

"I don't know. I'm just trying to get a read on the people who have popped up in my investigation. The Manning twins had opportunity and means. Do they have a motive?"

"Three million dollars is one heck of a motive, for anyone," Sonja pointed out.

"True. But is there a connection between Grace and the Mannings, or Sippi and the Mannings?"

She thought a minute. "I'd be willing to bet they all hate each other."

I barked out a laugh because she'd caught me unprepared. I could see her point, though. There didn't seem to be a lot of love lost between the main players of the Elvis festival.

"Do you think the belt is still in Tupelo?" I asked Sonja.

"I honestly don't know. I'm not willing to hazard a guess on that."

"If you'd stolen the belt, what would you do with it?"

"Oh, I'd take it home and hide it. Then I could look at it whenever I wanted. It is an incredible work of art."

"Yes, I saw it in the case. My fingers itched to touch it."

"That's what I'm talking about. People see it and just want to have it. For themselves. It's not about the money, it's about the artistic design. Sippi is a genius."

It hadn't occurred to me that someone would want the belt for their personal gazing pleasure. Art was meant to be displayed. At least that's what my parents had taught me. They'd valued the small museums and art galleries around the Deep South. There was fine art and performing art—the musicians and actors who made Mississippi shine. Then the culinary artists and those who crafted the perfect bar or hangout. My parents had been strong supporters of the libraries, many funded by the Carnegie family. Treasures were meant to be shared, not hoarded.

"If you had to name a suspect right now, who would you say?"

Sonja didn't hesitate. "Kent Madison. He's not a very nice man, and he was obsessed with that belt. Ask Grace, if she'll tell you the truth. He dated her for nearly a year—not exclusively—and I think it was all about getting close to that belt. His hands would sweat whenever he was near it."

Kent was a lead I hadn't followed as hard as I should have.

The bell over the door jangled and Coleman walked into the shop. I was watching Sonja's face and she gave an approving nod. "He's hot."

"Thank goodness, because it is freezing here."

We all laughed as the waitress brought Coleman coffee and he dug into a lemon-filled doughnut.

Sonja stood up. "Thanks for the coffee and fried dough." She gave Coleman a cheeky thumbs-up. "Good luck making this one obey the law." And then she was gone.

"She looked an awful lot like Priscilla Presley," Coleman said, following her with his gaze.

"Yeah, she does. I wonder if she's going to be in the amateur Elvis competition tonight." She would be hard to beat, based just on sentimental value. Folks in Tupelo still loved Priscilla. Several had mentioned to me that they would never accept Lisa Marie's untimely death.

"Grab those doughnuts," Coleman said. "They're really good."

I only shook my head and picked up the box while Coleman paid the bill.

Coleman and I left the doughnut shop and sauntered to the Arena Center, where we overheard two females talking about their belief that Presley's daughter, Lisa Marie, had not died but had been taken by aliens, was being held prisoner for a ransom, or was part of a future plan to bring Elvis and his daughter back to Tupelo. The conversation was wild, so I asked one of the women, "Where is Lisa Marie, if she isn't dead?"

"She's at Graceland. Watching over Elvis's grave. She's just fine." The well-dressed woman, in her fifties, looked at me as if I'd grown horns.

It was a sentiment I didn't want to argue with. A part of me hoped it was true. The loss of Elvis as a young man and Lisa Marie as a young woman was hard for a Mississippian to swallow.

The women moved on, and Coleman put his hand on my forehead. "I'm a little concerned about you, Sarah Booth."

"Why is that?"

"You left a warm bed, and that's not like you. And you're having conversations with people who believe aliens abducted Elvis Presley."

I gave him a grin. "I was interviewing a witness and I'm on vacation. Let's get back to the hotel."

"What are your plans for today?" Coleman asked.

"I need to track down Kent Madison. And Krystal Bond. The insurance agent is in this up to her eyebrows. What are you doing?"

"A little Christmas shopping." He gave me a bad-boy grin. "And then I'm going to talk to Yuma."

"Thank you, Coleman."

Back in the hotel, we knocked on the doors of all of our friends and delivered doughnuts and hot coffee. Then we got ready for our day. Coleman promised he'd call me with anything he learned. I grabbed Tinkie to help me corral Kent. We went straight to the mayor's office and found the assistant mayor in a meeting.

The secretary showed us to a comfortable waiting room, gave us more coffee, and offered pastries, which we sensibly declined.

After thirty minutes, we checked back with the secretary. She went to Kent's office and came back with a frown. "He's gone. He knew you were waiting, and he just left."

I blew out my breath. We'd wasted an hour on this. "Where did he go?"

"I don't know. He didn't say and he didn't leave a note." She bit her lip, then said it anyway. "He's a rude ass. I'm sorry."

"If he comes back, would you call us?" I asked, giving her a business card.

"I will. And I won't tell him."

At least we had an ally in the mayor's office. I didn't know how much good it would do us, but it was better than an enemy.

We left city hall and headed to the parking lot. A dark car idled at the end of the line of parked cars. My spidey sense kicked in and I looked the vehicle over. The windows were black, and I couldn't see inside. But the motor was running. Not all that sinister, but something to keep an eye on.

"Sarah Booth, do you think Kent Madison is involved in the theft of the belt? He's mad at Grace. He hates the Elvis competition. Maybe he hopes to return the belt and this is just an attempt to sabotage the Elvis event."

"That's really smart. It's possible. Maybe even probable. I wish the skunk hadn't ditched us so easily." I felt played, and I didn't like it.

Before Tinkie could say anything else, I heard tires boiling on the asphalt. The dark sedan roared to life and came right at us. For a moment I froze, unable to really comprehend what was happening. The car had to be going at least fifty miles an hour, and it was pointed right at Tinkie. At last, I moved. Using all of my body weight, I hurled myself at Tinkie and knocked her between two parked cars. I somehow managed not to fall on her and crush her.

"Damn!" Tinkie fought to catch her breath. I'd knocked the wind out of her, but if I hadn't pushed her out of the way, the speeding car would have killed us both.

Tinkie struggled to her feet and unloaded double middle fingers on the driver. "What a jerk! He almost ran us over. Is he drunk?"

"I think it was deliberate." Tinkie's angry gesture was a little compromised by the fact that her palms were bleeding. Otherwise, she looked undamaged.

I got off the pavement and brushed the grit and small rocks from the palms of my hands. My skin wasn't damaged, and my jeans had protected my knees, but Tinkie's festive holiday slacks were ruined.

"You really think he meant to hit us?"

"I do."

"I didn't even get a look at the license plate," Tinkie said. "Did you?"

"There wasn't one." I'd made it a point to look.

"We should call Yuma and report this," Tinkie said, and her reluctant tone reflected mine.

Nonetheless, I pulled out my phone. I dialed the police chief and was relieved when he told me Coleman was in his office. "My partner and I were almost run over. I think it was deliberate."

"We're on the way," Yuma said.

Well, great, he was bringing Coleman with him. Fun, fun, fun.

21

We didn't have long to wait. We were both sitting on the hood of my car when Yuma waltzed up and took command of the scene. Coleman swept me against him, holding me close as he whispered some low-key questions to me.

"I'm fine," I assured him. "We weren't hurt. Just our pride and a few scrapes." Yuma was examining Tinkie's torn slacks.

The chief dutifully took down our description of the car, but it wasn't exactly helpful. We didn't give him much to go on because there wasn't a lot. When he was finished, Yuma tipped his hat and left. But not before he gave Coleman a knowing glance.

"Did you get anything out of him?" I asked Coleman after the police chief was gone.

"Only that he feels Grace is responsible for this attack on you and Tinkie. He's pretty annoyed with her because the theft of the Elvis belt is overshadowing the Elvis competition. He said his affair with her was just sex, nothing romantic or serious. According to him, Grace and the ensuing scandal aren't good for Tupelo and he's ready to be done with both the festival and Grace, not to mention the aggravation of the stolen belt. And, yes, he said exactly that. In the back of his head, he thinks Grace is behind the theft."

"Why would Grace steal from herself? There wasn't insurance to collect."

Coleman shrugged. "Is Grace all there, mentally? Yuma implied she was not one hundred percent . . . reliable."

That stopped me cold for a minute. "I think she's fine. She's a bit . . . eccentric. And narcissistic." Grace was difficult—I wasn't trying to deny it. "But accusing her of stealing from herself is harsh. What an unpleasant thing to say, unless he has proof." Yuma really did seem to have an issue with Grace. He sounded more like a jilted lover than a former casual fling.

Coleman nodded. "He offered no proof, just his opinion."

Coleman didn't have a lot of respect for lawmen who operated on opinion or hunch. It was one thing to follow a lead, and another to brand someone as a thief or criminal without evidence.

Tinkie was on the horn talking to Oscar, and I had a minute to confer with Coleman. "Do you think Yuma is on the up-and-up?"

Coleman didn't answer immediately. He weighed his options. "I don't know," he finally said. "Yuma doesn't like Grace, and I get the impression he views you and Tinkie as interlopers in his town. Is he biased to the point he won't search for the real thief? I don't want to believe that. Not just the city, but the entire county depends on Yuma to uphold the law and protect the citizens. I will say he isn't taking the assault on you and Tinkie with the seriousness I would like to see. He isn't Grace's biggest fan."

I didn't say anything. I'd seen enough corruption in small-town politics to be wary of taking a stance. If Yuma was corrupt, it would make things harder for me and Tinkie, but we weren't the people who would ultimately suffer. The residents of Tupelo and Lee County were the ones on the line.

"This case worries me," I told him. "Someone in power had to allow this to happen. The heist was too smooth, too easy. The thief just walked out with the belt. All of the precautions and safety measures had been turned off. That's just astounding to me. Someone has attacked Tinkie and me, and Grace, too. Sure, we weren't seriously hurt, but we could have been."

"I see the same thing. This case worries me, too," Coleman said. "Something definitely isn't right here, but I don't want to point fingers without evidence."

I nodded. "Keep an eye on Yuma, if you will. You have a reason to hang out with him, talk to him, ask questions. He doesn't care for me or Tinkie."

"You only sleep with me because I'm useful to you in an investigation."

I looked up at Coleman and grinned. "That's right. So, if you want some action tonight, you'd better make yourself vital to the case right now and turn over some new information."

"What happened to the shy little girl who was more interested in playing touch football than charming boys?"

"I grew up and I learned the power of the feminine mystique." Laughter almost escaped, but I swallowed it back. I loved bantering with Coleman. "Women are in control of everything."

Coleman chuckled. "You're adorable. And wrong. It's a man's world, Sarah Booth." He tipped his hat and left before I could whip off a shoe and throw it at him.

Even though he was teasing me, I couldn't help that it got under my skin. Because he was mostly correct. It was still very much a man's world. But that was changing. Slowly but surely, and Coleman would be one of the men leading the change. But reforming the world was far out of my reach. Right now, I had Tupelo and a stolen piece of art to worry about. Not to mention someone who kept trying to turn me into a grease spot on the asphalt.

Tinkie signaled me with raised eyebrows that she was ready to move on. And she was a little aggravated. "Yuma really believes Grace stole the belt from herself," Tinkie said. "He's not going to be a lot of help for us."

"Coleman can work his magic on him."

"Good."

"Did he say anything interesting?"

Tinkie considered. "Only that Kent Madison has a rap sheet."

"What? For what crime?"

"Theft." Tinkie's blue eyes sparkled. "He was charged with stealing from a church."

"Damn." That was not a crime you wanted on your rap sheet. "What did he take?"

"Silver crucifix and some artwork hanging in the chapel. One painting he took was expensive. Not a famous work, but from a local artist who'd donated the painting to the church."

"Was that here in Tupelo?"

"No. It was in Biloxi, at the seaside church. In fact, why don't we call Janet and get her to check with the church if she hasn't left to drive up here?"

That was an excellent idea. Janet, Harold's honey, was a romance writer, but she had a nose for scandal and an itchy curiosity bone. She lived in Pass Christian, but Biloxi was only a hop, skip, and jump from her house.

I dialed Janet up and asked if she could check in at the church where Kent Madison allegedly committed his crimes. Yuma told Tinkie that the church hadn't pressed charges once the items were returned. But if Janet could track down the priest from three decades ago, it would help a lot.

"I'm in New Orleans," Janet said. "I can't check it now, but please tell Harold I'll be in Tupelo in time for the big impersonation contest for the men. I'd hoped to see you girls perform, but I'm on deadline. Sandra has a five-hundred-dollar bet that I won't make it, so I have to hand her butt to her and collect my money. After that, I'm all yours to spy."

I loved that the two coastal writers competed like teenagers. They were cousins and friends and constantly tried to one-up each other. It was part of their charm. "No worries. We'll track that rumor down later," I said before I hung up.

"What now?" Tinkie asked.

"That list of jilted men Grace has left scattered all around. And also, the contestants from her television show who might want to do her harm. Do you have a preference?" I asked Tinkie. Since there were two lists, she might as well take her pick. Many would have to be interviewed on the phone because they weren't local.

"I'm going with jilted lovers," Tinkie said. "The spleen might be delightful."

That left me with the names of the angry reality TV show contestants. Oh, joy!

22

Once I sat down with my phone, the list of names, and contact phone numbers provided by Grace's assistant out in Los Angeles, I was a little shocked at how many far-flung places the *Boyfriend Boot Camp* competitors came from. I had assumed, wrongly, that most would claim the LA area as home. I figured local contestants would be sought after, just as a cost cutting device. I was wrong about all of it.

The men and women who were willing to publicly humiliate themselves on national TV came from small towns and big cities all over the country—even two from Mississippi. Those were the ones I settled on first. Means, motive, and opportunity were big elements of a crime. Living near Tupelo certainly gave these two contestants the opportunity to steal the belt, and the show might have given them motive to harm Grace.

Coleman was still with Yuma, and Tinkie was in her room working the phone on the list of jilted lovers. She had one real possibility, but so far Rupert Crown, a banker from Jackson, wasn't answering. Tinkie was eliminating the other names.

My best suspects on paper were Bonnie Welford and Walton Reeves and Kayla Wingard and John Monroe. I found clips of the reality show on YouTube and I could see where both couples might want to have Grace's scalp on a pike. She'd been awful. She made the women look like the most unreasonable bitches on the planet, and the men had been reduced to groveling. Grace might be successful in showbiz, but she was even better at humiliating people and making enemies.

Bonnie and Walton lived on the outskirts of Tupelo, and I gave them a call first. A woman answered and identified herself as Bonnie. I didn't get three sentences into explaining why I had called before Bonnie went off like a jet-fueled rocket.

"I don't know why you're calling me about anything to do with Grace Land. She ruined my life. And almost ruined my relationship with a good man. You tell her if I see her, I'm going to spit in her face."

"I'm not here to defend Grace."

"And a damn good thing! She is indefensible. She is a monster. She is a woman who takes pride in destroying others."

I didn't try to explain that she was responsible, too. She knew what the show was and she went on it anyway. Grace was doing her job, as far as I could tell. "Bonnie, have you been in Tupelo for any of the Elvis festivities?"

"Not on a bet. Grace Land is all involved in that, and I don't ever want to see her ugly mug again. She is a monster." There was a pause. "Why are you asking all of these questions?"

"I work for Grace—"

"Well, then you are a damn fool. Or, as my grandmother would say, 'Bless your heart.' Which just means you aren't smart enough to put your own best interests first. Work for Grace and you deserve what you get."

"I realize you don't care for Ms. Land, but—"

"But nothing! Don't call me again."

"You can talk to me, or you can talk to the law." I finally got to finish a sentence.

"Bully for you, call the law. What is it you think I've done? Is Grace dead?"

There was such anticipation in her last question that I almost laughed. She truly hated Grace Land.

"You've undoubtedly heard that the replica of the expensive belt designed for Elvis Presley was stolen from the Arena Center."

"I heard. Are you saying Grace owned that belt?"

She sounded sincere. "She did."

"How much was it worth?"

There wasn't a reason not to tell her. It was in all the newspapers. "Three million dollars."

"Grace is out three mil?" She cackled with laughter. "Lord, my granny also told me that justice rides a slow horse. Well, it finally arrived at Grace's door."

"Bonnie, you should understand that you and Walton are suspects in the theft."

"Right. You get Chief Johnson and come on out to my

house. See how I live. If I had three million dollars, I'd be on a jet plane to Portugal. I wouldn't be hanging around here in Tupelo, Mississippi. You must think I'm a moron."

I didn't think she was a moron or a viable suspect. She didn't have sense enough to hide her dislike of Grace, and I figured if she'd taken the belt, she'd be bragging about it—from the balcony of a nice hotel in Portugal.

"May I speak with your boyfriend?"

"Husband. We got married, no thanks to Grace. Sure. Call him." She rattled off a phone number. "He's down in Brownsville, Texas, working on an oil rig. Been down there a couple of weeks."

I couldn't be certain, but it sure seemed Bonnie and Walton were dead ends. She wasn't subtle enough to pull off a robbery and he was out of town. Just to be on the safe side, once I hung up from her, I called his number, spoke briefly with him amid the sounds of men using heavy equipment. I also called one of his employees, who confirmed Walton had been on site for two weeks.

I moved on to the next names on my list. Kayla Wingard and John Monroe.

The Wingard/Monroes lived in Columbus, which was only a hop, skip, and jump from Tupelo. Kayla wrote a cooking column for the local weekly paper, and John was a middle school teacher. I caught Kayla at the newspaper. She was curious about the reason for my call, but if there was animosity toward Grace, it was well hidden.

"I hear Grace did a number on you and your fiancé on her TV show."

"Oh, she had a good time mocking me and John." I could hear the bustle of the newsroom in the background.

"Were you angry with her?"

"At first we were ready to cook her goose," Kayla said. "She did her best to make fools of us on television. But you know, Grace came across like a big bully."

"You don't sound all that angry with her."

"I got over it." She chuckled. "I'm sure you've seen the clip of John dumping that bucket of fish guts on her in downtown Tupelo last June."

I had not seen it. "Grace didn't file charges?"

"Oh, she threatened. But in the end, she didn't."

"Why not?"

"Fish guts are cheap and easy to find. She knew John would do it to her again. She let it go and John and I had a lot of good laughs over her expression when those bloody guts and fish heads rained down on her in front of the Episcopal church. No one would give her a ride in their car to get home and she had to walk a few blocks with about ten cats following her."

I was laughing, too. The mental image was too much to ignore. That would have burned Grace Land to a crisp, but the Monroes had the upper hand.

"John and I don't have time to carry a grudge. I work all over this region for the paper and John teaches. In a crazy way, Grace's humiliation made both of us wake up and realize our behavior was reprehensible. Both of us. Her actions were worse, but we weren't innocent. It was best to let it all go. We came home, made the changes necessary, and we have a fabulous relationship now."

"Do you have any idea who might want to steal that expensive Elvis belt that Grace owns?"

"Look, half the town has an issue with Grace. The truth is, the enmity felt for her has no boundaries. She has enemies in Mississippi and California, and likely all in between. I told John this morning that I would be willing to bet the belt shows back up on her front porch before this is all over. Someone just wants to make her suffer."

"I hope you're right." It was an interesting premise. That this whole thing was a stunt meant to make Grace feel the lash of unhappiness. My problem with the theory was that the person who took the belt, if caught, could face a long prison sentence. Just saying it was a payback prank wouldn't stop a criminal charge. And the heat was dialing up on Chief Johnson, whether he admitted it or not. Cece had informed us that several members of the national media were in town covering the theft. That was not a good look for Yuma and Tupelo. Maybe he would be a bit more cooperative now.

Once I'd ended the chat with Kayla Monroe, I worked my way down the rest of the list of eight names. All were out of state. Not a single person sounded like a potential thief. Time to check with Tinkie and hope she'd had better luck with the cheaters club.

When I tapped at Tinkie's room, I heard a little squeal and I tapped again, more loudly. Tinkie and Oscar couldn't be having all the fun! She came to the door with her blouse buttoned wrong. I only rolled my eyes and laughed as Oscar scooted away to "run an errand."

"Did you have any luck with the list of jilted lovers?" I asked her.

"No." She adjusted the buttons. "I did save the most promising one for last."

"You mean before Oscar distracted you?"

She only laughed. "Let's call Rupert Crown, the man who nearly lost his bank job for Grace, only to discover she was dallying with Sippi and probably Kent at the same time. Now, I'm not saying she was sleeping with them, but she was certainly leading them on."

That would definitely piss a man off.

Tinkie was still laughing when someone answered her call. She immediately dropped into professional mode and explained who she was and why she was calling. When I pinched her waist, she put the call on speaker.

"What do you think I can tell you?" Rupert asked once Tinkie had explained our involvement in the case.

"Who might want to harm Grace enough to steal the belt?"

"Oh, you mean like me?" Rupert asked. "If I'd thought of it, I would definitely have done it. But I wouldn't get caught and, to be honest, getting rid of that belt is going to be a nightmare for whoever has it."

"Any suggestions as to who that might be?" Tinkie asked Rupert.

"Kent Madison hated her guts. She had his nu—private parts in a vise. Found out he'd stolen some things from a Gulf Coast church, but old Kent turned the tables on her when he confessed his past to the mayor and made restitution. Grace didn't want to let it go, though. And he had it in for her. But then so did ninety percent of the men she went out with. She's an unpleasant woman who thinks no one else matters but her."

Well, that resolved our issue that Janet was going to check into for us. I'd text her right away to save her time so she could get on the road to come to Tupelo. "Kent is on our list already. Any other suggestions as to other potential thieves?" Tinkie asked him.

"Yuma Johnson. He and Grace were a hot, hot ticket last year. He even went out to LA with her."

This revelation shocked me into silence, but not Tinkie.

"What happened between them?" Tinkie asked.

"Oh, Grace will have to tell you that. I know Yuma tried to keep it a secret, but the local paper got hold of the fact that he was out in LA for weeks at a time. The citizens paying his salary were . . . disturbed. It's hard to enforce the law and protect the citizens when you're two thousand miles away."

"We can check this out," Tinkie said. "And if we have more questions, we'll be back in touch."

"Watch out for Yuma. He's a snake. He was dating Sonja Rivera at the time he took up with Grace. Sonja didn't take too kindly to Grace's involvement with her boyfriend. Look, I have to go. I'm just glad to be away from Tupelo, Grace, and all the lies and cheating. My life is one hundred percent better. Good luck with finding the thief."

Sonja was high on my list of people to talk to—again. She'd failed to mention her involvement with Yuma. For obvious reasons, if she'd been jilted, she didn't want to broadcast the fact. But I didn't think pride was her only reason for secrecy. Now, this was a bone with a little meat on it that I could gnaw.

23

Tinkie got off the phone and I waved her out of the hotel room and down to the parking lot, where we got in my car—thanks to Coleman. He'd driven my vehicle with Sweetie Pie and Pluto. I loved the electric crossover, but I missed my mother's Roadster, which was in the barn all tucked in for a rest. While I loved the convertible, it was a car that garnered a lot of attention.

"Where are we going?" Tinkie asked. She checked her watch. Our competition began at six sharp. I didn't want to be late because it would mess up everyone's plans. We had to make hay while the sun shone.

"First, I have to call Janet and relieve her of her duties tracking down Kent Madison's sordid past." I did just that and was glad to learn Janet would be headed our way soon. Then I took a quarter from my pocket. "Heads we go to Grace; tails we talk to Yuma."

I flipped the coin and Tinkie caught it, turning up heads. We were on the way to speak with our aggravating client.

"Oscar is taking Maylin for a stroll around town to meet all the Elvis impersonators," Tinkie said as I drove.

Oscar really was a terrific parent. He fed Maylin, changed her diaper, whatever she needed. Oscar had always struck me as somewhat fastidious, but when it came to Maylin, he was all in. Diapers, upchuck, the endless toil of raising a baby—Oscar never complained and never shirked his duty. I was impressed.

"Are we going to practice our song and performance this afternoon?" Tinkie asked.

"Oh, sorry, I forgot. We're meeting in my suite. Everyone else will be gone and I have the space. Cece has the music."

"Excellent. So, until then, we have time to work on the case."

"Yes."

Tinkie nodded. "Excellent. After rehearsal, though, I'm spending some time with Oscar and Maylin before we do our show."

"Are you going to drug Oscar so he can't record this?" I teased her.

"Not a bad idea, but it would be wasted effort since I overheard Coleman and Harold plotting to permanently preserve the moment so they can put it up on social media."

I wasn't a big fan of online platforms, where any fool could post an opinion, but with an election year coming up,

I accepted that both Coleman and I were going to have to become a lot savvier. Millie and Cece would help us get up to speed with our social media skills.

"We're going to be so fabulous tonight, we deserve to be recorded for posterity." I was trying to make the best of it because I knew I couldn't stop it.

"Posterior, more likely," Tinkie said under her breath.

I only laughed and pulled into the driveway at Grace's mansion. To my surprise, Grace answered the door.

"Where's the maid?" Tinkie asked.

"I had to fire her," Grace said, clearly peeved by the turn of events.

"Why on earth?" I asked.

"She was going through my jewelry case."

That stopped us all in our tracks. "Did she take anything?" I pressed.

"No. But she had all of my expensive jewelry out on the bureau top. I don't know how she opened the safe. That's what really upset me. She had access she never should have had."

"What was her name again?" I had my pad and pen out. I'd met her several times and she didn't strike me as the criminal type, but we had to track down all leads.

"Jessica Calvert."

"Was she really going to steal from you?" Tinkie asked.

"She said she wasn't going to. She said she was organizing my jewelry as a surprise." She frowned and looked down at her fancy stiletto shoes. "It is true that last week I threw a tantrum because my necklaces were all tangled."

Oh, there was more to this story than Grace initially wanted to tell. This was a pattern of behavior for her. "She may have been trying to do something nice for you?"

"Maybe."

Tinkie looked at me and rolled her eyes. "Grace, you admit she may have been helping you, and yet you fired her."

"I lost my temper."

Oh, I knew that feeling. I wanted to fire Grace on the spot. She was so careless of others.

"I should call her and apologize." Grace picked up her phone. I thought she'd go into another room to eat crow, but such wasn't the case.

"Jessica, I owe you an apology. Please come back to work." There was a pause. "Okay, tomorrow, then. With a pay increase of ten dollars an hour. I am very sorry I jumped to conclusions."

One thing about Grace, she knew how to make an apology. A pay raise was a smart move. It might not take away the sting of being accused of stealing, but an eighty-dollar-a-day pay increase would certainly help.

"Could we see your jewelry?" I asked.

"Why?" Grace was instantly defensive. Which made me instantly suspicious. My intention was to get her busy with a chore so I could drop the info about Yuma on her head.

"Why not?" I countered.

"Do you have something to hide?" Tinkie asked her.

"How dare you!"

"It's not fun being accused of something without evidence, is it?"

Grace harrumphed out of the room and signaled for us to follow her into her bedroom on the second floor. The house was huge. And eclectically decorated. Along with true works of art, velvet Elvis paintings lined the spiral staircase. While it might have been overkill in another home, it was perfect at Grace Land's house.

When she pulled out a tangle of beautiful gold necklaces in a huge snarl, I just shook my head. She held the bundle out to me and I nodded at Tinkie as I took it.

"Grace, you failed to mention that you were sleeping with Chief Johnson," Tinkie said.

Grace stumbled backward. "Where did you hear that?"

"No secrets are safe in a small town," Tinkie told her. "Now, why didn't you just tell us?"

"Yuma dumped me. Not my finest moment."

"Nor his," I said. "Conflict of interest."

She sighed. "I think he may have stolen the belt just to show me he could." She plopped down on the bed and began to cry. "I have the worst taste in men!"

She wasn't lying. She was one of those people who fouled her nest at every chance. "You haven't been honest with us at all, Grace." I was ready to throw in the towel.

"Please don't quit. I'll add another ten grand to your fee. Just don't quit on me."

Tinkie sighed and shook her head. "You have to stop lying to us. I mean it. One more lie and we're done. We'll return what you've paid us and move on with our holiday. Understand?"

"I do." She hugged Tinkie. "Thank you." She turned to hug me and I stepped back. I was still angry with her, though I agreed with Tinkie's choice.

"What about Rupert Crown?" I asked.

She flinched, but she didn't look away from me. "He was my beau for a while."

"Yes, he was on the list you gave Tinkie. Men you'd jilted or cheated or whatever. What's his story?"

Grace waved us out of the bedroom and down to the bar

area. She set about making us drinks, which I didn't want but didn't object to. We had a performance and I needed to get over my anxiety. One small drink might help. Maybe. Maybe not.

"What happened between you two?"

"I cheated on him with Yuma."

"Why?"

She shrugged. "I don't know. I do things all the time that don't make a lot of sense. 'Self-destructive' is what my shrink called me. It's like, since my mom abandoned me—"

"Abandoned you? I thought she was dead!"

"She abandoned me, and now I can't get enough love. Or attention. It's pathetic, isn't it?"

Okay, she'd brought out the big guns—her shrink and ownership of her issues. Which was another thing she'd failed to tell us about. I didn't really care, but it was another indication of her lack of forthcomingness. "How long have you been seeing a shrink?"

"Since I was fifteen."

"Seriously?" Tinkie asked, unable to hide her disbelief. "You were just a kid."

"Yes. The name thing really started to wreck me when I started high school. The way folks treated me." She hesitated. "I wasn't close with my mother, but I loved her. She's . . . different. And maybe a little desperate."

That was enough trauma to need professional help, for sure. "I'm sorry about your mother's death."

"Don't be. It turned out to be a lie."

"I thought your mother was deceased." Color me confused.

"She is to me," Grace said. "I have no idea where she is."

"So, she's not really dead?" I had to press this.

"I honestly don't know, but I think she's alive."

I could see sympathy on Tinkie's face. She had her own mother issues.

"When was the last time you spoke with your mother?" I asked. "And the truth, Grace. Seriously. I'm about done with your prevarication, omission, and just plain lying."

"It's been years since we actually talked. Last time we spoke she was in Reno. Married to a guy named Luther Abbott. He was headed to Los Angeles to try out for a soap opera role. She called to see if I had any contacts with talent agents."

"Did you help her?" Tinkie asked.

"I gave her some names. She got what she wanted, and I never heard from her again."

I refused to feel sorry for her. I wasn't going to be taken in, again. "Did this Luther fellow get a role on a soap opera?"

"He did," she said. "But I think my mother has been long gone from his sphere. Once a man isn't totally dependent on her, she's done. She can't make him jump through hoops if he has any independence."

I made a mental note to track down Luther Abbott. He wasn't a promising lead, but it might turn into something. We'd reported to Grace what we had so far, which amounted to mostly nothing. It was time to move along. "Tinkie and I have to go to rehearsal for tonight," I said, edging toward the front door.

"Oh, you have plenty of time," Grace said, making a grab for Tinkie's hand and missing. It was almost as if she was lonely. I had to beat that thought out of my head. I couldn't afford to feel sorry for a woman who lied as easily as she breathed.

"Nope, we gotta go." I caught Tinkie's arm and tugged

her toward the front door—which opened as I reached for the knob. I let out a little shriek and jumped back.

"Is everything okay?" Jessica the maid asked. "I came back to work right now since Grace apologized."

"Everything is fine." I pulled Tinkie out the door and onto the steps. "See you tonight, Grace." I closed the door and headed for the car with a full head of steam. Tinkie allowed me to drag her. "Step along," I said. "You act like you've got lead in your feet."

"You're desperate to get away from here," she said. "It's almost as if you're afraid of Grace."

I looked back to see the wide grin plastered on her face. She was gigging me. "Grace is a lying liar. I need to get away from her before I quit."

Tinkie laughed, and it was the sound of silver sleigh bells softened by snow. "You're too easy a target, Sarah Booth."

"Which makes you a bully." I was still a little cranky, though I had to fight hard not to laugh.

"Let's go grab a toddy before rehearsal."

"I figured you for a teetotaler when it came to public performance."

"You figured wrong, though a Diet Coke may be the order of the day." She linked her arm through mine and escorted me to the car.

24

We ordered drinks at the bar in the hotel and took them up to Cece's room. Of all my friends, she was most likely to know someone who might know someone at the soap opera where Luther Abbott worked. My hunch paid off.

"Luther Abbott is a Mississippi man," Cece said. "He's a bit older than we are, but we know people who had classes with him in high school."

"We do?" I'd looked up the handsome actor on the internet and I had zero recollection of him from my earlier years.

"Sure thing. Only way back then he was Luther Smith, a thin boy with thick hair, thick glasses, and a thick backwoods drawl. Luther Smith was the brainiac who could multiply and divide big numbers in his head. And he was a chess champ. He went on some game show when we were in grammar school and created a sensation. He was head of the Christmas parade in Zinnia back in the day. I remember him well. My family held him up as someone to emulate. I was such a bitter disappointment in that department."

"You've never been anything less than a superstar, Cece." I'd never erase the damage done by Cece's family, who'd refused to acknowledge her for who she was. All I could do was let her feel how much I loved and admired her. And change the topic. "So, what happened to nerdy Luther Smith?"

"He grew up," Cece said. "He's been the chief romantic lead on *The Secrets of Night* for the last five years. He changed his last name to Abbott because it sounded more serious. He does a good job with the melodrama."

So, Cece was a fan. "Do you know how to reach him?"

"Like I keep a file of soap opera stars?"

"Cece!" Tinkie chastised her. "You are the queen of celebrity gossip and juice. We need to speak with him. You do know how to reach him, don't you?"

"Maybe." She grinned.

"I have had it with Grace lying, and now you're withholding." I did sound testy and cranky.

"Just make the connection for us," Tinkie said.

"Right now? We have to rehearse."

"Right now." No one seemed to get it that Tinkie and I were working. We weren't just fiddlefarting around for the pleasure of it.

Cece whipped out her phone, sat down for a moment to go through some screens, finally hit dial, and handed the phone to me. It rang four times before a cultured male voice answered.

"Is this Luther Abbott?" I asked.

"It is. But you aren't Cece."

"No, I'm a friend." I gave him my spiel and then let him know I was working for Grace Land.

"Oh lord, that girl is crazy as an outhouse rat!"

I couldn't help it. I burst out laughing, and so did Cece and Tinkie—the phone was on speaker. "I agree, but she's still my client. Could you tell me where her mother might be?" I didn't bother to tell him I'd been under the false impression that Grace's mother was dead.

"I don't know, and I don't care as long as she leaves me alone. Grace is nuts, but let's just say that little acorn didn't fall far from the tree."

I'd just watched a few YouTube clips of Abbott on the soap opera, and he had no trace of a Southern accent. Now, though, he'd reverted back to his Sunflower County twang and heavy dependence on colloquialisms. On the TV show he played a big-city surgeon. He was a pretty darn good actor.

"We need to find her." I pushed a little.

"We broke up years ago and I haven't seen or heard from her since. She wasn't a woman who felt the need to drag a lot of baggage behind her. It was the best move for me. I've never had a problem dating older women, but she had some insecurities. She has no loyalty to anyone, so I guess she projects that onto everyone who makes her feel vulnerable."

"She dumped her daughter and never looked back."

"I didn't agree with the way she treated Grace, but no one—not even the good Lord himself—could move that woman off start once she was on the go line."

"She and Grace share a lot of the same characteristics."

"Why are you looking for Grace's mama?"

I glanced at Tinkie, and she shrugged as if to say, what's the harm in telling him? "Grace had a valuable piece of art stolen, and she hired us to find the person who took it."

"The Elvis belt," Luther said. "I read about that in one of the tabloid rags. Whooee! That was an expensive gewgaw. Any idea who took it?"

Either Luther was a really, really good actor or he was one of the dull knives in the drawer when it came to crime motivation. "We figure it was someone who wanted to hurt Grace."

"Someone like me or her mama?"

Well, he was sharper than I thought. "Yes."

"I've been working regularly. Long, twelve-hour days. Haven't left Los Angeles in the past nine months. My co-workers and the show producer will vouch for me."

Tinkie jotted down their names and numbers as Luther gave out the information. Checking alibis fell under proper investigative form, even when it seemed obvious.

"Have you seen Grace's mother?" I asked.

"No. I really haven't. And, like I said, I don't want to . . ." His voice faded to a stop as if he had something else to say but wasn't certain he should.

"But—" I encouraged.

"But I received several hang-up calls from a Mississippi number."

Now, that was interesting. I perked up and sat forward. "Who was calling?"

"I didn't recognize the number, and when I called it back it went straight to a dead line. It occurred to me that maybe it was her. That maybe she'd gone home and was rethinking things."

He actually sounded hopeful, which made me think he'd

really cared for Grace's mom. "Shoot me the number," I requested.

"Will do. Now I'm needed on set. Tell Grace I'm sorry her mom wasn't more maternal. It wasn't my idea that she skip out on Tupelo and Grace. I always liked the kid, you know. She had pluck."

He was about to hang up, so I spoke quickly. "Luther, do you know anyone who would want to hurt Grace by stealing that Elvis belt?"

"Lord, everyone in town thought she was a pretentious little thing. But that was her mother's doing, not hers. Still, folks found her hard to endure. Could it just be a prank? Maybe the thief will return the belt as soon as the Elvis contest is over."

"Maybe, but I don't think so. The belt is very valuable."

"Yes, I read that, too. If I think of anyone, I'll give you a call, Ms. Delaney."

"One more question. What name is Grace's mother going by?"

"Last time I heard, it was Brandi Beaumont. And I don't believe Grace was aware her mother was alive, at least for a number of years. Brandi never stayed anywhere long, and she changed her name often. I don't remember a lot of what Brandi told me over the time we were together, other than Grace had done okay for herself. Maybe check on a young woman named Sonja Rivera. She had a bitter feud with Grace. And there was an insurance woman in town. Hot, but kind of on the sleazy side. Krystal something or other."

"How do you know all this?" I asked. "You've been gone from the area for a long time."

"I have relatives in Tupelo. They keep me well informed. Good luck with your quest. Now, I'm wanted on set. It's the moment when I save the life of the town harpy and she jumps off the operating table and stabs me with a scalpel. It's going to be an Emmy-winning scene!"

He hung up and I looked at Tinkie and Cece.

"Sonja and Krystal," Tinkie said. "It's one or the other. I'm willing to bet on it."

A tap at the door reminded all of us we had to get busy. Millie was in the hallway, ready to start rehearsal for the amateur impersonator competition. We ran through the number four times and then called it quits. Cece had some heavy-duty makeup to apply. I ordered beverages for all of us, called the men to tell them to be at the Arena Center at six, and then we began the process of slithering into our Christmas tights and little elf suits, shoes, hats, and makeup. Tinkie would have to find family time after the show. Who knew being an amateur would require so much time and preparation?

Tinkie and I finished getting dressed and took a minute to make some phone calls. I was dying to grill Grace about Yuma and a number of other things. I was also eager to talk with Coleman. But first, I called Krystal. No surprise, she was as hostile as a rattlesnake in a burlap sack. She spewed venom at me and threatened to sue me if I contacted her again.

Tinkie didn't have any better luck with Sonja. The young Priscilla look-alike was a lot more civil, but she played it dumb before she got annoyed and told us to leave her alone "or else." Not the most explicit threat, but she made it clear she had no intention of talking to us about Grace, the belt, or the reason Luther Abbott thought she might be out for revenge against Grace. It was a little unsettling, because in the past Sonja had been pleasant. What had changed?

I drew Tinkie out on the hotel balcony for a chat and asked her that question.

"We found out about Yuma and Grace." She shrugged. "We found out someone deliberately tried to harm, if not kill, Grace by messing with the brake lines of her car. We were also targeted. We learned Grace is a terrible bitch to her employees and that numerous people from her past actively dislike her. I was going to say men from her past, but it is everyone. Even children, and maybe dogs. We found out Sonja may be involved in all of this. Her aggressiveness may simply be a protective maneuver."

I had to laugh, though it wasn't funny. Grace was headed toward pariah status in Tupelo. and probably in Hollywood. "Let's put the case aside until the competition is over. Tomorrow we have to make a focused effort to get some better leads. I'm putting my money on Yuma." The lawman had gotten under my skin. I didn't care much for liars, and he was a liar by omission.

Millie stepped out on the balcony and put an arm around each of us. "You girls ready?"

"Wouldn't miss it for the world. Let's go!"

25

The Arena Center had been magically transformed into a winter wonderland scene with fake snow all outside the building. Inside, a billion twinkle lights of all hues made me gasp with pleasure. I loved the multicolored lights, the tinsel, the smell of fir trees and fresh popcorn. My favorite Christmas carols were being performed by Elvis impersonators, and I stopped to listen to "White Christmas" being sung by a svelte young Elvis with a lovely voice.

We'd agreed that the men shouldn't see us in our outfits—which I thought were completely stunning. Cece and Millie had done a spectacular job with the elf makeup on Tinkie, Millie, and me. Cece had gone full Elvis in a blue spangled jumpsuit with a cape lined in silver with little bells on it that chimed merrily whenever she moved. With her hair spray-dyed black and swept back in a pompadour, at first glance she did favor the King.

I hadn't performed on a stage in a long time, and singing had never been one of my strong suits. I felt the familiar butterflies jittering around in my stomach. Why had I signed up to do this? But when I looked at my friends, I knew the answer. We were going to kill it and have fun at the same time.

For my prop, I had a bag of soft toys that I would throw into the audience from the stage. That was Millie's idea, but I had the best arm, so I got to play Santa. Tinkie and Millie had rehearsed some dance moves that were a bit tricky for me. And Cece, of course, would be the primary singer.

We took our places backstage and tried to calm down. We were number eight on the schedule of forty-two acts.

I didn't intend to watch the other contestants, but some of them were so original and fun that I found myself watching and applauding. We didn't have to win—just as long as we didn't humiliate ourselves.

In the blink of an eye, we heard our stage name—Santa's Little Helpers—called and we were being ushered onto the stage by the managers. For a moment I gazed out at the audience, which looked enormous, and felt like I was about to have a panic attack. I bit my lip lightly with disgust. I'd been on Broadway, at least for a few minutes in a walk-on role, and here I was about to collapse from nerves in Tupelo. I gritted down and found my courage.

Jaytee had engineered the music for our number, and as soon as it started and I caught Cece's eye, I was perfectly fine. We did our backup woo-woos to get started and then Cece was belting it out. She and Jaytee had added some bluesy music that fit the song and our act perfectly. We were rocking it, and I was having a blast. It was so much more fun than I'd anticipated.

Before I knew what was happening, a big man in a Santa suit leaped onstage and pulled Millie into some belly-rubbing dance moves that brought the audience to their feet. It wasn't planned—or at least I didn't know about it—but it was perfect. He kept yelling "Ho, ho, ho, my little fruitcake muffin!" And Millie shimmied and shook her breasts at him. *Dirty Santa* took on a new meaning. At last, he jumped off the stage and disappeared into the darkened house.

Right on cue, I tossed little stuffed Christmas figures out to the audience. Tinkie and Millie were dancing like they'd found a big stash of amphetamines. The bells on the curled-up toes of our shoes jingled in time with the bells on Cece's cape.

When it was time for the backup singers to get together and sing, I was right with them and singing my heart out. We brought the audience to their feet, clapping and applauding. Cece finished with a sweeping pose just like Elvis, and then she whipped her cape off and threw it into the audience. That was the final straw. The audience belonged to us! The joyous rush of performing came back to me on the sweet tide of Christmas music.

We joined hands and went to the front of the stage to take a bow. Then I heard something snap overhead. The space above the stage lights was dark. I bowed again, smiling at the audience as I stood up.

Another snap and pop from the darkness above.

"Encore! Encore!" The audience was shouting. Some flicked on cigarette lighters and held them up.

"We don't have another number rehearsed," Tinkie whispered.

"Encore!" The audience wasn't giving up.

"Cece, you sing another. Jaytee can accompany you on the harmonica," Millie suggested.

"Let's take another bow and just get off the stage," Cece said. "It isn't fair to the other contestants. We need to clear the stage."

She was right, and as we took one more bow, I heard the shriek of metal on metal and a loud pop. I looked up just in time to see one of the big stage lights coming down right on top of us. I pushed my friends out of the way, and we fell helter-skelter across the stage. The big, heavy light crashed down in a horrible sound of twisting metal and shattering glass.

And then all hell broke loose.

Grace rushed the stage, screaming for medics even though we weren't hurt. The backstage manager, Robbie, called 911 and Chief Johnson's office, demanding medical and law enforcement help. Coleman, Oscar, and Harold rushed to the stage to make sure we were okay. It was not the conclusion of our act that we'd anticipated.

Although we weren't harmed at all, Coleman, Oscar, and Jaytee insisted we get checked out by paramedics. While I was impatient, the delay also gave me a chance to scan the audience and examine the backstage workers who Coleman and Yuma had lined up like potential firing squad victims.

Grace sat with us, and for once she had the sense to keep her lips zipped. I don't know where she found plastic glasses, liquor, and a serving tray, but she got up and left for about fifteen minutes and returned with Cape Cods for each of us.

"Very Christmassy," I told her, noting the bright red drink.

"Only the best for my friends," she said. "That light came close to crushing all of you." She looked over at the big broken fixture that had fallen only twenty feet from where we'd all tumbled to the floor. "I'm tempted to say it looks deliberate."

"No kidding, Sherlock." I was annoyed. My knees were barked and painful. Tupelo had been hell on my body, from parking lot rug burn to now near death by stage light. Tinkie came to stand beside me. Her butt had taken the brunt of her tumble. Luckily we were both okay, as were Cece and Millie. They were mad but uninjured.

"We would have won that competition, too," Cece said bitterly. "I can't believe someone tried to kill all four of us."

The audience had been allowed to go to the lobby for refreshments until the show could continue. We were being held in the area in front of the stage while Yuma questioned us.

"Ladies, would you mind taking a seat?" Yuma asked us. "I have some more questions. I'm sorry to delay you, but it could really help."

I had some questions of my own, but it was the stage manager I was interested in talking to. Robbie looked like someone had kicked the wind right out of him. He sat glumly in the audience staring at the floor. I walked over and sat down beside him.

"Who was backstage that shouldn't have been there?"

He sighed. "Half the town. This is Tupelo, not New York City. Folks were running backstage to bring the contestants things and also just to be in the thick of it."

"Anyone that struck you as odd?"

He thought a moment. "Krystal was back there. And Yuma, who I didn't expect to be involved in the show at all. And some of the Elvis impersonators. But none of that is strange. It's just Tupelo. The only strange thing is that Grace Land *wasn't* back there. She's usually in everyone's business when it comes to any kind of event or performance. Other than that . . ." He stopped talking and looked away from me.

"Anyone in particular you'd like to mention?"

"Okay, okay. The Manning twins. I couldn't do my job efficiently because they were interfering."

"Can you show me where someone would have to be to bring those lights down like that?"

"Sure." He stood up and I hobbled after him. My knees were going to be a problem for the next day or so. But as I moved around a little, the tightness in the abraded skin eased.

While everyone else was busy, I ducked behind the thick curtains with Robbie and went to the back of the stage. There were ropes and levers and mechanical things used to set lights or bring the curtains up and down. There were moving dollies to change scenery. A longing for the stage hit me hard. I loved the trappings of the theater, but I was looking for something in particular. What I found was a pully with a bit of severed rope still on it. I picked up the end of the rope. The rope was cleanly cut, except for one bit that was frayed. I waved Robbie over.

"Damn, that's been cut," he said.

"Yes, it has." He was quiet and he'd gone completely pale. "Did you see anyone near this pulley?"

"I was stage left helping line the contestants up and keep

them in order. I wasn't even looking over here. We'd set the lights up yesterday so that Sonja, in the control booth in the back of the theater, could manage the lights and the curtain."

"Who else was working backstage?"

He motioned for a young high school student to come over. "Did you see anyone near the ropes and pulleys?" he asked her.

She started to cry.

"You have to tell us," Robbie said gently. "Please. It's important."

"Chief Johnson was back here walking around, and I saw him by the lights. But so was that Allan Malone guy, the one with the TV show about singing Barbra Streisand songs. He had his dogs back here and one of them was pulling on a rope. That little bratty dog tried to bite me, to boot. Allan was trying to catch her, but she had a rope and she was giving it everything she had."

Was it possible that my friends and I were almost obliterated by a dang pug with an underbite and a bad attitude? That thought infuriated me.

"Anyone else?"

The high schooler shook her head and wiped her tears. Robbie sent her on her way, then turned back to me. "Sonja Rivera was back here right before the show started. She was making sure the light board worked with all the spots and colored lights. Like for the number you did, Sonja hit y'all with that blue light that made the song even better." Robbie shrugged. "Look at the rope. It looks like it's been cut almost all the way through. Someone could have just cut it and left a tiny strand holding the lights up. Then the dog was chewing that."

"Then they wouldn't know exactly when it would fall."

"Technically, that's true."

The would-be murderer wouldn't know who the lights might fall on. Maybe it wasn't directed at me and my friends. Maybe it was just meant to wreck the show.

"Anyone else back here?" I just kept asking.

Robbie slapped his thigh. "Yeah! Kent Madison, the assistant mayor, was back here. He was whanging on about how he hated the impersonators and how they were going to screw up Christmas for the 'people who really celebrated the season for the right reasons,' whoever those people are and whatever the right reasons may be."

"Did he show any interest in those lights?"

"In fact, he did." The stagehand patted his pocket for his cigarette pack. He motioned me to follow him outside.

It was tough when he lit up—I was a reformed smoker—but I stood strong and didn't bum one. "What did Madison say?"

Robbie sighed. "He wanted to know how the lights worked. He said he was going to help Sonja Rivera at the light board." He frowned. "But I never saw him there. I guess he got busy with that Krystal woman." He laughed. "I thought she was going to gobble him up the way she was kissing him with that big old mouth of hers. They were going hot and heavy back here."

Not the mental image I wanted in my brain, but there it was.

"Thanks." I looked out in the audience to see Coleman signaling me over. He'd been talking with witnesses, but now he was helping Yuma handcuff Kent Madison. I looked closely to be sure Madison's head wasn't concave from Krystal's tender mercies.

I strolled over to Coleman. "So, Yuma thinks sleazy Kent is the guilty party?"

"Yep. The assistant mayor is denying it, but there were several witnesses who saw him by the rope-and-pulley system. He's responsible for that light falling and almost killing all of you. Yuma is positive, and I agree."

That took the wind out of my sails for a moment because, as much as I disliked Kent, I wasn't certain he was guilty of this particular event. I didn't trust Yuma. "Do you think Madison was trying to kill us?"

Coleman considered. "Maybe. Or maybe he was just trying to kill the Elvis impersonator show. He hates it so much. It's like a personal affront to him."

That last statement was revealing. Madison clearly hated the Elvis thing, but why? It was a boon for Tupelo, no matter how he tried to deny it. "You think killing the Elvis contest is truly his motivation?"

"I don't know."

Any further thoughts were interrupted by Grace, who'd taken center stage and had a microphone.

"Ladies and gentlemen, if you haven't already, please go to the lobby and grab a complimentary glass of wine and then return to your seats. As soon as the broken glass is swept up, the show will continue. Nobody, and I mean *no-body*, is going to stop my Elvis show! Sit down, drink up, and get ready to be entertained."

The house lights were turned up as young volunteers cleaned up the broken glass and debris. I had to admire Grace and the people of Tupelo who refused to be cowed by evildoers. I also felt more than a twinge of relief that Yuma thought the near-death experience wasn't aimed at me or the girls.

We got some wine, took our seats, and Cece grasped my wrist. "I don't agree that this was only meant to stop the show."

Her words and the expression on her face chilled me. "You think it was meant to hurt us?"

"I do. If Madame Tomeeka were here, she would confirm this. You and Tinkie were absolutely the target. Millie and I are just collateral damage."

My gut told me she was right. As much as I wanted to believe it was a coincidence that the lights had nearly fallen on us, my instincts told me it was deliberate. But how had the culprit engineered the timing of the lights falling? A frayed rope wasn't exactly a scientific way to create an on-demand disaster.

I excused myself and stepped around Cece to slip into the aisle. Coleman was busy with Yuma as they hustled Kent Madison out the door and hopefully to a jail cell. I headed to the light booth, where Sonja was working. She might know more than she'd let on.

As I reached the booth, the house lights went down and the stage was brightly lit. Grace announced the next act, a duo from New Haven who sang "O Holy Night." Not a lot of Elvis in the song, but it was beautifully performed.

I waited until the act was done to approach Sonja. When I spoke up from behind her, she nearly jumped out of her skin.

"What do you want now?" she demanded.

"The truth."

She looked around as if she intended to rabbit on me. "Don't do it. I'll have to catch you, trip you, and hurt you. I'm tired of the runaround and crazy bull hockey in this town. Why would Kent Madison try to kill me and my friends?"

She sighed. "He wasn't aiming to kill you. Only stop you and the show. The lights were supposed to fall as you came on the stage. Not after you finished your act."

Sonja looked like a very sad Priscilla Presley. "You knew this and didn't warn us?"

"He told me about the plan. Honestly, Kent is all talk and no action. I didn't believe he'd go through with it. And he assured me the timing was perfect. I think Allan Malone's little pug got hold of the rope and tugged it enough that it didn't break when it was supposed to."

"He might have killed me or my friends." My voice was low and harsh. I was angry.

"But he didn't." Sonja had no remorse. "You're fine. Kent was arrested. What else do you want?"

"Where is the Elvis belt?"

She pressed her lips into a thin line and pushed at her beehive hairdo. "I don't know. I don't. I'd tell you if I knew. I'm sick of all of this. All of the Elvises will be gone by Sunday, but this whole stolen belt thing is going to go on forever. Grace will be the center of attention, just like always. It will ruin the holidays for everyone here."

"What do you know about Yuma and Grace and their affair?"

"They had a torrid encounter last year. 'Affair' is a bit too generous. It was just a fling for both of them when Grace was home for a few months from Hollywood. They had it bad. They couldn't keep their hands off each other. It was kind of disturbing. And if you're asking if they could conspire together to steal the belt, Yuma would be the perfect partner in crime, wouldn't he? The man hired to pursue justice? That would be a real kicker. But why? I heard the belt wasn't insured. Why would Grace want to go through all of this commotion and look like a dunderhead for not having insurance? Folks in town don't like her and now they think she's stupid."

"Maybe they just hate Grace enough to do it for the hell of it. And maybe people like you let it happen."

Sonja's hands hovered over the light board. "You might want to have some evidence before you say that again. I don't have the money Grace does, but I'm not going to let anyone slander me. Got it?"

"Loud and clear."

26

It took a few acts, but finally the audience relaxed and settled into the night's entertainment. There were several terrific performances, but none matched Cece's powerful vocals or our fetching costumes. Not to mention the mysterious Dirty Santa, who'd danced so lewdly. We had brought the Christmas joy to Elvis's "Blue Christmas."

At last, the competition was over and Grace took center stage to award the trophy to the winner. The girls and I sat on the edge of our seats. It was peculiar. I hadn't given winning a lot of thought, but I discovered I really wanted to win. Badly.

When our names were called, I whooped and jumped to my feet. We trooped up onstage like invading locusts, and

Cece grasped the beautiful silver statue of Elvis in her hand and held it up. "For all the contestants," she said.

"This is a pity win," Sherman Manning called out from the third row. "Just because you almost died in a freak accident doesn't mean you deserve to win."

"So come up here and take it from me, wussy boy," Cece said.

Before things got out of hand, Jaytee and Oscar joined us onstage. Coleman was nowhere to be found. He'd vanished into the audience. Neither Oscar nor Harold had a clue where he'd gone, but Yuma was gone, too. And when Grace left the stage after giving Cece the award, she disappeared, too.

I was about to have a conniption when I caught sight of long blond hair and a body to die for. Sippi Salem was in the house. He lingered in the back by the light board, talking to Sonja, before he started to slink out the back door.

"Come on!" I grabbed Cece, because Tinkie was talking with Oscar and Pauline, who'd shown up with Maylin. My partner had her hands full.

"What's up?" Cece asked. She was hanging on to her trophy like it had been presented by the Academy.

"Sippi. You wanted to meet him. Let's go. We'll bird-dog him and see what he's up to. I never expected him to show up here."

"That man is a bane to womankind," Cece said, but she was hot on his heels, camera out and snapping.

"Did you get good shots of the competition for the newspaper?"

"A ton. And Harold was kind enough to photograph our act and the falling lights. He captured it perfectly."

I made a mental note of that. I wanted to look at that footage ASAP. I might learn something new. But right now, bird-dogging Sippi was my primary goal. And we needed to pick up our pace or else he would give us the slip.

We followed him out of the Arena Center into the night. It was colder than I remembered, and I pulled my jacket around me more snugly. The bells on my little elf shoes were a dead giveaway, so I snatched the jinglers off and discarded them. Cece, as the primary singer, had worn sexy black thigh-high boots and no bells except on the cape she'd thrown into the audience. She didn't jingle as she racewalked after Sippi.

I hung back—thinking if Cece caught him she might have more sway with him. He'd already met me and knew I was a PI. Cece looked like a supermodel lost in a small Mississippi town.

Sippi managed to avoid all of his many fans who would have swarmed him if they'd seen him. Somehow the tall, attractive man was able to blend into the night. An interesting talent for a well-known artist.

He left the grounds of the Arena Center and headed downtown. The bars were still hopping and music blared. Several Elvises were on street corners. Sippi slowed to hear one with a lovely voice sing "Silent Night." I was glad to stop and catch my breath. The little elf shoes were not all that substantial, and my feet were freezing. Not to mention that I only had on tights and a skirt so short folks could see my lacy green and red pantaloons. I wasn't dressed for the Tupelo night.

Cece didn't even ask. She slipped off her jacket and handed it to me. "I have a heavy sweater," she said. "I'm glad I grabbed it. I thought we might go barhopping or something fun where I might need a warmer coat. You remember fun, don't you?"

"This is a perfect evening. And seeing as how we barely escaped being crushed by a falling light, I'd say just walking down the street is fun."

"No, it isn't. Man, your fun standards have fallen into a pit." She pointed and forestalled my response. "Look, he's on the move again."

And so were we.

Sippi moved down Main Street, stopping again to listen to an Elvis crooner perform "Jailhouse Rock" with a near-perfect hip swivel. He tipped the performer and moved on beneath the multicolored lights. Another Elvis sang "God Rest Ye Merry, Gentlemen." I thought I might have to drag Cece away to keep up with Sippi, who was a block in front of us. Thank heavens for the crowds out in the street. Some sang along with the Elvises as they ran through the carols that made Christmas such a special time to me.

"Remember that time in high school when we were both in chorus?" Cece asked.

Sippi was setting quite a pace, so when I answered, I was panting a little. "You mean the time when we both got kicked out of chorus?" Oh, I remembered. I looked behind me to be sure Aunt Loulane hadn't risen from her grave to box my ears. She'd been really angry with us.

"That would be the time." Cece laughed.

She'd been Cecil then, and some of the more ignorant kids gave her a really hard time because she loved fashion and movie-star gossip and didn't play football. They'd teased her mercilessly backstage at chorus. To get even, Cecil and I had come up with a scheme. Several of the worst offenders were boys who'd camped out regularly at our favorite swimming hole. Cecil and I slipped up to the campsite and poured ipecac in the liquor bottles. Those boys nearly puked their guts out.

When Cecil was questioned about it, she admitted it and kept my name out of it. But I'd stepped forward, too, unwilling to let her take the fall for a stunt I was also involved in. The end result was that both of us were jettisoned from chorus, even though Cecil had an incredible voice. It was a punishment to her, but not to me. I could carry a tune, but I didn't have the pipes she did. The chorus teacher stayed mad at her for the rest of the year.

"What made you think of that?" I asked her.

"Listening to the Elvises sing. I never let on, but being kicked out of chorus really hurt. That class was the one I really enjoyed. The one where I could just sing and feel the emotions of the songs. I didn't have to justify it to anyone. Not a living soul. When that was taken from me, I felt lost."

I hadn't fully considered how much performing meant to Cecil. "I'm sorry. I would have taken all the blame, but you jumped ahead of me."

"I was guilty. You were missing your parents and looking for a way to act out. And you were standing up for me. You shouldn't have been punished."

"But I didn't love chorus like you did, so it wasn't all that much of a punishment to me. But it hurt you."

Cece put her arm around my shoulders. "Lord, let's climb out of the gully of memory lane! Next thing we'll be weeping in our beer."

It was a good decision, since Sippi suddenly ducked behind

a building. We hurried forward, but by the time we got there, he was gone. We stood staring at the empty street. I listened for the sound of footsteps echoing, but there was only silence. We'd left the more populated areas of Tupelo behind us, so the quiet was eerie. In the distance I could vaguely hear some carolers singing "Deck the Halls."

"Where'd he go?" Cece asked.

"This is the last of the business area. Down that way it becomes residential." I picked up my phone and texted Coleman to let him know Cece and I were fine, but on a lead. I wasn't ready to turn back, but I didn't want to worry Coleman or my friends.

"Let's walk down a little farther," Cece suggested. "If we don't pick up his trail, we'll turn back. I just have to wonder what he's up to. And where'd he go? Did aliens pick him up and teleport him somewhere else?"

"I wish we'd picked up Sweetie Pie. And Chablis." I didn't want to leave the little dust mop out. She was tiny, but fierce and a good tracker.

"That would be helpful. Call Harold."

I did as she suggested, and within two minutes Harold, in his fancy pickup, found us. Sweetie was in the front seat with him. Chablis was with Oscar, Maylin, and Pauline, waiting for Tinkie to finish at the Arena Center. I knew Tink would get more out of Yuma than I could—and she was also well aware that Yuma was a prime suspect. Still, I had a fleeting regret that I'd left her there. Not alone, but without me.

Sweetie Pie seemed to realize that stealth was in order, because she held back on her signature baying and put her nose to the ground. She struck a trail almost immediately, and we were off. The little elf shoes had now become not just unpleasant, but a major pain in the butt. My toes were so cold they might have broken off. I had no way to tell without removing the shoes, which was not going to happen. The only thing to do was move forward with as much speed as possible and hope we ran Sippi to ground in some place warm.

Harold was right with us as we cut behind buildings and ended up going through the backyards of a fancy residential area. It reminded me of the night that Tinkie had given birth to Maylin in the Moran backyard. The doctor had feared complications, and yet the only real help Tinkie ended up having was me. Maylin had been born into my hands—an amazing, perfect little girl!

When Sweetie led us out on the sidewalk, I realized we were at Grace Land's home. A tall, dark shadow was slipping in the window of her house. Was it Sippi? Had he come to steal something else?

Cece pointed and hissed. "It's him."

I nodded. "Harold, go to the front door and knock, please. I'll wait in the back for Sippi to try to leave. He won't want to be caught in that house, so he'll likely come out the back and I'll tackle him. Cece, get the camera ready in case he bolts. Sweetie will help me bring him down, if necessary."

It wasn't a great plan, but we didn't have more time. We separated and took our places. I was just outside the window where Sippi had gained illegal entry, assuming he'd likely bail out from that same location.

Harold pounded on the front door, and I listened, waiting for footsteps headed for an escape.

Crickets.

Harold pounded harder.

Nothing.

If Sippi meant to flee, he wasn't showing his hand. I told Sweetie Pie to wait for me, and I threw a leg over the open window frame and slipped into the house, following in the artist's footsteps. I'd just gotten into the house and let my eyes adjust to the darkness when I heard a *glissando* on a finely tuned piano.

I froze in place. Something told me Sippi wasn't primed to give a concert at the piano. Who was in the house with me? I didn't think I was going to like the answer. Before I could move, I heard a familiar tune and a male voice singing "I'll Be Seeing You." He had an excellent voice, and his mastery of the keyboard was unparalleled.

The piano stopped, and a man in a heavily sequined suit stepped into the hallway. The sequins caught the light from another room in the house. We stood, squared off. I had no idea who he was, but I knew neither of us was supposed to be in the house. The man was not an Elvis impersonator. He was somebody familiar, but not Elvis. I glanced around to see if Cece might be coming in the window. Maybe she could get a photo.

"Who are you?" I asked.

"You don't recognize the world-famous Liberace?" he asked.

I didn't miss a beat. Oh, I knew who it was and there was going to be hell to pay. "Jitty, you are going to die. Again. You've scared the snot out of me for no good reason." I hurried to the window to check outside to be sure Cece wasn't coming in. And I heard Harold knocking on the front door. He was losing his patience, judging from the length and power of this knock.

"Entertainment is always a good reason to turn people's

expectations upside down," Liberace said. "Besides, you're the one who broke in here, not me."

"You broke in here, too," I reminded Jitty. "Just because you're invisible to everyone but me doesn't mean you can break the law."

"Try and stop me."

Jitty was full of prissy bravado. "Where's Sippi?"

Liberace only grinned. "You know, I had my own television show. I also played piano in strip clubs back in the years of the Depression. My mother was appalled, but I wasn't. Because of my versatile piano skills, I was able to support my family through very hard times. It made me the musician I am today. I had a varied career."

"I don't care."

"You should care. Varied career might be a clue, Sarah Booth." Liberace was slowly shifting into my favorite haint.

"Wearing my clothes again, I see."

"Of course. After all, we share so many things, why not your clothes." Jitty was fully her beautiful self, wearing my jeans and heavy barn jacket. She also had the good sense to wear my riding boots instead of stupid little elf shoes.

I knew better than to ask her to trade. "Why are you here?"

"You need time to prepare yourself for what you're about to see."

"Okay, I'll bite. What am I going to see?"

"Continue down the hall. Open the door on your right. Good luck."

The grin on her face was particularly aggravating. She knew a secret, and was having the time of her life rubbing my nose in it. "What am I going to see?" I asked.

"You're the gumshoe. Find out for yourself."

She was gone and I was curious. I walked softly down the hall to the door she'd indicated. I turned the knob slowly, wondering if I would find the Elvis belt back in Grace's house. Maybe the whole thing had been a publicity stunt. If that was the case, I might have to do something violent to my lying, annoying client.

The door creaked open, and I stepped into the darkened room. To my surprise, a light snapped on.

I screamed and the man in the bed screamed, too. He jumped up, buck naked, and froze. I should have looked away, but Sippi Salem was not a vision any normal woman would be able to tear herself away from. I loved Coleman, but dang, Sippi had some bountiful assets. I finally covered my eyes.

"What are you doing here?" Sippi asked as he pulled the bedsheet around himself.

"Protecting Grace," I said.

"From what?" he demanded.

"From . . . you! Did you steal her Elvis belt?"

"Dammit, it isn't the belt that I want from Grace. I want her attention. I want her time. I want her support and love. I want her to marry me." He reached under his pillow and brought out a jewelry case. I walked toward the bed and reached for the black velvet box. As he handed it to me, the sheet slipped.

"Oh, Aunt Loulane, save me from impure thoughts," I mumbled as I turned away from him with the box in my hand. While he grabbed his sheet, I opened the jewelry case. A beautiful blue diamond winked at me from the box. Sippi had been planning on asking Grace to marry him. The parameters of my case were now totally upended.

27

I gave him back the diamond ring before I stepped out of the bedroom and called Coleman. "I'm at Grace's house. Hurry. There's a naked man with a diamond ring in her bed."

"I'm not going to ask any questions until I get there. Keep your clothes on."

"Not funny." I was almost insulted.

"Sarah Booth, you sound awestruck. Who's there?"

"Sippi Salem. And Harold is about to beat the front door in. Cece is outside somewhere. Just hurry and get here. Please."

"I'm on the way. Keep Sippi there. Use whatever means necessary." He was laughing at me. I was not finding the situation all that humorous.

"Are you with Yuma?" I asked him.

"I am, but I'll ditch him unless you need his arrest powers."

"I think Sippi and Grace are hot and heavy. She won't press charges, so leave Yuma behind if you can. I have concerns about him."

"Me, too. I'll be pulling up out front in two minutes."

In less than two minutes, my phone beeped. It was Coleman.

"I'll bring Harold inside with me. He's about to blow a gasket."

Coleman had a lead foot when he needed to get somewhere fast. It pleased me that he was coming to rescue me from a naked artist. I didn't need his help, but it was sure nice to know it was there.

"Some people are here to talk to you," I told Sippi.

"I'm going home." He picked up his pants from the floor.

"Nope." I snatched them and held them behind my back. "You need to talk to Coleman and help us find the belt. Grace was almost killed. My friends and I were almost killed. This has to end, and you need to help."

Sippi sat down, leaned back against the headboard, and put his feet up. His long legs poked out from under the sheet. "Can I have my pants if I say I'll stay?"

I considered, but Coleman was coming up the walk with Cece and Harold. Sippi could just wait. "After you talk with Coleman."

"Who?"

"My significant other and the sheriff of Sunflower County."

"He has no jurisdiction here," Sippi pointed out.

"True. But very soon he is going to have your pants. So maybe wise up and help us."

Sippi leaned his head back and laughed loud and hard.

"You are too much, Ms. Delaney. A new interrogation tactic—holding a man's pants hostage. Maybe you just want another look at what I have available." He started to toss the sheet aside.

I went to the bedroom door. "Coleman, get in here fast!"

Sippi was still laughing when Coleman and his entourage stepped through the bedroom doorway.

"The front door was open," Coleman said, giving me a wink at his lie. He slipped past me and sat on the bed by Sippi's feet. Harold and Cece leaned against a wall. "Where's the belt?" Coleman asked.

"I don't have it. I've never had it."

Coleman assessed him. "Make me believe it."

"I know who has the belt."

If Sippi was lying, he surely was a terrific actor. I believed him. "Who has it?" I asked.

"Chief Yuma Johnson."

I had suspected Yuma, but it was still hard to believe that the primary law officer in the county was a jewel thief. "Can you prove it?" I pressed.

"I saw him with it myself," Sippi said.

I glanced at Coleman, who was watching Sippi like a chicken watches a grub.

"That's easy to say and hard to prove," Coleman said. "Where's the evidence?"

"Maybe you should search Yuma's house."

"And why would Yuma do something this stupid?" Coleman asked.

Sippi shrugged. "Grace. It's all about Grace. They had a thing. She threw him over and took up with me again. Yuma isn't a man who likes to play second fiddle to anyone." He sighed and looked truly puzzled for a moment. "Grace is like a virus. She gets into your blood and you can't get her out. I couldn't tell you why, either. She's a liar, a manipulator, a narcissist, and a walking puddle of ego. But I keep coming back. There's just this . . . vulnerable sweetness at times."

"You really believe a sheriff stole a valuable piece of art to get even with an ex-girlfriend?" I didn't need to point out that not only would Yuma lose his job, he would likely go to jail if he was tried and convicted.

"I wouldn't put anything past Yuma. Or that wretched Kent Madison. Lord, he never got over Grace dumping him. And he's such a smarmy chamber of commerce guy." Sippi didn't hold back on the competitors for Grace's affections.

"What's Grace's relationship with Allan Malone?" I asked.

"He's a wart on her butt. She pretends that he's okay, but she hates his guts. And those dogs of his. Grace has fantasies of sending them to the pound."

That wasn't entirely shocking, but I hadn't realized the animosity ran that deep. Then again, Grace seemed to be a polarizing force. People loved her or hated her. Well, they mostly hated her.

"Sippi, she didn't pay you for the work you did on that belt. Part of the value of it is your craftsmanship. Doesn't that make you angry?"

"It did for a while but, to Grace's credit, she was plenty generous in telling everyone I did the work. That alone has brought in at least two dozen commissioned works. So, I can't be too much of a hypocrite, can I?" He flipped his long blond hair behind his shoulder.

I heard someone with a key at the front door and couldn't suppress a grin. What would Grace say when she saw me,

Coleman, Harold, Cece, and Sippi in her bedroom? Yikes! It was going to be a scene to remember.

"What a day!" Grace said as she slammed the front door behind her. I heard one shoe, then the other, hit the floor as she kicked them off. It had been a long and grueling day. And, had me and my friends not intervened, Grace would be getting ready for some bedroom fun.

I waited for Sippi to call out to her, but he didn't. He turned off the bedroom light and waited. He was a skunk, for sure! Though I couldn't really blame him. This moment was going to be priceless.

From the noises, I deduced Grace was getting a glass from the cabinet. Likely some alcoholic tonic after the craziness of the Elvis competition. Any minute she'd come to the bedroom. We were all standing in the dark like it was some Halloween horror show.

Grace came around the corner and walked into the darkened bedroom.

"Hey, baby," Sippi said in a voice so silky and sexy I felt chill bumps dance.

Grace shrieked and tossed an entire glass of red wine on Sippi. I was hit with some back splash, and when Sippi turned the light on, Grace screamed four more times. I guess once for each of us.

"Get out of my bedroom. What are you doing here? You are a bunch of pervs and sickos. Sippi, you get out, too."

Grace was hopping mad—and terrifically entertaining. I couldn't help it. I started laughing. Cece joined in. Then Harold and, finally, Coleman. Grace was not amused. When Sippi started to laugh, she picked up a book on a table and threw it. She clocked him in the head.

"This isn't funny," she said. "What are all of you doing

here? How did you get in? If you broke into my house, I'm going to press charges. I don't care who you are or what you claim to be up to."

"Sippi has a really serious question to ask you," I said, hoping to divert her ire with that big old diamond.

"What?" She was about as gracious as a coiled snake.

"Could we have a moment alone?" Sippi asked.

"No, hell no. Spill it. If you have something to say, spew it out right now."

Sippi stood up and dropped the sheet. I was prepared, but Cece gasped out loud. Harold muttered, "Oh, dear lord."

Coleman looked at me. "You shouldn't be in here," he muttered.

I didn't disagree, but nothing was going to drag me away from this scene.

Sippi dropped to one knee. He held up the ring box. "Grace, will you marry me?"

For all of the fact that it was completely insane, I eagerly awaited her answer. Yes, it was a crazy question, asked in one of the most bizarre proposal scenarios I'd ever heard of. But it was a marriage proposal, nonetheless.

All eyes were on Grace.

She opened the box and looked down into Sippi's eyes. "You really want to marry me?"

"I can't live without you," he said.

"Hogwash," Grace said. "This is some kind of ploy to keep me from pressing charges against you. Did you steal that damn belt?"

"No and no. I came here with the purest of heart and the dirtiest of mind," he said. "You're the hottest woman I've ever known. I'm ready to settle down."

"Yes!" Grace rushed toward him and leaned down for a kiss that quickly turned very passionate.

"Get the fire hose," Cece said, laughing. She took Harold's hand and eased him toward the door. Coleman grabbed me and pulled me along.

I couldn't resist a parting shot, though, at both of them. "Aren't they doing something illegal?" I asked Coleman loud enough for them to hear.

"The only people committing an illegal act is us," Coleman muttered, herding me ahead of him.

Grace's response was to slam the door with everything she had. Coleman took my arm and we walked into the living room together. "We can't stop them, and we aren't going to watch them," he said, laughing. "Let's go find the others and have a drink." He edged us out of the house and onto the front lawn.

"What about the person who tried to kill us?" I asked.

"Yuma has arrested Kent Madison and Allan Malone. He's claiming Allan's pugs were at fault and the falling lights were accidental."

"Do you believe him?" I asked. I had my doubts, but it was always good to check with the man with the badge.

"Nope. I don't believe anything anyone in this town says."

28

I didn't know how Coleman planned to play the information that Yuma might be our prime suspect. Aside from being the sheriff, Yuma was the foremost law enforcement authority in Lee County. Coleman had no authority to arrest him—unless a warrant had been issued. In some states the coroner could arrest a sheriff. Or a mayor could arrest or fire a police chief. Or a justice of the peace had some powers. But Mississippi's laws were confusing, and though I'd researched them, I didn't know how far Coleman might legally be able to go, if push came to shove. Right now, I was just happy to get out of Grace's house before I went off on her and Sippi. They were so busy canoodling, they didn't even care that we could still hear them even though we were outside. Whatever he was doing had Grace begging for more. I thought my ears might bleed.

I had to accept a hard fact: either Grace didn't believe Sippi was involved with stealing the belt, or she just didn't care.

"Did it ever occur to you that Grace may have stolen the belt from herself to get Sippi's attention?" Cece asked. She edged toward the door.

"Yes, it's crossed my mind." The possibility made me anxious and angry. I was getting paid one way or the other. But the idea that I'd spent the days before Christmas being a pawn in Grace's foolish game of love and manipulation didn't sit well with me. I had to remember, though, that I had no proof.

"Thanks for helping me, guys." I was a lucky person to have such great friends. But I was freezing and tired, and my friends had loved ones and responsibilities. "Let's head back to the hotel. It's too cold to stand outside."

Cece gave me a weird look, but she didn't object.

Coleman eased down the sidewalk. "I'm going to the courthouse to talk to Yuma. I'll catch up with you in a bit. Yuma needs to give me contact information for a judge. It's too late to run one to ground tonight, but tomorrow . . ." Coleman was aggravated. A lawman acting unprofessional drove him nuts. He felt it reflected on the whole profession, but he took the time to blow me a kiss.

I was hoping for some romantic time with my fella, but obviously that wasn't going to happen. At least not yet. "Take care of Yuma; I need to talk to Allan Malone."

"Be careful, Sarah Booth." Coleman was serious. "Allan seems harmless, but I'm not so sure. He's a big, strong guy.

And he has vivid feelings about Tupelo, Elvis, Grace, and so much more."

"His pugs are his weakness." I didn't underestimate Allan, but he truly loved those dogs. I couldn't believe he'd do anything that might put them—or himself—in jeopardy. Allan might be a prima donna, but he was aware he couldn't care for Lovely Katherine and Avery from a jail cell. Also on his plus side was the fact he'd offered Cece a chance to show off her singing talents on his television show. I wanted that for her, which meant I was hoping he wasn't a thief and general villain.

Now, Krystal Bond, on the other hand—she smacked of larceny and bad actions.

"After Allan, I need to talk to Krystal. And the Manning brothers. And Kent Madison."

"All of that tonight?" Tinkie asked.

She was right. I was biting off more than I could chew. But I wanted to find the belt, close the case, and go home to Zinnia with the trophy for Best Amateur Elvis Impersonation Group with a Christmas Song. It was a long title, but we deserved it! And we hadn't had any time to celebrate our win or the holiday.

"No. Not tonight. Right now, let's go to the Hound Dog and get a drink." I was eager to move.

"Right on." Cece dangled a set of car keys. "Coleman left these for you."

"Is he walking to town?" That didn't seem right since I knew he was going to talk to Yuma about possible criminal behavior. While I was talking to Tinkie, Coleman had disappeared.

"A patrol car came by and picked him up. He's fine. Let's

just go. I can't take another minute standing out here on the lawn, knowing Grace and Sippi are about to shag at any second."

It was a disturbing possibility. I didn't want to see it or hear it. I followed Cece to the car. In no more than ten minutes we were at the hotel bar, waiting on a round of vodka tonics and for Millie and Tinkie to join us.

"Tinkie is with Oscar and Maylin," Millie said as she pulled up a chair at our table. "She looked heartsick and tired, so I told her to spend a little time with her family."

"Good plan." I filled Millie in on all that had happened at Grace's house.

"You saw Sippi Salem totally naked?" Millie was breathing fast and shallow.

"I did."

"I miss all the good stuff." She was suddenly glum.

"Hop in the car, and I'll drive you over there. I'm sure they're still going at it like honey badgers. One of them might lose an arm, but they won't notice."

That made her laugh, and we sipped our drinks.

"Where's Coleman?" Millie asked.

"I think he's at the jail." When I told her about the possibility that Yuma was a thief, she didn't say much. She finished her drink and then nudged my foot under the table. I looked over at where she was staring and saw Sonja Rivera and Allan Malone walk in the door. Obviously, Allan had been released. He had his little pugs in his arms, and the minute he set them down, they came over to my table barking. Since I'd hidden Sweetie Pie under the table, I was less than pleased. But if they let Allan have his pugs in there, I was keeping my Sweetie Pie.

The barkeep may have noticed the pugs and Sweetie Pie, but he had no interest in enforcing any anti-canine rules. He made us another round of drinks and took a tall, yellow fizzy thing to Allan and a whiskey neat to Sonja.

I waited until they finished their first round before I went over and sat down with them.

"No one invited you," Allan said.

"Too bad. Allan, have you considered who will care for your pugs when you're in prison?"

"Don't be ridiculous."

"You almost killed me and my friends. You took responsibility for *your* dogs bringing down the stage lights. That's criminal assault. We're going to press charges. Better make arrangements for those dogs while you're sitting in a cell at Parchman prison."

I had no intention of pursuing charges, but it got Allan's attention. I turned to Sonja. "Be careful, or you'll go down with him. And, just so you know, we're in the process of making sure Chief Johnson has nothing to do with this case. We've called in the Mississippi Bureau of Investigation and the FBI."

I could spin a lie, too, and I was tired of being the target of grievous personal injury.

"I swear to you, the thing with the stage lights was a complete accident," Allan said. He snuggled his pugs to his chest. "I can't leave Lovely Katherine and Avery. No one knows how to cuddle and care for them the way I do. They would die without me." He actually sounded a little worried. "I wasn't the only one by that rope. I know Avery was tugging on it, but Chief Johnson was back there fiddling with the ropes and the weights."

He dropped that bomb like it was a dud instead of a live

grenade. "Are you accusing Yuma of sabotaging the light cables?"

"Yes." Allan didn't flinch. "Yuma has a thing for Grace. Bad. She got under his skin like an infected splinter and he could never dig her out. Believe me, he tried. Grace knew how he was struggling at times, and she took delight in reeling him back in and then tossing him away. When she took up with that artist, Yuma was beside himself. The whole time Grace has been planning the Christmas Elvis festival, Yuma has been hanging out in the Arena Center, wandering around the theater, hoping she'd show up so he could spend a little time with her." He rolled his eyes. "He's been backstage a lot."

"Did you see him messing with the ropes that held the lights?"

"Not specifically. But if Yuma was playing with the idea of bringing those lights down on top of anyone, it would probably have been Grace."

His factual delivery chilled me. But he had a point. Why harm me and Tinkie when killing Grace would solve the root of this problem? If he was the thief, that is.

"Yuma strikes me as a man who would do anything for love," Sonja said. She licked a bit of moisture off her upper lip in a gesture that was almost as deadly as Tinkie's lip pop. Sonja's beehive hair might intimidate some men—until they saw that lip thing. It was good she and Tinkie lived on opposite sides of the state. The male population of either Zinnia or Tupelo wouldn't have survived both of them.

"Sonja, you were in the Arena Center the day the belt disappeared. Who did you see there?" Tinkie asked as she came over to the table.

"Everyone in town. I mean, literally, everyone. We'd all

heard stories about the Elvis belt that Sippi Salem created, but we'd never seen it."

Interesting. "She would have been smarter never to display the belt."

"She teased folks about having it. Saying she did, then saying she didn't. Saying it was in a bank vault. Saying it didn't exist at all. Grace loved to change the story to whatever suited her at the time." Sonja signaled for another round of drinks. "To be honest, I assumed that belt in the Arena Center was paste. It never occurred to me that Grace really owned a multimillion-dollar piece of art or that she'd put it on public display in a situation so unsecured. And uninsured! Man, the hair dye she uses must have penetrated her brain."

"Even if the belt had been insured, the company might not have paid out because of the poor security."

"Unless Yuma guaranteed the security," Sonja said with one arched eyebrow.

Excellent point! Had the sheriff lured Grace into a false sense of security in order to rob her—either for the money or a payback for years of torment?

"Did you ever know Grace's mother?" I changed tactics. Keeping someone off-balance was often the best way to learn things.

"Why are you asking? She's been dead for years." Sonja's interest was piqued.

"Just something I heard," I said. "A lot of people have told me that Grace is so . . . vindictive because of the way her mother treated her."

"It sucks to lose a parent. At any age," Sonja said. She glanced at Allan and, in that split second, I wondered if she knew Grace's mother was alive.

"How are you holding up with all of this, Sonja?" I asked.

"Why do you ask?"

I shrugged. "You're such a perfect reflection of Priscilla Presley's style from the 1960s, it's hard for me to remember that you're probably under thirty." Flattery was always a good tactic when the option presented itself.

"Thank you. I'm older than the legal age and able to take care of myself."

"Did you grow up in Tupelo?" I asked.

A wary look crept into her eyes. "What's it to you?"

"Maybe you grew up in New York City. Or Los Angeles. You have cosmopolitan . . . flair."

"I was born in Brooklyn," Sonja said, patting her bouffant hairdo. "I grew up in foster care, but my foster mom was great. She adopted me. She was a hairdresser. We moved here to Tupelo when I was eight. Mom worked at the Clip and Blow until she passed of cancer."

Sonja hadn't had an easy life. I'd assumed—an asinine thing to do—that she'd been allowed to playact into adulthood. I was wrong. Was her Priscilla persona an attempt to carve out her own niche in a life where she'd never truly known who she was? Or was it a fantasy escape? Either way worked for me.

I felt a vicious pinch just below my shoulder blade and jumped. When I looked behind me, Tinkie was standing there, lips pressed tight.

"What?" I asked.

"You look like you were off in la-la land, daydreaming." She looked at Sonja and then Allan. "Have your little dogs bitten anyone lately?"

"How dare you!" Allan stood up, his hands curled into fists.

"At least he loves his dogs," I said to Tinkie, easing her back from a confrontation. "Allan was just telling me all about Brandi Beaumont."

That was it. Perfect. Allan looked as if he'd been gaffed. "What are you saying? What are you talking about? I didn't say a word about . . ."

"I know a lot more than anyone thinks I know. Where is Brandi?"

"Who's Brandi?" Tinkie and Sonja said together. They honestly sounded sincere.

I pulled out my phone. "I think it's time for the law to show up." I dialed Coleman instead of Yuma. "Sheriff, we need you here at the Hound Dog Hotel bar right away. I do believe we have some Tupelo residents involved in an insurance scam. You know, collecting life insurance policies on people who aren't really dead."

"I hope you aren't pulling my leg," Coleman said. "I'm on the way."

29

Allan scooped up his dogs and stood tall. “I’m leaving.”

“I think you should stay,” I said. When Sonja put her hands on the table to push up, I put my hands on her shoulders, pressing lightly. “Stay a spell. The law is going to want to talk to both of you.”

Sonja was indignant. “Take your hands off me or I’ll charge you with assault.”

I removed my hands and stepped back. I couldn’t physically stop them from leaving. If they ran, we could track them to see where they went. If they stayed, Coleman would grill them and might pull out some good information. Folks like Allan and Sonja responded better to a man with arrest powers, even if those powers derived from another county. It was win/win, as far as I could see.

My cell phone rang, and I glanced down. Someone at the insurance company Krystal Bond ran was calling. Since she was the only employee—because she was too cantankerous to keep a receptionist—it stood to reason it was her. I answered warily, shocked when the voice was male.

"You want to know who has it in for Grace Land? It's my brother. He's planning on killing her. You'd better stop him if you can."

"Who is this?"

"Sherman Manning. Wilbur has a gun and he's headed for Grace's place. He says he's going to put an end to her meddling and false allegations once and for all."

"Why does he want to kill her?" I asked. Everyone in the room was listening to my conversation.

"He said she's destroyed Elvis's reputation. But that isn't the real reason. Not at all."

I couldn't fully grasp what he was saying because it made zero sense. "What is the reason?"

"The real reason he intends to kill her is because of that infernal television show. Wilbur says that Grace has contributed to the destruction of the American family and the role of the male as patriarch. By mocking men and reducing them to objects of ridicule, she's bringing America to her knees."

Now that, officially, was the craziest thing I'd heard in a while. I wasn't a fan of reality TV, but to say Grace was single-handedly destroying America was a bit strong. "Do you really think he's going to harm her?"

"He will if he can. He's dressed to kill, if you know what I mean."

Again, he wasn't making sense. "I don't!"

"He's in his leopard-print Elvis outfit. He has a gun

strapped on beneath his cape. You'd better stop him or at least get her somewhere safe. He's looking for her now, hoping to find her alone. But he'll take her out in public if that's his only opportunity."

I honestly couldn't believe this was happening. A grown man dressed as Elvis Presley was on a moral rampage against a reality TV show host. "Do you know where Wilbur is?"

"He's not at the pawnshop, where he's supposed to be working. And he took a gun from the store. I'm only calling to give y'all a heads-up. I'm out of it now. I've done all I can do."

"He's your brother. You can't just turn your back on this."

"I can and I am. Wilbur has gone off the deep end. He's a dangerous man."

Wilbur had always struck me as the more sensible of the twin brothers. "Did something trigger him?"

There was a pause on the line. "Maybe."

"Care to expound?" Pulling information from Sherman was worse than extracting a chew toy out of Sweetie's mouth.

"Wilbur got a phone call. After that, he wouldn't talk to me at all. He was acting all nuts and hefting the guns to see which one felt best in his hand. I knew he was disturbed, but until he just walked out of the store with the gun in his hand, I didn't know how bad he was. I followed him home and he changed into the Elvis outfit and walked out the door."

"Do you know who called him?"

"It was a woman. Sounded . . . mature."

How politically correct of him not to say *old*! "Who was it?"

"I don't know. Wilbur has a lot of older widows who adore him. They come in the pawnshop just to bring him slices of cake and pie. Maybe one of them told him something that torqued him up."

Talking to Sherman any further was a waste of time. And as I looked out the window, I saw Coleman heading toward us. "Thanks for the heads-up. Gotta go." I hung up and rushed outside to meet Coleman. "Hey, Sherman Manning says his twin brother, Wilbur, is on a tear to kill Grace Land. Says he has a gun."

"Does this day get any better?" Coleman said. "I don't have any authority here and I don't trust Yuma. In fact, I actively suspect him of being involved in the theft of the belt."

"What are we going to do?"

He signaled me to follow him. "Let's go find Wilbur and talk him out of acting rash. Tinkie, contact Yuma. Explain what's happening."

"How are we going to find Wilbur? Do you know where he might be?" I really wanted to ask him what had happened with Yuma, but he'd spill the beans when he was ready. Right now, Wilbur Manning was our biggest worry and the problem we needed to address—pronto.

"I'll handle Yuma," Tinkie said. "You two see if you can find Wilbur."

Coleman led me out into the parking lot of the hotel. "Do you have a plan?" I asked him.

"We're going to follow Allan and Sonja."

"But what about Wilbur?"

"Yuma can take care of him. Let's go."

We had vehicles available to us. It was doable. "Great."

"You take Allan," he said.

That was a curious choice. "Why him and not Sonja?"

"If Allan threatens you, you'll tear his head off and take his dogs back to Dahlia House to love. Sonja, you might hold back on her. But I won't. Speak of the devil, here she comes."

The Priscilla look-alike came out the door, one hand grasping at the big bouffant hairdo that caught a brisk wind. The bubble of hair lifted and fell, lifted and fell on the wind, as if it were going to take flight all on its own. Watching that beehive bobble in the breeze, I wondered if she'd pull a Mary Poppins and just float off. This wasn't the first time I'd had the sense that supernatural forces were at work.

"Sarah Booth, are you with me?" Coleman asked, giving me a long curious look.

Now wasn't the time for self-doubt or out-there theories. "I'm on it," I told Coleman, and I darted among the shadows to get in my car. There was only one real option—to wait for Allan to come out and follow him.

When Sonja pulled out, Coleman, in Harold's truck, was behind her—just far enough not to appear to be tailing her. All I could do was wait for the singing host to make a move.

I wasn't certain how following either of these people would help us find Wilbur Manning, but I trusted Coleman's judgment. Maybe Yuma had revealed something to Coleman that I didn't know. I picked up my phone and then put it away again. Not being able to talk to Coleman about Yuma was driving me a little bit crazy! Still, I couldn't risk calling him.

Allan pulled out of the lot and headed downtown. Likely, he was going to some bar to have a drink. Dutifully, I followed. To my surprise, Allan didn't go in the direction I anticipated. And he wasn't heading to his Tupelo home either. It took a few minutes of tailing him to realize he was beating a path to the insurance company. My watch showed it was after midnight. What was Allan up to?

He pulled in behind the insurance building and I drove past, hoping I could find a place to park quickly and tail him on foot. I ditched the car on a side street and scooted around the corner of the building just in time to see him go in the back door. A sharp bark of laughter escaped through the open door—Krystal Bond's signature cackle—telling me they were both in the insurance office. Whatever Allan was up to, he had a confederate to help. I had to get inside there where I could listen to their plans.

The back door was locked and solid steel. Though I put my ear against it, I couldn't hear a thing. I crept around the building and went to the front. It was an ugly little cement-and-glass office building, but I was in luck, because the front was all windows. The blinds had not been drawn. I could clearly see Allan and Krystal hunkered over a desk, looking at some papers. The two little pugs were running around, barking and tearing up paper that Krystal—or someone—had thrown on the floor. The dogs were shredding the heck out of pages and pages. I was desperate to see what they were destroying. It might be documents relating to the Elvis belt. I didn't trust Krystal—or Allan—at all.

Suddenly the dogs whipped around and looked right at the window where I was standing. They bolted across the room and began barking. I knew they'd seen me, and I stepped back into the shadows. Allan called to them, but he mostly ignored them, a reminder to me to always pay attention to Sweetie Pie and Chablis.

I thought of Sweetie. She was safe with Harold, but I sure wished I had her with me. When the pugs withdrew from the window, I eased forward again. It was silly to risk being seen, because I couldn't hear anything and I certainly couldn't view the details of the papers on the floor or see what Krystal and Allan were now arguing over. What had seemed to be a good working arrangement between the two of them now looked like a mafia war. Krystal was shaking her finger in Allan's face and he reached out and grabbed it, bending it back. She slapped him and pulled her hand free. Yikes! If they were partners, one of them was likely to beat the other up, and my money was on the insurance agent. Krystal seemed to give as good as she got.

Allan scooped up the pugs, which was my cue to withdraw back to the parked car. I'd tail him again when he left Krystal's office.

The front door unlocked and was pushed open. I barely ducked behind a column before Allan came out the front. He yelled through the open door. "You're a real bitch, Krystal. I should have let Avery bite you."

"That little smush-faced rat would never have bitten anything else. And I would have sued you."

"You deserve whatever Grace does to you," Allan said. "I hope she cleans your clock."

"Bring it," Krystal said. "If you're smart, you'll drag your butt back to Hollywood and leave decent people alone."

"Decent people who screw their own clients out of a payoff?" Allan asked.

Here it was. This was worth every bit of freezing to death out in the cold a few nights before Christmas. I thought to click record on my phone and held it out. I didn't know if it would pick up, but it was worth the chance.

"I didn't screw anyone. Grace failed to renew her policy. That's not on me."

"You knew it was due and you did nothing to help her."

"I'm not required to help any of my clients. The notice was sent. I have email proof. She either ignored it or didn't pay enough attention. That is not on me. End of story. And if I hear you're saying otherwise, I will sue you down to your last penny. Not even Barbra will be able to save you."

"So bold, Krystal. So bold. I wonder if convicted felons are allowed to sue other people."

"You don't know anything about me."

"I know enough," Allan said. "I know plenty about you and Grace and Sippi. The unholy trinity."

I was afraid Allan would hear my chattering teeth as I hugged the column. When the lights of an approaching car brushed over me, I thought I was done for. But the car kept going. As it drew abreast of Allan and Krystal, gunfire rang out. Four shots. Allan fell to the ground and Krystal lunged back into her office. Two of the windows shattered.

"Call the cops," Allan ordered Krystal. "Now!"

I couldn't see her on the floor, so I assumed she hadn't been hit. I had to clear out of the area. If Yuma arrived, I would be toast. Besides, I just had a line on where Wilbur Manning might be. I was pretty sure he was the shooter.

30

While I was waiting for a break to get to my car, I texted Coleman the bare details of what had just happened. I didn't know where he was, but I hoped he could drive by and follow the shooter's car. The taillights were fast disappearing into the black Mississippi night. The urge to simply run to my car came over me, but I beat it back. Allan and Krystal did not need to know I'd been outside the building while they argued—and revealed pertinent details. I had to bide my time, hoping I could make my getaway without being detected.

When I heard the wail of the sirens approaching, I ran around the back of the building and made it safely to my vehicle. Krystal and Allan had gone back inside the office building. I was free to try to catch up to the shooter. And

I sure didn't want to hang around to give a statement to Yuma. The less he knew about what I was doing, the better.

My phone was on the passenger seat of my car, but no word from Coleman. I sped away from the parking lot and headed in the direction the shooter's car had gone. I had been able to tell it was a dark sedan, but I hadn't gotten the make, model, or tag number. The only thing I had going for me was the fact that the roads were virtually empty. Tupelo was shut down, like most all small Southern cities, after nine o'clock at night.

I drove straight down the highway, speeding, hoping for a break. Up ahead, I saw the taillights of a vehicle that had slowed. Once upon a time in America—the car capital of the world—I would have been able to distinguish the taillights of one make and model from all the others. Now, all the cars looked alike, for the most part; nothing distinctive, except the price tag. I could only hope this was the car I meant to pursue. It was behaving strangely. I followed.

The car was barely moving down the road. As I got closer, the whole thing creeped me out. The sedan was idling down the straight shot of highway. I followed, hitting my brights to try to illuminate the cab. It appeared empty. Which didn't make a lick of sense.

When we came to a curve in the road, the sedan kept going straight, right off the side of the road and into a ditch. There was no attempt to brake or correct course. When the sedan stalled against the side of the ditch, I got out with a flashlight. The driver had to be injured. If there was a driver. Every awful horror movie I'd ever watched flashed through my memory. I took all precautions, even though I'd seen no indication that anyone was actually in the car.

I approached slowly. The motor was still running, but the

car was just pushing into the ditch. I eased up to the driver's window and flinched. There was blood on the window. I used my flashlight to illuminate the interior and gasped. A middle-aged woman was lying on the front seat, a bloody wound on her temple. I'd never seen her before, but it was clear she needed medical attention.

The car wasn't locked so I opened the door and reached in to check her pulse. She was alive. And the head wound wasn't as severe as I'd feared. She was breathing regularly. When I gently touched her shoulder, she started to come around.

"I'm going to call an ambulance," I said. "Can you sit up?"

She did, looking around as if she were lost.

"What happened?" I asked.

"That bastard clocked me upside the head after I gave him a ride. That'll teach me to be a good Samaritan."

"I'm going to call for medical help. Don't move."

"Don't call! I don't want any help. Just get away from me and my car." She tried to pull the car door out of my hand and shut it, but I held firm. I wasn't certain she was in her right mind. And she surely didn't need to be driving.

"Hey, you need to get checked out. You hit your head."

"I didn't hit anything, and when I get my hands on Wilbur, I'm going to give him something to think about."

"Wilbur Manning?"

She finally really looked at me and her eyes narrowed. "Get out of my car. Now."

I shook my head. "Can't do it. Who are you?"

"No one." She tried to push me out the door and into the ditch, but I had the advantage—I was younger and stronger.

"What's your name?" Something niggled in my brain.

She looked vaguely familiar, but I couldn't place her. Was she from Zinnia?

She reached across the car and tried to escape out the passenger door, but I grabbed her arm and hauled her back in. I couldn't tell if she legitimately wanted to escape the car or if she was delusional from the blow to her head.

I grasped my phone. Holding her with one hand I called Coleman with the other. "I'm on the highway headed north out of town, about three miles, in a car in the ditch. There's been an accident. Could you come and send an ambulance?"

"On the way." Coleman didn't waste time talking.

The fight suddenly went out of the woman. "Why'd you have to do that?"

"You may be injured."

"I'm not. But Wilbur Manning is going to be hurt when I catch him."

"What happened?"

"I saw him and offered him a ride. At first, I didn't see the gun. He got in the car with me, then forced me to drive him by the insurance place, where he took some shots at Krystal Bond and Allan Malone. Then when I tried to resist driving him to Grace's house, he clocked me in the head."

"You know Wilbur and Grace? Who are you?"

"Brandi Beaumont."

There it was—the reason I halfway recognized her. She looked like Grace. "You're Grace's dead mother."

"Oh, for pity's sake. Don't start that crap. I did what was best for Grace. Don't make it sound like I'm a coldhearted criminal who abandoned my only child. I got out of her life and she was free to tell everyone I was dead. She got the insurance payout, which saved her. Eventually she knew I was okay. And she had money and security. And just so you know, I paid the insurance company back. Nothing illegal was done."

There were a million things I wanted to say, but I didn't. My job was simply to hold her in place until Coleman and the posse arrived. Thank goodness I didn't have to wait long.

Coleman pulled up behind her, effectively blocking her retreat. I remained in the driver's seat until he opened the passenger door and assisted her out. "Are you hurt?" he asked her.

"I'm not, but that nosy biddy there had to jump in the middle of my business."

Coleman looked over at me in the dim interior of the car.

"Coleman, this is Grace's mother, Brandi Beaumont," I said. "She was driving Wilbur around town while he took shots at people."

"Oh, you make it sound like I did that willingly. I was held at gunpoint," she said. "I didn't have a choice."

"Why are you back in town?" I asked her.

"That is none of your business," she said in an imperious tone. I could see where Grace got her overblown sense of self.

Coleman frowned at her. "Does your daughter know you're alive? I'm confused. Didn't Grace imply her mother was dead?"

"I'm a long way from dead. Now get out of my car. I haven't done anything wrong. Where is Yuma Johnson?" She reached onto the floorboard and brought up a phone. "I'm calling the police chief right now."

"Call Yuma. I have some questions for him, too," I said. Once again, Yuma was implicated in a situation that seemed the opposite of professional law enforcement work.

He must have known Brandi was still alive, yet he'd never mentioned it. Yuma Johnson was looking dirtier and dirtier each moment that passed.

"You'd better get in my vehicle," Coleman said to her. "We'll go to the sheriff's office and you can talk directly to Yuma."

"And who are you?" Brandi asked Coleman. "I don't remember seeing you around these parts, and believe me, I would have remembered."

So now she was hitting on my guy? This was unacceptable. "She hit her head pretty hard. I think she must have scrambled her brains."

"Ignore her," Brandi said to Coleman, putting her hand on his chest and running her fingers lightly down his torso. She was a bold hussy! "Help me into your vehicle. I'm cold. Maybe you can warm me up."

"I'm happy to drive you to the sheriff's office, where we can sort all of this out." He assisted her out of the car. "Sarah Booth, would you grab the keys from the ignition?"

"Sure thing, lover boy."

Coleman's chuckle seemed to linger in the night as he put Brandi in his vehicle and signaled for me to follow them back to town. I assumed the wrecker would handle Brandi's vehicle.

Tinkie joined me at the sheriff's office, with Grace in tow. When they walked in the door, I was eager to watch Grace's reaction to her mother. The whole orphan thing had been a great sympathy card to play, but now that the Brandi cat was out of the bag, it was only going to make people dislike Grace more than ever.

Brandi was sitting at a desk, her back to the door, when it creaked open and Tinkie and Grace walked in. Grace's face registered shock, and then anger. "What are you doing here?" she demanded as she strode up to her mother. "You swore I'd never have to look at you again."

Yeehaw! That was not what I was expecting.

"Wilbur Manning happened to me. And then her! She's been very mean to me." She pointed at me.

"Wilbur Manning?" Grace looked truly confused.

"He abducted me at gunpoint."

"What are you doing here in Tupelo? You promised me you'd stay in California if I set you up. And I did. Now you've broken your word."

Wait, wait, wait! I wanted to hold up my hand and pause the conversation so I could rewind back to a place I might be able to understand what was really happening. Grace and her mother were far more intent on tearing into each other than clarifying the facts.

"I heard about the belt being stolen. I came to check on you."

"Everyone in town thinks you're dead—that was our deal. You got what you wanted and I got you out of my life. Now you show up, and who's going to look like the idiot. Me, not you."

That wouldn't be the aspect of this situation that I would be harping about. Her mother was alive. What I wouldn't give for the chance to discover my parents alive and well. Yeah, I'd be really angry, but happiness would outweigh anything else. Grace was shockingly selfish and awful. And to be fair, Brandi wasn't any kind of prize, either.

Tinkie glanced at me, her blue eyes round with shock and

disapproval. "I have totally had it. I mean it." She turned to our client. "Grace, we quit."

That short statement silenced everyone.

"You can't quit," Grace said.

"Oh, yes we can." I was on board with Tinkie's assessment. Grace had lied to us one too many times. Now it was time to hit the highway. We still had one more night in Tupelo that we could enjoy as average citizens. I was ready to leave Grace behind in my rearview.

"You can't quit on her," Brandi said, standing up so fast she almost smacked Yuma in the face with her head. "My daughter needs your help."

"And I did tell you Brandi was alive," Grace insisted. "So, I didn't really lie."

"Tough." Tinkie was digging her heels in, and so was I. We'd never quit in the middle of a case. But this was the perfect client to abandon.

"Ladies, let's talk this through," Yuma said. He had moved to stand beside Grace.

"We can't work for someone who lies all the time," Tinkie said. "Chances are we could have solved this case yesterday if Grace hadn't fed us a pack of lies. Now I'm tired of it. We're both tired of it. And we're going to enjoy the last little bit of our stay and then head home. Good luck, Grace. We'll refund half the retainer you paid and not a penny more."

The door to the sheriff's office opened and Sippi Salem entered the room. Tinkie closed her eyes and sighed deeply as Brandi slowly rose to her feet. "Sippi," she said. "It's good to see you."

"I never believed you were dead," Sippi said. He then looked at Grace and asked, "Where has she been?"

"California. And she simply couldn't stay out of my

business." Grace threw up her hands. "Sarah Booth and Tinkie are quitting the case."

"Ladies," Sippi said. "May I speak with you in the hall?"

Oh, I didn't want to do this. I could feel the noose tightening around my neck. He was going to talk us into staying on the case. Tinkie rolled her big blue eyes at me. She saw it coming, too. We excused ourselves and stepped into the empty courthouse hallway. "What?" I asked.

"Don't let her down. Everyone has let her down. Everyone. Grace can be very difficult, I concede. But she's been hurt too many times. Her mother pretending to be dead and deceiving her for several years—that took a toll on her. She's not a bad person."

"Maybe her mama left her because she's an impossible liar." I hated to be pushed into a corner.

"I promise you, Grace didn't know Brandi was alive for a long time. I'm serious. Brandi needed money for a new life. She'd been seeing a doctor and he'd dumped her. Brandi developed the whole dead scheme to get insurance money on a life policy. She gave the money to Grace, to set her up. Grace had a fat check, but it tore Grace up. And, to be clear, I learned that Brandi paid the life policy back. They aren't bad people."

He was playing the sympathy card hard. "Sippi, Grace is a pathological liar. Brandi is no better."

He nodded. "Lying is a survival skill. Never let anyone see the hurt or pain. Look, she's difficult. I know that. But she really needs your help. She won't admit it, but that belt is important to her. She acts like she's wealthy, but I think that was a big part of her future security."

He knew how to hit all the right buttons. "We really can't continue with a client we don't trust."

"Please."

That was it. I looked at Tinkie and knew our gooses were cooked. "This is wrong of you to ask us."

He grinned, and it was so sexy I had to laugh out loud. The man should have had his own TV show. "You tell Grace she has to come clean about everything. Every tiny thing."

"I'll make sure of it. From now on, only the truth. And thank you."

31

Grace and Brandi refused to talk until they were alone with me and Tinkie. Coleman and Yuma decided to make a pot of coffee in the back of the sheriff's office to give us a chance to get everything straight with Grace. I could tell by the way Coleman held his shoulders he wasn't happy about the turn of events, but he also was smart enough to know that keeping an eye on Yuma was the biggest help he could be.

Tinkie had just stepped into the hall to call her husband when Brandi signaled me over to a corner. Grace was going through her list of phone contacts.

"What?" I asked Brandi.

"Grace isn't involved with the theft of the belt. I am."

Her confession was totally unexpected. And unbelievable. It was obviously a Hail Mary in an attempt to redeem herself as one of the worst mothers of the year. "So, where is the belt?"

"I can't tell." She looked just past the side of my head. I wasn't great at reading body language, but Brandi was practically screaming that she was lying. This was not an auspicious start to our "new" partnership.

"Cut it out, Brandi. You're not half the liar Grace is."

She slapped her palm on the top of Yuma's desk. "You are going to get her killed," she whisper-hissed.

"What are you saying?" I wasn't in the mood for double-speak and lies. "Just spill it."

"Grace didn't have anything to do with the belt being stolen. I had planned to steal it and ransom it back to her—hell, she should be wallowing in dough. She makes nearly three hundred thousand dollars a show. Anyway, I didn't see the harm." She shrugged. "But someone got to the belt before I could."

"Was Grace in on this plot?" I couldn't believe a mother would steal from her daughter, but I'd seen a lot worse in some of my cases. It just hurt my heart, and though I didn't want to, I felt sorry for Grace.

"No, she didn't know a thing. I was really sneaky. See, I was going to give the belt back and I didn't want to fall out with Grace over any of this. I thought I'd—"

"Blackmail? Cheat? Scam your own daughter?"

"Pretty much." She looked down at the floor. "Pretty much. I was desperate."

"Did you ask Grace for a loan or a gift?"

"Never." Her head came up and her green eyes were defiant. "I would never ask for help. Never."

"But you would steal it?"

"Somehow, that seems more honorable."

Call me nuts, but that didn't make any sense to me. My thought must have registered on my face.

"I wasn't a very good mother to Grace. I abandoned her while I ran off to find myself. Turns out what I found wasn't all that terrific."

Brandi was eating a lot of crow, and it didn't appear to agree with her. But I was curious. She'd confessed to trying to steal from her only child. What else had she done?

"Just tell me everything. I told Grace and I'm telling you. One more lie, and Tinkie and I are off the case."

"Okay, okay."

"Who has the belt?"

"I honestly don't know."

"How were you planning on stealing it?"

"What difference does that make now?" she asked. "I didn't even get a chance. That belt was gone the first day it was on exhibit."

"Who was helping you? The truth. Now."

"Kent Madison arranged to have the security measures disabled. I was going to give him a cut of any money I got from Grace when I ransomed it back." She sighed. "Like I said, someone beat us to the belt before I could grab it."

"Have you been in Tupelo all this time?"

She nodded. "I was staying at Kent's place. He's got a burn on for Grace. He feels like she treated him unfairly and dumped him."

"And you? Why would you harm your daughter in this way?"

"Look, I figured the belt was insured. I mean, Grace isn't a dum-dum. She's a smart businesswoman. So if I took the belt, and she filed a claim on the insurance, then she'd have a cool three million cash and I'd take one million as ransom. That would leave her with two *and* she'd have the belt back before too long."

"That's a federal crime. You would be guilty and so would she, unless she told the truth."

Brandi shrugged. "I've walked on the shadowy side of the law before. Grace, not so much. She could have handled it any way she preferred and just left me out of it."

"You are going to break her heart." I just said it. "What kind of mother does this?"

"I gave Grace every chance I could when she was growing up. I gave her a name to live up to. A name that was both a person and a place. A tribute to the greatest singer ever born."

"You know the other kids made fun of her." I was suddenly defending a client I didn't really like.

"It taught her to be tough. To stand for something. I did her a favor."

"And now you were going to fleece her. Terrific parenting."

"Do you have any children?" Brandi asked.

"No, but I had great parents. I know the difference. Why did you abandon Grace?"

She sighed and motioned to a chair. We walked over to a table and took a seat. Tinkie came up and joined us.

"I had a life insurance policy on myself. Grace was the beneficiary. I was struggling to provide for her, and I certainly couldn't give her the leg up in life she deserved. So, I faked my death and the lawyer helped her cash in the insurance policy. My action gave her the life she has today. I don't regret it, and I'll bet Grace doesn't either. And by the way, I paid the insurance money back when I made good out in

LA. I saved Grace. She could have grown up to be ordinary and simply married a man, worked at the bank as a teller, or whatever. Instead, she has a brilliant life with a television show and is highly regarded. That name gave her the drive to do all of this."

"And do it all alone," Tinkie said softly.

"What?" Brandi frowned at her.

"She is alone. Did you ever stop to consider maybe she hasn't settled down with a man because she doesn't trust that they won't leave her, too?"

It was a well-put question, and one that hit Brandi in the solar plexus. She turned slightly green. "That wasn't my intention."

"Likely not. But it doesn't matter what you intended. There are consequences for every action. Grace has suffered. From what I can tell, she doesn't have any friends here in Tupelo, or out in Hollywood. Folks admire what she's accomplished, and they want to be part of it, but they don't care about Grace."

Tinkie had landed a blow. She spoke from her own pain of feeling abandoned by her mother, and it walloped Brandi.

"I wanted to give her success, achievement, not sorrow."

"Brandi, who stole the belt? Do you know?"

She shook her head. "I don't know. I swear. Someone who must have known the security would be turned off."

"Who else would Kent Madison have told about that?" I asked.

"Sonja Rivera or Krystal Bond. Or both of them. When he couldn't get Grace to care about him, he took up with both of those women. Either one is capable."

It became clear to me that we would spend the rest of the week going in circles if we didn't do something drastic. I signaled Tinkie to step with me into the back of the office. "Let's call this quits. We're not getting anywhere. Let's just go back to the hotel."

"What are you up to, Sarah Booth?"

"We need to set a trap."

Tinkie's blue eyes sparked. She loved a good trap. "Yes! We need to take action, not hang back waiting for something else to happen."

I nodded. The only problem was that I didn't know how to set a proper trap. What would lure the thief out into the open? The whole town knew the bejeweled belt had been stolen and everyone was on high alert. It would be difficult to pull off.

"We need some bait," Tinkie said.

"Exactly. Any ideas?"

Tinkie's grin was both wicked and mischievous. "Maybe."

"Care to spill?"

"Let me think about it. I need to ask Oscar first."

She had my curiosity aroused, but I didn't press her. Tinkie would share when the time was right. As for now, I checked my watch. It was late. I was tired. And aggravated. The best thing would be to go back to the hotel, catch a few winks, and see what Tinkie had to share in the morning. Tomorrow would be our last full day in Tupelo. Saturday morning we would get up and head back to Zinnia to prepare for Harold's big Christmas Eve party. It was tradition. We had just under forty hours to find the belt and close the case. It sounded impossible. And it probably was. But Tinkie and I weren't quitters.

I left Coleman in the sheriff's office to talk to Yuma. The police chief had a real burn on for Tinkie and me, so it was best to let Coleman talk to him. And maybe find out something interesting.

Sippi, Brandi, and Grace all left the courthouse with us, but they turned off to head to Grace's place. Whatever Grace was feeling or thinking, she was keeping it to herself. Again, I felt a twinge of sympathy, but I squashed it. I wanted a bed and my boyfriend. It wasn't a lot to ask for on a cold December night.

I met the girls in the lobby, but I didn't stop in the hotel bar for a nightcap. We said our good-nights in the hallway and went to our respective rooms. I had just closed the door and snapped on the light when I heard the wonderful bay of Sweetie Pie Delaney. There was a note on the bed.

"I figured you'd want your hound for the evening. See you in the morning. Harold."

My good friend had delivered the incomparable Sweetie Pie to the hotel room. Somehow, he'd sneaked her past the clerk at the desk. Harold was full-on furtive when he took a notion. I jumped in the bed with Sweetie Pie and waited for Coleman to arrive. He was in for a surprise.

32

Coleman was much later getting back to the hotel than I'd anticipated. Sweetie gave a soft sigh of recognition when he slipped into the room, discarding clothes as he walked toward the bed. I'd meant to stay awake for a special holiday greeting, but my eyelids had slipped shut, and I was snuggled under the covers with my hound for company. Coleman had missed his opportunity for canoodling with one of the famous "Blue Christmas" singers of Elvis fame. This little elf was over the rainbow and needing sleep.

"Sarah Booth?" Coleman whispered.

I mumbled and snuggled up against him. He was warm and strong and made me feel safe.

"Sarah Booth?" Coleman whispered in my ear.

He knew that drove me crazy. "What?" I asked without opening my eyes.

"We need to talk."

"Right now?"

"Yes, right now."

I rolled over, snapped on the bedside lamp, and sat up. Sweetie Pie gave me a withering look before she let her head flop down, ears dangling off the side of the bed. Sweetie Pie took her beauty rest seriously.

Coleman gave Sweetie some cuddles as he settled in the bed. "Yuma arrested Wilbur Manning."

I woke up. This was good news. Great news, in fact. I hadn't believed Yuma had it in him to arrest anyone. "Where'd you find him?"

"He turned himself in."

That made me sit up and take notice. "You're kidding, right?"

"No. He walked right in the door of the sheriff's office and turned himself in."

There was more to the story. I could hear it in Coleman's voice. "Did he say why he tried to kill those people?"

"He did." Coleman was about to pop.

"You'd better tell me before I have to beat it out of you."

"I quake with terror."

I pulled the pillow from behind me and hit him with everything I had. He responded with a laugh. "You'd better come up with something better than that."

"Please tell me." I wasn't above finding a weapon, but I'd have to get out of bed. "Please!"

"He said he was under the influence of a spell cast by a witch."

"What?" It wasn't that I hadn't met a few witches in my day. Or that I didn't believe some of them had interesting . . . powers. But for a grown man to use that as an excuse. It was cockeyed.

"He insisted that Grace had visited him in the dead of night and put a spell on him, making him behave irrationally. He said she forced him to get his gun and take some shots at Krystal and Allan."

"And Yuma believed this?"

"Not sure." Coleman's grin was wide. "Wilbur is in the pokey, though. Locked up tight. Unless a witch comes along and gets him out of jail."

"He said Grace was the witch who put the spell on him?"

"Weird, right?"

"Yep. Weird." Was the whole shooting a plot to try to get Grace arrested as an accomplice? But I couldn't see any lawman buying into the whole spell-casting witch explanation. "Did Yuma seem to be putting any stock in what Wilbur said?"

Coleman kissed me on the forehead. "I'm afraid he was."

I thought for sure Coleman was teasing, so I sat up and turned his face toward me. The bedside lamp gave me a clear view of his blue eyes. "He really believed it?"

"To some extent."

"And you?" I felt like the floor had dropped out from under me. Lawmen didn't believe in witches or spells or ghosts or curses. A good law officer believed in facts, evidence, and legwork.

"Wilbur was very convincing. I don't know what happened to him, but I believe he believes he's being controlled by a magical person."

"Are you sure it wasn't the ghost of Elvis?" I asked sarcastically.

"Funny you should say that."

I slapped my forehead. "What?"

"He said Grace was with the ghost of Elvis when she cast the spell on him."

Try as I might, I couldn't detect if Coleman was pulling my leg. Surely he didn't believe any of this. He wasn't superstitious. Yet he was laying it on thick.

"What did Yuma say?" I asked.

"He's genuinely afraid of Grace. Whatever she's done, she's convinced him that her powers are . . . preternatural."

"I've never heard anything more ridiculous in my life." That was a truthful statement.

"I'm just telling you what happened." Coleman yawned and snuggled deeper beneath the covers. His eyes started to close, but I was wide awake.

Grace dressed up as a spell-casting witch running around with the ghost of Elvis Presley was something else. It deserved more exploration.

I rolled out of bed and grabbed my jeans from the floor. It was cold outside. And late. I didn't relish going anywhere, but I would do it.

"Where are you going?" Coleman sounded concerned.

"Going to check Grace's closet to see if I can find a broomstick. If she's a witch, she's bound to ride a broom, right?"

"We'll check when it's daylight," Coleman said, reaching for me.

I dodged his hand. I was a little aggravated that neither Coleman nor Yuma had checked this out and put the foolish rumors to rest. No, I had to do it. And do it I would!

I palmed the keys from the bedside table and whistled up Sweetie Pie. She could go with me. "I'll be back as soon as I can." I tried not to sound aggrieved or whiny. It was my case, not Coleman's.

"I wish you'd wait until daylight. It won't be long."

"I wish I felt I could do that." I slipped out the door and closed it after me and Sweetie Pie.

Tupelo slept under the waxing December moon as we crossed the parking lot and got in the car. In a matter of minutes, we pulled up in front of Grace's house. What I really wanted to do was to gain entry and snoop around the house. If she'd dressed up as a witch and somehow drugged or messed with Wilbur Manning, surely there would be evidence.

Instead, I knocked on the door. Grace was my client. I couldn't break into her home and search for evidence that she was, yet again, lying to me.

Lights were on in the upstairs bedroom, but no one came to the door. I knocked again. When I tried the doorknob, it turned and the door soundlessly coasted open. The hair on my neck and arms stood on end. Beside me, Sweetie Pie bristled, too.

Something was definitely wrong.

We slipped in the door, and I noticed the alarm on the wall. It hadn't been set. Was it possible Grace had fallen ill? Or simply fallen? I started toward the stairs to go up and check when I heard something in the back of the house.

Footsteps.

I didn't believe in witches, but I had to admit I was a little spooked. I hadn't brought a weapon, so I picked up a poker from the fireplace in the front parlor. Sweetie Pie was moving toward the back of the house. I wanted to call her back, but I didn't. She was smart. And powerful. She'd have the element of surprise. I had to trust her to take the lead.

The door to the kitchen was closed, so Sweetie waited silently for me to push it open. She rushed into the kitchen. Glass shattered and a woman screamed so loud that I thought my eardrums would burst.

When I hit the light switch, Brandi Beaumont stood at the sink, a gigantic butcher knife in her hand. She came toward me but stopped when she realized who I was. Sweetie Pie sat on the floor and wagged her tail.

"What are you doing here?" Brandi asked. "You made me break that decanter!"

Sure enough, a once-beautiful leaded decanter was shattered on the floor.

"I came to check on Grace. And you?"

"I had nowhere else to go. Grace tried to dump me outside a fleabag motel, but I had enough money for an Uber. The maid let me in. She's a bit surly, but she did have a key."

"Does Grace know you're here?"

Brandi frowned. "No. She might not let me stay. She's pretty mad at me."

I understood why. "So, where is Grace?"

"She's upstairs. Sleeping, I hope."

"Try again." Grace stood in the doorway with a gun in her hand. "I should shoot both of you." Grace was fully dressed. I took note of the fact that she was wearing hiking boots. When I looked behind her, Sippi Salem stood in the shadows.

The doorbell rang and before anyone could answer it, Tinkie sailed into the house. It was a dang house party. I thought I was hallucinating, but while I was looking at Sippi and Tinkie, Chief Yuma walked in and stood behind him.

Grace turned around and brandished the gun at Yuma. "You can just leave right now. Why are you here?"

"Checking to make sure you aren't flying around on a broomstick," Yuma said.

He was pretty but not very bright. Grace didn't shoot him, but she grabbed a can of peas out of the cupboard and threw it at him. The can smacked into the door and left a dent in the solid wood. Lucky she wasn't a very good pitcher.

"Grace, honey, he's doing his job," Brandi said. "Come sit down at the table. Watch the glass!"

Grace slipped into a chair at an old farm table while Brandi swept up the broken decanter. "All I wanted was a shot of bourbon," Brandi said, mopping up the liquor once the glass was picked up. "I should have stayed at a hotel. It would have been smarter."

"And easier on me," Grace said, displaying her total *lack* of grace.

"Take it easy," Yuma said. "You've got some questions to answer. Were you anywhere around Wilbur Manning this evening?"

"What are you talking about?" Grace addressed Yuma. "I haven't seen Wilbur."

"Wilbur says differently," Yuma said. "In fact, he says you're responsible—"

"Stop it." I broke into the conversation. "This is ridiculous. Grace is not a witch and she hasn't been flying around on a broom, casting spells on people."

"What?" Grace stood up. "Is Wilbur claiming I, what? Put a spell on him? Visited him on a broom? And you are taking this seriously, Yuma?"

"He believes it." Yuma looked at the floor instead of Grace.

"To what end?" Grace asked. And that was the question. There was no benefit here for Grace. Getting Wilbur to shoot Krystal Bond might give her a modicum of satisfaction, but it wouldn't change the fact her insurance policy on the Elvis belt had lapsed. And how exactly was Grace supposed to have transformed herself into a witch?

But I had an idea. I motioned Tinkie to lean in. "Come with me."

"Where are we going?"

"To Wilbur's house. I have a plan."

While Yuma was arguing with Grace and Brandi, Tinkie and I slipped out into the night with Sweetie Pie. We drove to Wilbur's place. The door was locked but the windows were not, and we easily got into the house. I led Tinkie to the kitchen, where I found a Crock-Pot of spaghetti sauce on the counter. I had to admit, it smelled delicious. Lifting the lid, I peered at the slowly bubbling sauce.

Mushrooms. Just as I suspected. It was the only thing that made sense. Unless Wilbur had deliberately taken hallucinogens, which I did not believe was the case, then he was dosed in another way. I turned the pot off. Even with a Crock-Pot, Wilbur was lucky he hadn't burned his place down.

"This is the culprit." I pointed the mushrooms out to Tinkie.

"You think those are . . . magic mushrooms?"

"It's the only thing that makes any sense," I said. "Someone laced Wilbur's supper with psilocybin mushrooms."

"Why?"

"They somehow suggested to him that Krystal and Allan needed to be shot. Wilbur did his best to take them out." I looked at Tinkie. "Someone is cleaning up the loose ends of their crime wave."

33

As I expected, my conversation with the police chief was tense. Yuma wasn't thrilled at what we found, but he had to take it into consideration. And when he went back to the jail to talk to Wilbur, the effects of the mushrooms were already wearing off. Wilbur was contrite and unable to fully explain his conduct.

Krystal and Allan didn't press charges, and Yuma said he would release Wilbur early Friday morning. He was, after all, scheduled to participate in the big Elvis finale.

It was our final day in Tupelo. Christmas was almost upon us, and the town was rocking to the music of Elvis Presley as performed by dozens of impersonators. It was as if some madness—perhaps more mushrooms—had gripped the town.

Tinkie and I were on the case of finding where the mushrooms had come from. If we could find proof of whoever had slipped them to Wilbur, we'd be closing in on the person responsible for so much of what had happened in the town.

"Do you think it was his brother?" Tinkie asked as we walked across the parking lot to a health food store at the south end of town. Tinkie had wisely suggested that we check to see if they sold fresh mushrooms. It was possible the magic mushrooms had gotten mixed in with others by accident.

"Why? Why would Sherman try to get his brother charged with murder?"

"Because he wanted Krystal and Allan dead? I don't know. Then who? Wilbur's security kind of sucks. It's true almost anyone could have had access. But why?"

"Look!" I pulled Tinkie down behind a car and pointed across the lot to the door of the health food store. Sonja Rivera hurried across the asphalt and got into her vehicle. In a moment she tore out of the parking lot.

We hustled inside to talk to the clerk in the store. I spent a few minutes softening her up, but Tinkie had no patience. "Do you sell mushrooms here?" she asked. "Specifically psilocybin."

"We don't sell drugs," the clerk said flatly. I'd scoped out the store and knew they had a fine supply of shitake, white, portobellos, button, and other fungi. Some were fresh. Others dehydrated.

"Where could a person get those mushrooms?" I asked the clerk, showing her a photo on my phone of the mushrooms bobbing in the spaghetti sauce.

"Any cow or horse pasture, though it's been pretty cold for mushrooms this time of year. I'd think maybe someone was cultivating them in a greenhouse situation. A lot of healers are using shrooms now to treat depression and anxiety. It's big business. That and Special K, too. Recreational drugs are finding real medicinal uses."

"Any names of health care practitioners you'd care to give us?"

"Chief Johnson would know. In fact, he has cows and horses. The mushrooms grow naturally in the poop. People come in the store and buy a lot of stuff, but since we don't sell the shrooms, or Special K, or any narcotics, I have no idea who is using them medically. And if I did know, I wouldn't rat out my customers."

I didn't really blame the clerk. "Do you know this woman?" I showed her a photo of Grace.

"Sure. Grace Land. She has an awesome TV show about training men to be good partners. They damn sure need some training. That Grace, she gives those little man babies hell."

At last, we'd found someone who liked Grace's TV show. "Has she been in this store lately?"

The clerk frowned. "She was here a couple of days ago. I saw a ticket charged to her account."

This was at least information that might be helpful. "What did she buy?" I asked. Tinkie had drifted over to the register. She signaled me to lure the clerk away.

"I wasn't working so I don't know. I just happened to see the ticket on the stob." She pointed to a spike where a number of sales receipts fluttered. "It's kind of old-fashioned, but then we can put all the sales into the computer at the end of the day. The store owner likes to keep the paper copies, too. He doesn't believe anything is safe in the cloud. The fact is, we're a week behind in entering the sales." She sighed. "It's a job I hate, but I need to get after it."

I shared the owner's skepticism about the safety of the cloud, but I didn't go into that. "I'd like something to sleep," I said. "Could you help me find something? Not melatonin. That doesn't work for me."

"How about some hemp gummies? Lots of people say that helps."

"Show me what you have."

For ten minutes the clerk went over the benefits of different types of CBD gummies and the different flavors. I settled on a small bottle of mango chews. I seldom had trouble sleeping, but I'd kept the clerk occupied while Tinkie slipped behind the counter and went through the tickets stuck on the large spike. She'd photographed several, and when she signaled to me that she was done, I went to the counter to pay for my purchase.

"I hope they work for you," the clerk said.

"Me, too." I couldn't wait to get outside. "Thanks for your help." I picked up my package and headed to the door. Tinkie was hot on my heels.

"What did Grace buy?" I asked Tinkie as soon as we were clear of the store.

"Mushrooms."

I thought for sure she was kidding. "Uh-uh. You're lying."

"I wish I were." She showed me the photograph. Grace had bought a pound of cremini and a pound of portobellos. Along with some sleep aides and pine nuts.

"Do you think it's possible she bought those mushrooms but ended up with the magic ones?" I asked.

"Maybe, but that still doesn't tell us how she got Wilbur to cook them," Tinkie said. "Did she make the spaghetti sauce? If so, that's a pretty clear indication it was a deliberate act. Not like Wilbur picked them in the woods not knowing what he was doing."

Tinkie had a point. But even better, I had enough information to talk to Wilbur and make him tell the truth.

"I'm going to find our homicidal spaghetti eater. Why don't you pick up some doughnuts and take them to the gang? Buy me a little time to grill Wilbur."

"You don't want me to come?" she asked.

"Have a late breakfast with Oscar and Maylin. I can do this. I won't be far behind you."

I dropped her at the doughnut place near the hotel, and I went on to the police chief's office. Yuma hadn't come in yet, but I was in luck. I learned Wilbur was asleep in a cell. He wasn't under arrest—he just hadn't been physically able to go home. I talked the deputy into letting me ask Wilbur some questions. I couldn't help but feel sorry for the wannabe Elvis, who was still dressed in his leopard spandex outfit. When he saw me, he jumped to his feet, chomping at the bit to get out of his cell and begin preparations for his act. The cell wasn't locked, but I didn't bother to tell Wilbur that. I needed his cooperation.

"Where'd you get the mushrooms for your spaghetti sauce?" I asked Wilbur.

"How did you know I had spaghetti . . ." He pointed his finger at me. "You broke into my place."

"I'm trying to help you. I think someone spiked your marinara sauce with hallucinogenic mushrooms."

"Who would do—" He whipped around. "I'm going to kill Sherman."

"Your brother? You think he would do this?"

Wilbur sank onto the bunk in his cell. "I don't want to believe it, but . . ."

"But what?" He needed to talk and fast. This case was like an octopus with eighty tentacles. I couldn't keep up with the insanity happening on all fronts.

"The truth is, I sing a little off-key."

I reached through the bars for his throat. I meant to grab him and choke until he squealed like a pig or passed out. "Your brother would dose you with magic mushrooms and send you out on a mission to kill two people because you lack singing talents?"

He shrugged but wisely stayed out of my reach. "Sherman is serious about winning this contest. He has ambitions. He only let me be in the group because I paid for all the leopard-print spandex jumpsuits. See, if I'm in jail, I can't perform tonight, now can I?"

I could have told him he wasn't under arrest, but I didn't. In the way that a lot of crazy stuff in Tupelo made sense, this did, too. It was possible his brother had dosed him in an effort to get him off their Elvis foursome. Sherman struck me as a man intent on winning the competition so he could reach for the golden ring of an Elvis show in Las Vegas. He may not have meant for Wilbur to go nuts and shoot at people. Then again, he might have sent him on that mission. I wondered if I could talk Yuma into arresting the other Manning brother.

"Wilbur, where did you get the mushrooms?" I asked him in a gentler tone.

"They were left in a brown paper sack on the doorstep with a note that said 'enjoy with your favorite marinara sauce.'"

"And you didn't question where they came from?"

He looked at me like I'd sprouted four eyes. "This is Tupelo. Neighbors are . . . neighborly. Everyone knows I love to make spaghetti sauce. I have it every week. And there are folks in town who pick mushrooms fresh for me and leave them for me." He shrugged. "I don't have enough money that anyone would want to hurt me for some kind of profit. Who else would want to harm me?" He glared. "Other than my fame-obsessed brother."

"I don't know. But what if you were being manipulated? Did you see anyone around your house?"

He thought a minute. "Rufus Trilby was walking down the street yesterday. He was walking Lily, his dog. You know he's a member of the leopard-print Elvis quartet. Do you think Sherman put him up to trying to poison me? Rufus wouldn't do that on his own, but Sherman might have talked him into it. Rufus is kind of suggestible."

I didn't think that was the case, but I didn't bother to say so. "Is Madison part of the group?"

"Kent used to be, until he got the big head and decided he was solo-act material. He is awful." He rolled his eyes. "He's going to sing the 'Little Drummer Boy.' Bring your pillow and blanket, because it's a yawner for sure. His hips don't move like Elvis. He's more like the Tin Man in need of an oil can."

"Wilbur!" I snapped. "Who else was around your house?"

"Rufus Trilby. I told you. I don't remember seeing anyone else around."

"Why did you want to shoot Krystal and Allan Malone?"

He shook his head. "I wish I knew! I love Allan's TV show, *Who's Singing Barbra*. It's superior TV." He looked like he was going to cry. "I don't know why I did it. I don't.

Could you ask Yuma to let me out so I can participate in the competition tonight? I really want to sing with the group. I've rehearsed and rehearsed."

I couldn't help it. I felt sad for Wilbur. He had been practicing. And he loved his Elvis outfit so much. Also, it seemed clear to me that he was a pawn in the shooting. "I'll speak to Yuma." It was making me cringe not to tell him he was free, but I had to get every bit of info from him I could. "But only if you tell me the total truth."

He nodded. "I didn't know what I was doing, Ms. Delaney. I swear it. I've never harmed anyone in my life. I don't even know where I got the gun."

"You have a pawnshop full of guns."

"True, but I didn't buy it." His eyebrows shot up. "Did I steal it? Man, Sherman is going to be really pissed."

"I'll be back in a bit." I had an idea. The pawnshop did have cameras all over the place. Yuma hadn't thought of how Wilbur got a gun. Maybe he hadn't gone up there to check the store cameras and tamper with the evidence—if that was his inclination. "Keep practicing your part for the competition. I'll do my best to get you out of here."

"Ms. Delaney, you are an angel sent down from Heaven to help me this Christmas. I'll bet you even have wings."

It was hard to be mean to someone who seemed so genuinely sweet—but I wanted to give it a try. I was more imp than angel, and I knew it. I didn't have time to show Wilbur the true me. But I did stop and mention to the deputy that Wilbur was up and ready to leave. Soon he would know he was free to participate in the contest—but not before I had a chance to do some investigating.

I hauled boogie out of the sheriff's office, making sure no one was watching me, and drove out to the pawnshop on the highway. Tinkie would be annoyed that I didn't swing by for her, but I'd make it up to her. The sign on the door read CLOSED. I figured Sherman was down at the Arena Center, making sure everything was in order for his performance. It was now or never.

The front door was dead-bolted, and the back door was also locked. I didn't have Tinkie's skill with lockpicks, but I did find a rock and broke the window glass. I creaked the door open slowly, ready to run if an alarm went off. Nothing. Only silence. I was in!

I found the cameras—and yes, I was being filmed. I could put an end to that! For a store without an alarm system, the interior cameras were somewhat sophisticated. Wireless. I found a small office behind the counter and searched. The recording device that the cameras fed into was high on a top shelf. I unplugged it and took the whole thing. I needed Cece or Tinkie. They were much smarter with electronics. I was about to head out the back when I heard something in the front of the store.

I peeked around a doorway and stopped in my tracks. A gorgeous woman stood behind the gun counter. She held a Glock and pointed it right at my face.

"Going somewhere?" she drawled in a passable Mississippi accent.

Her hair was reddish blond—classically a strawberry blond—and poufed up. Her makeup was stellar. She was gorgeous, and she oozed sex appeal.

"Who are you and how did you get in here?" I hadn't seen her when I first broke in.

"You can't come to town and mess with the memory of the man I love."

"Wilbur? You're in love with Wilbur?" I thought another moment. "But he isn't dead."

"You are an idiot!"

Something in the phrasing of that sentence gave me a clue. I stepped toward the counter to get a better look. The woman was breathtaking, and I now recognized her. Ann-Margret, Swedish-born actress and costar with Elvis of *Viva Las Vegas*. She was a megastar of film, stage, and TV, had topped the Billboard charts as a singer, and had been a live performer at Las Vegas and other venues. She was loaded with talent and a gun, but the first question I asked was "Why didn't you marry Elvis?" I'd wanted to know this question my entire life. Who could *not* have married that handsome, talented, kind man?

She put the gun down and a tear slipped down her cheek. "I don't know. If I could go back in time . . . That's not even true. I believe everything happened just as it should have. As it turned out, I had a wonderful husband. I had a full career. I thought I could be a better friend to Elvis. Honestly, I think back, and what happened to Elvis doesn't make any sense to me."

Ann-Margret had had a spectacular career. Five Golden Globes out of ten nominations, Oscar nominations, Emmys, Grammys, and numerous other awards for her musical work and singing and dancing. She'd been a busy lady on the stage, the big screen, the little screen, and musical venues. She was an international star, much like Elvis had been. The biggest difference was that Ann-Margret was very much alive and still working.

"It's remarkable you recovered from that tragic fall in Las Vegas." She'd fallen twenty-two feet from a raised platform to the stage. It would have been a career ender for many people, but after lots of surgery she was back onstage, still a triple threat, and she went on to achieve even more fame.

"I had great surgeons and lots of support. I was lucky."

"And determined to get back to work."

"Yes, that, too."

I knew the apparition in front of me wasn't the real Ann-Margret. The movie star was working down in Florida, the last I heard. She wasn't in Tupelo, Mississippi. "Jitty, why are you here?"

"To encourage you in your stage ambitions."

"A little late for that." I didn't have the grit or the talent that Ann-Margret had. And I had accepted that. As Jitty had wisely said only moments before, I, too, believed that things had happened as they'd been meant to. "My shot at acting fame has come and gone."

"Maybe. Maybe not."

Jitty loved to be cryptic. "Seriously, what are you doing here in the pawnshop?" I checked my watch. I had to clear out quickly. I didn't want to get caught here before I had a chance to review the tape on the recorder I was holding in my hand. As typical with a visitation from Jitty, what had seemed like ten minutes was only a few seconds. She could manipulate time like that.

Jitty did a runway turn and looked over her shoulder, so glamorous and so totally in control of her image. "You know, I have a real belief that I'll get to perform with Elvis again. We'll both be young and have the time of our lives." She looked at me for a long moment. "Never give up your dreams, Sarah Booth. Even the ones that seem way out of reach."

Her words sent a chill through me. I didn't know if it was because they gave me a lifeline to a long-ago dream, or because they sounded so much like something my mother would have said. "It's hard to know the difference between a ridiculous dream and real possibility."

Ann-Margret smiled. "I will perform with Elvis again. I know it."

"I hope so." It was a thought that made me happy, too. "But not too soon. Not too soon." The talented actress needed to live a long time.

"Agreed."

Jitty did a twirl that sent the spangles on her outfit sparkling, and then *poof!* she was gone.

I had the recorder in my hand and I fled out the back door before Sherman—or the police chief—could arrive. It was always better to beg forgiveness than ask permission. Neither Ann-Margret nor Jitty had to tell me that. I knew that truthful tidbit all on my own.

34

I drove like a bat out of hell back to the hotel room. Coleman wasn't there, and I didn't know where he was. But Tinkie was sitting on ready. She came over to my room as soon as I called her. I plugged the recorder into the TV—with a little help from my partner—and we sat down to watch. There wasn't a time stamp on the footage, but in the end I didn't need one.

After the Manning brothers had closed, locked up the store, and left, the front door opened again. A slender figure dressed all in black with a ski mask covering the face entered the store. It was likely a woman or a very slender man. I couldn't tell who it was, but I would recognize the gait of the person if I ever saw them again.

The figure went to the counter where the guns were

displayed, slipped behind the case, and removed a Glock. After admiring the gun and picking up some ammunition, the figure went back out the front door and locked it.

"That's the person who gave Wilbur the mushrooms?" Tinkie said. "Do you know who it is?"

We watched it twice more. "I believe it's a woman."

"Me, too." Tinkie bit her lip. "I'd say about five-eight, maybe a hundred and twenty pounds. Nice defined arms. Slender neck." My partner had keen observation. "Who fits that description?"

I could think of only two women who might have a stake in manipulating Wilbur. Sonja Rivera and Krystal Bond. When I said their names, Tinkie nodded.

"It's one of them."

"But which one?" I asked.

"That's what we're going to find out. And then we're going to put this case to bed so we can enjoy the show tonight and head home tomorrow with a clear conscience. I can't wait to tell Maylin about Santa Claus and the reindeer. She's too young to remember, but you never know what a child retains."

"I second that plan." It wasn't a lot to ask. Not really.

"Are you going to show that to Yuma?" Tinkie asked.

It was a problem. I'd have to admit to breaking into the pawnshop if I showed him. "Maybe I'll just show Coleman and let him handle it."

"That man deserves a Purple Heart for getting involved in your cases."

I had to laugh, because she was only being truthful. I texted Coleman and asked him to view the footage. "Let's go talk to Kent Madison."

"Why Kent?" Tinkie asked.

"He hates Grace and Sippi. And probably Krystal and Allan. He has motive and opportunity, and he's clearly implicated in several aspects of this case. I mean, he had the codes to the security cameras that were shut down. He knows something."

"Maybe he won't tell even if he does. He's a toad."

"That's why you're going to break him, Tinkie. Use your plump full bottom lip that pops out of your mouth . . ." I made a disgusting sound. "Bring on your man magic and force him to heel!"

"Eeww. That sounds sick."

"Yes, and oh, so powerful!"

"Leave me with Kent and I'll bleed the info out of him."

Her look was more predatory than sexy. It was another disturbing image, but I had to laugh. Tinkie, for all of her ladylike ways, could be graphic when she took a notion.

As much as I loved singing "Blue Christmas" with my friends—and escaping certain death on the stage—I was glad our performance was over. The coming evening's activities were purely spectator for us. No worries, just pleasure. I could focus totally on closing this frustrating case.

I started to call Cece and Millie, but I hoped they were sleeping in. They both worked full-time jobs, on the clock, and seldom got to sleep late. I decided to give them a pass until later. And the truth was, Cece and Millie had a newspaper column to write, too. There'd been plenty of excitement at the Elvis festival to report on, and I knew for a fact the two journalists had some terrific photos of the performances, the decorated town, the fun events and activities. Not to mention a lot of handsome Elvis impersonators. It was best to leave them to their own devices to finish their work. After all, it was almost Christmas. We'd get back to Zinnia tomorrow in time to finish wrapping gifts, then we were due at Harold's place for supper and a gift exchange. This year would be a blast with Maylin. There was nothing like a child to bring the real joy of Christmas home.

"Are you growing to the spot or are we going to confront Kent?" Tinkie asked.

"Limber up your lip, big girl. First Kent, and then you can take your shot with Wilbur."

She rolled her eyes and picked up the keys to her car. "What about Oscar?" I asked. "He may need a ride."

"Coleman can haul him around. Or Harold. Oscar can manage on his own."

We were out the door and into the bracing December day. I didn't have a good feeling about solving the case in the time we had left, but I kept my doubts to myself. It was, after all, Christmas. No point dumping gloom on everyone else. We could continue the case after the holiday was done. Not very satisfactory, but it might be our only choice.

We pulled into the parking lot at city hall. Sure enough, Kent was in his spacious office, his back turned to the door, talking on the phone.

"I don't know what you expect me to do. I've told you my hands are tied."

Tinkie and I both stopped in the doorway. Sure, we were eavesdropping.

"Don't threaten me!" Kent leaned forward in his chair. "I won't put up with this. I know things, Krystal. I know plenty. Things you don't want me to tell."

Oh, this was better than I had any right to expect.

"You'd better rethink the way you act." He slammed

the phone down and turned around. When he saw us, he turned pale. "What are you doing here?" he demanded, standing up and coming toward us.

I held my ground. "We have some questions for you."

"And I have an answer. Get out of my office now."

Tinkie stepped right up to him. She only came to his chest, but she was not afraid of his bully posturing. "Answer our questions or Yuma will grill you at the jail."

"Screw Yuma. All he cares about is Grace Land and covering his own butt."

"I'm sure he'd love to hear your opinion of him," Tinkie said. "Come on, Sarah Booth. We came here to try to help old Kent out, but he's not smart enough to take advantage of our generous offer."

"I don't need your help. I haven't done anything." He was still bowed up, but he stepped back two paces. And he didn't sound as certain as he should have. Kent Madison was guilty—I just couldn't pinpoint of what.

"We know you were backstage last evening. You were seen messing with the ropes that control the stage lights," Tinkie said. "That's attempted murder, Kent. Yuma may not want to charge you. He might want to protect you. But there are other lawmen on the case now. Yuma will cover his own butt before he risks everything to protect you."

Tinkie's words elicited an angry response from Kent.

"You don't know anything. You think you do, but all of your suspicions are ridiculous. When you finally figure out Sippi—" He stopped, his eyes wide.

"Sippi what?" I asked softly.

"Leave me alone. You're going to get me killed."

"Are you saying Sippi Salem will kill you for talking to

us?" I asked. I wondered if he knew Grace still had a soft spot for Sippi. And a warm bed.

"Sippi wouldn't harm a fly. Hell, he doesn't have to do anything mean. He just charms those women right out of anything he wants." He shook his head. "You don't understand any of this. Just know that I'm in a bind, and so are other people. Keep meddling and you're the one who'll be responsible for someone getting hurt."

Tinkie looked at me. "Grace thinks you may be responsible for stealing her Elvis belt."

"I know. But I didn't take it."

"But you helped someone else do it, didn't you?" Tinkie asked.

"Not like you think." He walked to the window of his office and looked out on the cold December scene. "Not deliberately."

"So, tell us how you accidentally played a role in this."

"You won't believe me."

Probably not. I didn't look at Kent as a paragon of truth and virtue. But I needed to hear what he had to say. "Give us a try."

"The evening the belt was stolen, I did turn off the cameras and the lasers. Because Grace asked me to. She said she was going to substitute a fake belt for the one on display because she was worried it would be stolen. I guess she didn't get around to doing that. I did what she asked because I love Grace. Maybe I wasn't very smart, but I didn't harm anyone, nor did I steal that belt. If you're looking for the guilty party in this situation, look no further than your lying client."

"Who stole the belt?" His self-serving denial almost had

steam coming from my ears. Grace! Once again, she'd lied to us about her involvement. She was the worst client we'd ever had. I was ready to drive straight to her house and string her up by the thumbs.

"I don't know. I don't know why Grace didn't make the exchange like she said she would."

"Do you think she meant to have the belt stolen to collect the insurance money?"

"But there wasn't any insurance," Kent reminded me. "And that crazy Krystal, running around leaving magic mushrooms for people. I guess she hoped to provoke an action that would take the heat off her."

So now we knew where Wilbur had gotten the fungi. At this point in the case, Wilbur didn't figure into the ending.

"But maybe Grace didn't know that," Tinkie said. "If she has that belt hidden somewhere . . ."

That would be an ugly scene, for sure. But I couldn't believe Grace would hire us to find something she had hidden somewhere.

"If Grace doesn't have the belt, who does?" I asked Kent.

"How would I know? It isn't me."

"Someone took advantage of you," I pointed out. "They used you to turn off the security for the belt. That's going to come back on you, Kent. Whether you were part of the robbery or not, it looks like you were. That's prison time. Doesn't that make you angry? Why protect someone who doesn't care how much you pay for doing a favor for a friend?"

I could tell I was getting under his skin.

"If we recover the belt, it could make things a lot easier for you." Tinkie was leaning in, too.

"I honestly don't know. I believe that Grace truly meant

to swap the belts. I don't know why she didn't do it. Maybe she didn't get a chance. She's more than a little ditzy."

That was a question only Grace could answer. "We'll speak with her. But if you have any information, you'd better spit it out now. With us or with Yuma. And you're still going to have to answer for the lights falling on the stage. We were nearly killed."

"You might talk to Allan Malone about that. His pugs were chewing on that rope backstage."

"You're accusing two little pugs of trying to kill us?" Tinkie asked.

"I'm accusing Allan of not keeping up with his dogs. He lets those little ankle biters run wild. Because he loves them, he thinks everyone else should. But they are bad. They are always into things, and they were tugging on the rope." He looked straight at me. "Or maybe it was deliberate. Maybe Allan meant to take you out."

I didn't let on that Kent had finally gotten to me. I had to talk to Grace and right away.

35

"I have no idea what you're asking." Grace rang her little bell for the maid. "Would you please make Bloody Marys for us?" she asked Jessica. "And for Mother, too."

Brandi Beaumont walked into the room. The tension between the two of them was electric. We'd obviously interrupted an argument between mother and daughter.

"Why are you here?" Brandi asked me.

"We need to ask Grace some questions."

"No, you don't." She stepped between us and her daughter. "Grace is tired and upset. She needs peace and quiet. You should leave."

"Grace, we know about your scheme to replace the Elvis belt with a replica."

She blew out her breath. "Yeah, so what? I wasn't doing

anything illegal. I realized it was risky to leave the real belt up at the Arena Center. Boy, was I right about that. I didn't even get the belts swapped, so what I planned to do and what I actually did are two different things."

"Why didn't you follow through and change out the belts?"

"Because Allan Malone showed up here, raising hell about my TV show, and he wouldn't leave. He let those little pugs loose in the house and they chewed the corners off my brand-new kitchen cabinets. Those little dogs are terrorists. I think he had them trained by ISIS."

She wasn't really exaggerating about the dogs. They were Allan's secret weapon. "I suspect they played a role in nearly killing me and my friends with that stage light." I didn't know this for a fact, but it was a great gambit to keep her talking.

"See. They're agents of evil."

"So, Allan was here with you the afternoon before the belt went missing."

"Yes. Pretending we could do a crossover season between our shows. The idea is ridiculous. The men I have to train on my show don't sing or dance or do anything amusing. That's why they have to be trained to perform chores and make life easier for the women."

I didn't want to get into a debate with Grace about how men should be trained. "Grace, I don't think we're going to be able to find out who stole your belt before we have to leave in the morning."

She sighed. "I know. It's okay. I don't think I'll ever see that belt again."

"It's worth three million dollars!" Brandi said. "You have to find it or the people who stole it."

"Believe us, we want to do just that," Tinkie said. "But

Grace hasn't been truthful with us, and we've wasted a lot of time checking into people who aren't even viable suspects."

"So, who is viable?" Brandi asked.

"You. Sippi. Allan. Krystal Bond. Kent Madison. In fact, all the suspects we had initially are still suspects. We haven't been able to eliminate anyone." Tinkie just put the facts out there.

Grace stood up and paced. "I'm beginning to believe I should just let this go. Pointing the finger at people won't bring my belt back."

"But Allan should pay for nearly killing us." Tinkie's cheeks were pink. She was angry, and so was I. Grace and Brandi acted like attempted murder was nothing as long as it was directed at us and not them.

"Let's find the belt and then, I assure you, I will make Allan pay for his sins," Brandi said. "With pleasure."

I didn't trust her any more than I trusted Grace. They were both professional liars and manipulators. "Tinkie, we should go to the Arena Center and check out some things." I really just wanted to get out of Grace's house. "Maybe some of the workers will remember something."

I didn't give Brandi or Grace a chance to stop us. We were out the door in record time.

"What's at the Arena Center?" Tinkie asked.

"Nothing. Not a thing."

"We don't have any other leads. We might as well check it out."

While Tinkie talked with the workers—young people responded better to her than to me—I went to look at the office where the cameras had been feeding into. Someone had made a fresh pot of coffee, and I opened some cabinets looking for paper cups. It wasn't until I started on the bottom cabinets that I stopped. The edges of the wooden doors were chewed. Grace had said Allan's dogs chewed her cabinets. It was pretty thin evidence, but it was better than anything else we'd unearthed. It was solid proof Allan and the dogs had been there at a time when no one was watching them.

The young worker, Darcy, came in the break room and stopped. "What are you doing in here?"

"Coffee." I pointed out my steaming cup. "Darcy, when were these cabinets chewed?"

"Oh, goodness. The assistant mayor has almost had a stroke over that. No one knows who or when it happened. The volunteers are going to get the blame. You can bet on that."

"I don't think y'all were down on your hands and knees chewing the wood."

She laughed out loud. "Good point, Sarah Booth."

"Has Allan Malone ever had his pugs in here?"

"No." She frowned. "No, but it does look like a dog chewed it. Yes, it does." She looked at me. "Dogs aren't allowed in here. What if someone is allergic?"

"Thanks, Darcy. By the way, you should call the mayor and report all of this," I said. "Be the hero. I have to run some errands."

I might not be able to prove it hard enough to charge him with the theft, but I knew Allan was involved. For whatever reason, he'd been in the Arena Center with his dogs when the belt was taken. He'd been on site when me and my friends were almost killed by a falling stage light. Grace had been run into a ditch—after Allan came back to Tupelo for the Elvis festival. We'd almost been run down by someone. In both instances, Yuma had been less than helpful. It was almost as if he weren't trying. But there was no getting around that Allan had either been on scene or very close to the scene of all the crimes circling Grace.

The one thing I'd noticed in Tupelo was that wherever Allan went, Krystal Bond wasn't far behind. I'd assumed their relationship was either professional or romantic. But what if I was wrong? What if it was criminal?

Tinkie and I didn't have the chops to get an order to examine cell phone messages. Yuma could do it if he wanted. But I knew in my heart he wouldn't help us. Whatever was going on in Lee County, Tupelo police chief Yuma Johnson didn't want to get in the middle of it.

"What are we going to do?" asked Tinkie, who had joined me in my room.

We didn't have a box full of options. We needed Allan's phone to check his messages. Since we couldn't legally obtain it, there was only one thing to do—steal it.

Tinkie looked at me. "Okay."

"I didn't say anything."

"You don't have to. I know that look. So how do we set Allan up so one of us can steal his phone?"

"He wants Cece to do his show about Barbra Streisand. She can distract him while we look for his phone."

"Yuma will put us in the hoosegow if he catches us."

"Yep."

"Can Coleman get us out?"

"Probably not." Coleman would try, but if Yuma was corrupt, as I suspected, professional courtesy to another lawman would have no impact on how Yuma dealt with us.

"So, when do we do this?"

"Now." We didn't have more time. It was now or never. "After the competition tonight, Allan will likely go back to Hollywood. If he has the belt or knows who does, he'll take that information with him. He'll be far from our reach."

Tinkie nodded. "I have a problem." Her blue eyes filled with tears. Tinkie was *not* a crier. She was tender and kind, but she was not a person who cried unless it was serious.

"What?" I put my hands on her shoulders. "What is it?"

"I can't do this." Tears moved down her cheeks. "I can't go to jail and miss Christmas with Maylin. I just can't."

It hadn't occurred to me, but I understood. "That's fine, Tinkie. I'll steal the phone. Cece can distract Allan. There's no reason for you to even be in the vicinity, and if I get caught, I'll say you had nothing to do with this plot."

"And you'll take the punishment for something we did together."

"Oh, for Pete's sake, it won't be a federal case. I'll play it off as an accident or something. Like the phone just jumped right into my back pocket. All by itself."

My plan to get Tinkie to laugh was working. If she was laughing, she couldn't cry, and I could not bear to see my loyal friend distressed and upset. Especially not over something that made perfect sense to me. Coleman would miss me at Christmas if I went to jail, but he wasn't a child. He could emotionally understand what was happening. Maylin could not. Whatever else happened, I could not risk having Tinkie go to jail.

"It isn't fair for you to take the risk." Tinkie's jaw was set. She could be stubborn when she put her mind to it.

"Oh, you'll have to take a risk. While Cece and I are

doing this, I want you to find Sippi and convince him to tell us everything he knows."

"You're just trying to make me feel like I'm useful."

"Tinkie, you could probably get more info out of him than Coleman and I could with truth serum. Please?"

"Okay, but it isn't fair."

"When Maylin is grown and in college you can take all the risks from then on."

She huffed. "By that time we'll both be too old be private investigators."

"I have great genes. I'll be working, and so will you!"

"Okay." She was reluctant to let it go, but she had to put Maylin first.

"I'll get Cece and talk it over with her."

A knock at the door made me laugh. "That's her. She may be psychic."

Tinkie opened the door and Cece stood there in a winter green jacket, black leggings, and boots. "What are you up to?"

"We need your help," I said as I drew her into the room and began to lay out my plan.

36

The goal was clear, but the route to achieve it was not. How in the world was I going to trick Allan into leaving his phone out so I could grab it? And then what? If it was locked, how would I get into it to read his messages?

"As soon as we find him, you need to call him while I'm talking with him," Cece said. "He'll pull out his phone to check to see who is calling. I'll do my best to get him to put the phone down somewhere."

"But how would we open it?" I was still trying to work through the scenario. I obviously wasn't a very good phone thief. "Could we send some kind of false alert or someone pretending to be a software person?"

Cece laughed. "We'd first need to have some expertise to sell that bit of fiction."

She was right. "Okay, once we get the phone, we'll just have to figure out how to open it, then."

"I have an idea," Cece said. "But we'll have to work quickly."

It would be so much simpler to have a law officer do this, but I knew Yuma wouldn't help us and Coleman had zero authority. And the minutes were ticking away. I wondered when Allan would head back to Hollywood. Soon, if I had to make a guess.

"What's your idea?" I asked Cece.

"Best you don't know." She picked up her purse. "Let's find Allan. We need to corner him in a private setting, not in a public place."

"How about we get Grace to invite him to her house?" I asked.

"It's the best we've got, I suppose. Though it may put Grace in a tough spot."

I shrugged. "What's the other option?"

"Call him." Cece had made up her mind. "Tell him to meet us there immediately. I'll call Grace and get her and her mother out of the house. That should help."

"What are you—"

"Don't ask and I won't tell. Now get busy."

I called Allan, who answered on the fourth ring.

"Yes?" He sounded testy.

"I need to talk to you at Grace Land's house right away. It's urgent," I said. I was likely cooking my own goose, but I had to get him to cooperate.

"I will never set foot on her property again. And neither will my precious babies. Grace doesn't even like dogs. She's not a nice person."

"I'm not going to argue that, Allan. But we need to talk. Please."

"I don't know anything about her Elvis belt, and I'm busy. I'm leaving in the morning to head back to Los Angeles. Once this festival is done tonight, I'm gone."

"I have Cece with me. She wants to sing for you." It was the only lie I could come up with. And it wasn't really a lie. Cece did want to perform on his show. And she could do it. She could really sing Barbra. It would be great for her and Jaytee, because he would play the harmonica with her, except that Allan might be looking at a long jail sentence. Other than wasting Cece's time to sing for him, I didn't see a real issue. And if he wasn't guilty . . . win-win.

We arrived at Grace's just as she and her mother were getting in the car. She'd left the front door open. "Don't let him steal anything. And don't let those dogs in the house. They're terrorists in fur coats."

"Got it!" I gave her a thumbs-up and hustled Cece inside to encourage Grace to drive away. She did just that, only a few minutes before Allan arrived. He had the pugs with him. I was faced with confronting him about the dogs or simply doing my best to make sure they didn't destroy Grace's house.

"Where's Grace?" Allan asked. He stood at the passenger door of his car, deciding whether to let the dogs out or not.

"She had to run an errand with her mom."

"Brandi is still in town? I figured Grace would either ship her out or kill her."

He wasn't being funny. I ignored his dig at our client. "Come in. Cece wants to sing for you. Since you're leaving in the morning, it's now or never. You need to hear her sing."

"Did she bring her music?" he asked.

"She's going a cappella, just for the audition."

"She'd better be good if she's going a cappella." He glanced at Cece. "I heard her sing when y'all won the amateur impersonator contest, but I'd like to hear only her. I guess I can take a few minutes." He opened the car door and the dogs came out like buzz saws on four paws. They barked at me, barked at Cece, and scratched the front door to go inside. It eased open and they were in. I had to try to keep an eye on them.

Allan followed his dogs into the house; Cece and I were right on his heels.

"Let's go into the front parlor," Cece said. "The acoustics in there are pretty good. That's why I wanted to meet you here. And Grace gave permission before she left."

"I'm going to put some coffee on," I said. I had to trust that Cece could get him to put his phone down somewhere I could snatch it up. I needed to be in the kitchen to call him, but if I disappeared right before he got the call, he would know it was me! Damn. My plan was flawed.

But I could fix it.

I dialed Millie. "Call Allan, please." I gave her his number. "Tell him you're looking for Cece. That you need her for an article for the newspaper."

"What—"

"Please, just do it right now. I'll explain when I see you."

"Will do."

A minute later I heard a phone ring in the parlor. Allan answered. "Who is this?"

There was a pause. "Yes, she's here but we're busy. I'll

have her call when we're done." He was all business when it came to auditioning for his TV show.

"Allan, what do you think about this?" Cece began belting out "Evergreen."

I was stopped in my tracks. Cece could sing, but this was a new aspect of her vocal talent.

"I wonder if Kristofferson would join you." Allan sounded suitably impressed. "That would be a freaking coup! You must come out to Hollywood. Promise me that you will! I can build an entire show around you."

Red alert! Red alert! Allan was trying to steal my friend out from under me. It was true. Cece could carry her own TV show. But then she would be out in Hollywood and not in Zinnia, keeping an eye on the local crooks and hucksters. The community needed Cece's reporting. We couldn't do without her. And then I remembered Allan was likely going to prison. Whew!

I slipped into the parlor. Cece had managed to get Allan into the far corner, where he was transfixed by her singing. And she was putting on a show with dramatic arms and dance twirls. Sure enough, his phone was on the sofa table. I tried to open it up, but it required Face ID. We were screwed. Even if I slipped it in my pocket and took off with it, I couldn't open it. Cece was watching me and I pointed to my face. *We need Face ID*, I mouthed at her.

She nodded. As she twirled by a small desk, she picked up a bookend. With three strides, she was right by Allan. She sang and twirled and clocked him upside the head with the heavy bookend. He went down like a sack of potatoes.

"Cece!" I was shocked.

"Get the Face ID!"

I held the phone so it registered his face, but it wouldn't

open. I punched in codes and tried the Face ID again. "It isn't working. His eyes are closed. It doesn't recognize him." I tried from several angles. With Allan laid out on the floor, he looked quite dead. The phone was having none of that. "Damn. What now?"

"Try again." Cece knelt beside his head and used her fingers to open his eyes. "This should work."

I had my doubts, but I maneuvered the phone, hovering over his face. To my astonishment, it worked. I was in his phone. "Got it."

"Hurry, Sarah Booth. I don't want to have to hit him again and he's moaning like he's coming around."

I didn't want that either. I went directly into his private messages and stopped cold. He must have had a million contacts and people who messaged him every three minutes. The phone dinged, signaling an incoming message, as I held it in my hand.

"I'm waiting." That's all the text said.

"Delayed," I typed back. The contact was KB with a Mississippi area code. It had to be Krystal Bond.

"Don't try to double-cross me" was the response.

"Never. Give me a few minutes. I'll be there." He wouldn't and it made me happy to think Krystal would be inconvenienced.

"I want this finished. It's dragged out too long. We're in a dangerous place. Where are you?"

Oh, I wanted to ask questions. Many questions. I didn't owe Krystal any answers, but I played along. "On the way. Be there fast. Wait for me." I wanted to ask where she was. I needed to ask that. "Could we meet at the Hound Dog Hotel instead?"

"Fine. Just hurry."

At least now I knew where she would be. But I had bigger fish to fry. I needed to read the texts between Allan, Krystal, Grace, Sippi, Brandi, and Yuma—and anyone else who might be implicated in the theft. But most especially Krystal.

"Did you find anything?" Cece asked. She was checking Allan's pulse.

"Yes." I scrolled to the top of the exchange with Krystal and Allan, and there they were. All the texts between him and Krystal. They'd plotted and planned the whole thing, from the theft to the disposal of the belt by removing the jewels and melting the gold. They'd been communicating long before the Elvis impersonator Christmas festival. They'd been plotting since October. I was stunned at the volley of texts that laid out the whole scheme—to the point that Krystal admitted she'd allowed Grace's policy to expire so that she could purchase her own policy! She was going to split the money with Allan.

I was in a pickle now. I couldn't very well steal Allan's phone—Yuma would put me in jail instead of Allan. But the proof was on the phone. And I couldn't let it go to sleep again—I wouldn't have access to Allan's face for very much longer. How could I preserve the messages?

"Copy and send them to your phone," Cece said, knowing I was technology challenged. "Here, give it to me."

I handed over the phone and knelt beside Allan. He was moaning and coming around. He'd be pissed, for sure. While he was a Hollywood pretty boy, I imagined he could land a nice punch if he decided to try.

"Look, you press these two buttons on the side and it will take a screenshot. Then message the screenshot to your phone."

"Won't he know we did that?" I asked.

"He'll know *someone* did it. And he'll suspect us. But I don't see another option if this is really evidence."

She was right and I was wasting time. I started screen-shotting the texts and sending them to my phone. Allan would clearly be able to see what I'd done . . . unless. I had my own devious plan.

I copied everything I could between Allan and Krystal. When I started looking through other exchanges, I heard Allan start talking.

"What the hell happened?" He hadn't opened his eyes yet.

"Get out of here." Cece pushed me toward the door. "Go! Let me handle this. Take the phone."

That was one solution. It would delay Allan's discovery of how we'd hacked his phone, but only for a little while. The records of my transfers would be there when he got his phone back. Or got a new one. Still, it was a slice of time that was better than nothing.

As much as I hated to leave Cece there, I knew she could handle it. And handle it far better if I wasn't around. I hurried out of the parlor just in time to hear a giant crash in the formal dining room. Allan's little pugs had caught the table runner and pulled place settings of plates and crystal to the floor. Oh, they were little demons. Grace was going to be furious. And I had to beat it out of there and find Tinkie. Now that we knew who had taken the belt—or who had engineered it—we had to figure a way to get it back. And to punish Krystal and Allan.

I was at the front door when I heard Allan begin to curse. He had regained consciousness much faster than I'd anticipated. I should have tied him up or something. Grace would be home any minute. I had to act quickly.

"I'll get you!" Allan said, and there was the sound of a table crashing. The two pugs were barking and growling. Would they bite Cece because they realized she'd hurt Allan? My Sweetie Pie would have figured that out—and even Pluto would have defended me with all of his might. I couldn't leave my friend in peril.

I rushed back into the room to see Allan staggering toward Cece. The dogs had her cornered. The little pugs, despite their destructive natures, obviously loved Allan and were going the extra mile to protect him.

Allan's back was to me and I slipped into the parlor, dodging the antique sofa. The bookend was right where Cece left it. I picked it up and eased behind Allan. Cece saw me and nodded. He was brandishing a heavy candle holder like a club, threatening to hit Cece. I clocked him on the back of the head. Not too hard, but hard enough. He went down to his knees and then fell over. I had an almost irresistible impulse to yell out, "Timber!" But I restrained myself. The little pugs hurled themselves across the room toward their fallen daddy. Avery and Katherine were on him—licking his face, whining, trying to wake him up.

I grabbed Cece's hand. We had to get out of there. Pronto!

"We can't just leave him here in Grace's house!" Cece kept trying to break free and go back to Allan.

"Why not?"

"He's going to think she knocked him out."

"And?" That sounded like a terrific solution to me. Grace could take the blame. She'd figure out a way to lie herself out of it. I had faith in her.

"He'll press charges against her," Cece insisted.

"Better her than you." I was steadily dragging my friend to the front door.

Cece finally got her hand free. “I’m staying.”

“Why?”

“I need photos, and I’m going to control the narrative of this event. Go, Sarah Booth. Prove that Krystal and Allan are the culprits and let’s blow this Popsicle stand.”

I loved it that Cece knew catchphrases from the ’70s, but I hated leaving her. I chose to honor her choices. The same as I’d want my friends to do for me. “I’ll bail you out when you’re arrested.”

“I know you will. Now, go!”

37

I tore out of Grace's driveway, not a moment too soon. She was coming down the road with her mama in the front seat. Luckily, they were so busy arguing, they didn't pay any attention to me passing them. I just kept driving. Cece could manage them. I had full faith in her.

I pulled into the Hound Dog Hotel parking lot and called Coleman.

"I know who took the Elvis belt, and I have the evidence."

"Have you told Yuma?" he asked. He didn't whisper, but it was clear he didn't want to be overheard.

"No. I don't trust him."

"What's the evidence?"

"An exchange of text messages between Allan Malone and Krystal Bond plotting the caper."

"How'd you get those texts?"

That was the question I dreaded. But I'd decided I would not lie to my man. Trust, once broken, was hard to restore. "Cece knocked him on the head with a bookend. I took his phone and opened it via Face ID. Then I copied the messages and sent them to my phone."

"Did you steal his phone, Sarah Booth?" There was wariness laced with amusement in Coleman's voice.

"I took it when he was done with it. He put it on an end table."

"He dropped it because he was struck in the head?"

"Well, no. He put it down before that." It was an important distinction, the way I looked at it.

"Should I send an ambulance to pick up Allan?"

"I don't think so. Cece is still with him at Grace's house, and Grace and her mama were arriving home when I left." I hadn't admitted to hitting him a second time, but I'd work through all of that when I found out how much Allan remembered. Hopefully, not much. I loved Coleman and the trust between us was vitally important. I also was not a fool—I wasn't going to confess to something that might never come up.

"I have to call Yuma and relay this information to him. If you have the evidence, he'll have to make the arrests."

I sighed. "Can you delay it a little while? I'm meeting Krystal at the hotel. I hope to get her to confess, but I can't do that if Yuma locks me up."

"An hour."

It wasn't much time, but it was better than nothing. "Okay. I'll be at the hotel. Drinking heavily."

"Forward those text messages to my phone, please,"

Coleman said. "That way we absolutely have a record. Just in case Yuma confiscates your phone and shirks his duty."

Ah, Coleman, my handsome, smart law officer. He saw what Yuma was. His first impulse was to protect me and my evidence. "As soon as I hang up."

"Just so you know, I have a good friend who lives here in Lee County. I'm going to encourage her to apply for police chief. I think this part of Mississippi is due for a change."

"We'll support her however we can. You're right. The people of Tupelo and Lee County deserve better."

"Go grill Krystal, but do *not* hit her on the head with anything."

"I'm not making any promises."

Coleman laughed. "If Yuma puts you in jail, I may have to leave you until after Christmas."

"Oh, try that. Jit—I'll make sure you suffer." I'd almost slipped up and mentioned Jitty.

"Who, or what, is a Jit?" Coleman asked.

"When you bond me out of jail, I'll tell you." I wouldn't tell him about Jitty, but I could make up a story he'd love. "Now I'm going to get Tinkie and clear this case."

We were seated at our favorite table in the bar when Krystal walked in. She was dressed to the nines, in a bejeweled silver jacket and black slacks. Despite the bling, she looked haggard, as if she'd aged ten years.

"What do you want?" she demanded. She stood at the table, ignoring the chair that Tinkie indicated she should use.

I made a big production of sending the last text message I'd stolen from Allan to Coleman.

"Oh, we don't want anything *from* you. We have something to *show* you," Tinkie said, her tone a perfect inflection of Daddy's Girl graciousness.

"Whatever it is, keep it. Not interested." Krystal started to walk away.

"This is your text to Allan. 'Kent has assured me the cameras won't be working.'" I read the text aloud.

Krystal whipped around. "I don't know what that means. Why are you reading me some stupid text from *your* phone?"

"Because you wrote it. To Allan."

She simply stopped moving. It was like she'd magically been turned to stone. At least a minute passed before I saw her swallow. Her eyes darted back and forth, and she slapped the table really hard. Everyone in the bar turned toward us.

"Big deal. So, you have a text. I lost my phone several weeks ago. Anyone could have sent a text. What do you think that proves?"

"I'm sure it proves that you and Allan plotted the theft of the three-million-dollar Elvis belt, and that you both carried out this crime. Have a seat, Krystal. We want to talk about the insurance policy you took out on the belt. Have you collected yet? Maybe not, but you've filed. I'm sure Yuma wrote up the perfect police report. Clever. I have to give it to you. You cheated Grace out of her insurance money, but you're going to collect it. A scheme worthy of Rasputin. Or maybe one of those televangelists with huge compounds, private jets, and all kinds of ill-gotten gains."

"If you really had proof against me or Allan, you wouldn't be sitting here in the hotel bar. You'd be at the police chief's office showing Yuma this pretend evidence. But you know he'll see through it. And how did you get Allan's text messages?"

"Maybe he's working with the law," Tinkie said sweetly. "He's smart enough to cover his own ass. Now it's just yours hanging out, flapping in the breeze, if he makes a deal and leaves you holding the bag."

"You two meddlers." She leaned down into our faces. "I'm going to get you."

"And how do you think you're going to do that?" Tinkie asked.

"Those stage lights—that was a close call. You would be dead if I'd been in charge of that. It isn't safe for you to walk on the sidewalk here in Tupelo. Remember that, and maybe clear out of town. Before you leave in a coffin."

"Is that a threat?" I asked, frowning at Tinkie. "Is she threatening us?"

"Maybe." Tinkie gave her a thumbs-up. "Work a little harder to make me believe you're serious. Details might help. Do you think you can put me in a coffin? Better bring an army."

She suddenly reached for Tinkie's hair, but I slapped her hand away. "Watch yourself, Krystal."

"Or what?"

"I don't threaten people. And maybe you shouldn't either."

"I'm going to screw over both of you. I'm going to hit you so hard and strong you'll never recover. You'll be in the hospital for six months. That is, if you live."

I didn't dare glance at Tinkie, who was recording the whole conversation with her phone beneath the table. If our glances met, we'd both start laughing. Krystal was way too easy to manipulate.

"Just tell us about the heist," I said. "Cooperate and save

yourself. Because if you don't, Allan surely will. Did you think of stealing the belt, or did Allan? It must have been you. Allan has a successful TV show. He doesn't need the money. But you do. Three million, or is it six with the insurance policy you wrote up for yourself? That's a nice little nest egg for you, even if you do have to cut some people in."

She didn't bother denying anything, but she stepped backward two steps. "You don't know anything. I had nothing to do with that belt disappearing. Grace probably still has it. That's probably why she isn't raising hell about the insurance being canceled."

"Oh, you mean the policy you deliberately let run out—after you destroyed Grace's payment. She found the copy of the check in her checkbook. You tossed her payment out. I mean, you couldn't write two policies for the same piece of art, could you?"

She shrugged. "You can't prove that."

"Oh, we can and we will."

She took two more steps away from us. She was going to make a run for it.

"Don't do it, Krystal." Tinkie moved to flank her.

"You can't stop me from leaving."

That was exactly the wrong thing to say. Tinkie was aggravated because she wanted to be with her baby. I was agitato because I was tired of the lies and greed. We'd worked through our entire Christmas vacation. We had one event left and, by damn, we were going to have fun and not deal with thieves and attempted murderers.

"If I have to tackle you, tie you up, and put you in the trunk of a car, you are going to Yuma's office. What he chooses to do is up to him."

"You wouldn't dare!" But Krystal didn't hang around to

stand up to her taunt. She ran. Hard and fast. She was out the door and in the parking lot before you could say Jack Sprat.

That was it. Tinkie just snapped. She ran full tilt at Krystal. The insurance agent didn't stand a chance. Tinkie was out the door, tracking her into the parking lot and gaining on her. Once she was a few feet away, Tinkie hurled her body into a flying tackle. I watched in amazement as my partner stretched out, long and lean. Her shoulder caught Krystal right at the knees. Krystal buckled and went down with Tinkie on top of her. When Krystal hit the asphalt, I heard her go *whoof* as all the air was knocked from her lungs.

She was gasping and struggling for breath as Tinkie got off her.

"Go to your room. Let me handle it from here," I whispered to Tinkie. I already had a call in to Coleman. He was going to have to intervene. Tinkie had crossed a line, and I knew it. But I applauded her athleticism. She was tiny, but tough.

"I'm not going anywhere." Tinkie was defiant. When Krystal tried to sit up—her breathing heavy and harsh as she gasped for air—Tinkie rounded on her. "Stay down!"

Krystal looked at me, an appeal for rescue. "Not a chance," I said. "You racked up this bill and you're going to pay it."

"She'll kill me." Krystal was truly afraid of Tinkie. Good. It would save mayhem in the long run.

"She may," I agreed. "And the world will be a better place."

When Krystal started to get up, Tinkie stomped her foot at her. "Stay down!"

For once in her life, Krystal did the smart thing and reclined on the cold asphalt.

I put in another call to Coleman. “Bring Yuma to the Hound Dog Hotel. We have Krystal under control. Hurry, Coleman. We don’t want to have to hurt her.”

“What about Allan?” Coleman asked.

“Cece has him at Grace’s house. I don’t think he’s going to be a serious problem. At least for the moment.”

“I see trouble down the road,” Coleman said, but his voice was jolly. He liked a good set-to when the right people won.

38

As I had suspected, Yuma was not pleased with our citizen's arrest of Krystal. Before any complaints could be lodged against Tinkie, Yuma handcuffed Krystal and took her to the city jail. Coleman, Tinkie, and I hurried to Grace's house to see what had occurred with Allan.

The first thing I heard were howling dogs. Not dogs in distress. But dogs that were singing the blues. I had no idea pugs could harmonize like a pack of hounds. Their song was coming from Grace's house. I could only imagine how much she hated that.

Before I could even knock, the front door flew open. Grace, in a state of total upheaval, glared at me. "This is all your fault. All of it."

Coleman smothered the chuckle that escaped. "What's up, Grace?" he asked.

"This!" Grace stepped into the middle of the room. I entered a disaster zone. Pillow stuffing, ragged tears of cloth, what looked like blueberry jam, and perhaps some little doggy accidents that someone had stepped in and smeared everywhere littered the foyer. When I walked farther into the house, it was even worse. The parlor was a disaster. Tables were overturned, beautiful glass that had broken spilled across a stained carpet. A single bottle of raspberry ginger ale spun slowly in a circle on the floor, spewing red, sticky soda in all directions. I covered my mouth to stifle the laugh.

"What happened?" I asked.

Two buff-colored streaks of destruction hurtled into the parlor. Lovely Katherine and Avery jumped onto an upholstered antique sofa and went nuts. They tore at the fabric and the stuffing. The savagery was amazing.

"They really hate that upholstery pattern, don't they?" Tinkie asked. "It is kind of tacky." It was almost my undoing. I bent over, pretending to cough to disguise the laughter. It was rude to make fun of our client, but dang! She'd driven us almost insane with her lies. We could have resolved this whole thing several days ago if Grace had been truthful with us.

"Where's Allan?" Coleman asked, helping to cover my amusement.

"He's a little tied up." Grace was being clever, as I could clearly see Allan sitting on the parlor floor with his hands and feet tied with an old extension cord. He leaned back against a big wing chair, his face almost white with anger.

"Get me out of here," he said. "I'm suing everyone. Every single one of you. I will ruin you."

"These people make a lot of threats," I said to Coleman. "All hat, no cattle."

"He doesn't look in a position to do anything bad to anyone." Tinkie nudged his foot with her toe.

"Let me up." Allan's pale face was slowly flushing red. Not a good sign.

Coleman pulled out his phone and dialed. "You'd better have Krystal in jail, and you'd better come over, or send a deputy, to pick up Allan Malone at Grace Land's place. Sarah Booth and Tinkie say Krystal and Allan stole Grace's Elvis belt. Like it or not, Yuma, it's up to you to convince them to tell you where they stashed it. Oh, and Yuma, I'm watching to be sure you don't let these people go before the belt is found."

Coleman had had enough of the lawman, too. "Is Yuma crooked?" I asked him once he'd hung up.

"I don't know," Coleman said. "And it doesn't matter. All that is important is that he arrests these two and squeezes them until the truth comes out. If other bodily fluids leak out, too, so much the better."

"That's my favorite part," I said. "Watching the squeeze go into effect."

"Call my lawyer," Allan said.

"Get those damn pugs out of my house! I'm not calling you a lawyer, but I am calling the dog catcher." Grace put a hand to her forehead. "Those vile creatures have given me a migraine."

Tinkie knelt down beside Allan. "Tell us what we want to know, and I'll take the pugs until you can get them. I'll take good care of them. Otherwise, they're going to the pound."

It was absolute genius! Threats of jail and punishment wouldn't move Allan, but the care of his pugs . . . now, that was powerful ammunition.

Coleman had started forward to pull Allan to his feet, but he stopped. "Grace, why don't you and your mother make me a cup of coffee, please?"

"I have a maid for those things," Grace said. "I want—"

"Black would be fine." Coleman took her arm and maneuvered her out of the parlor and toward the kitchen. Brandi followed. Coleman was giving Tinkie and me a chance to close our case. He was the man!

"I don't make coffee. The maid does that." Grace's complaints were muffled when the kitchen door closed.

"Spill your guts," Tinkie told Allan. "Now."

He sighed. "You promise to take care of Lovely Katherine and Avery?"

"I promise. I have a dog and a cat. They'll get the best care and a farm to play at while you resolve these issues."

"How can I trust you?"

Tinkie shrugged. "What's another option?"

She had an excellent point. But I had another to add. "And, Allan, I believe I can convince Cece to host your show for a few weeks until this is cleared up. Of course, that depends on what role you actually played in the theft of the belt and everything else that's transpired."

"'Played' is the operative word," Allan said, defeat clear on his face. "I was played big-time by Krystal Bond. What was supposed to be a prank, a little bit of teeth grinding for Grace, has turned into a criminal case. This wasn't what I signed on for."

Tinkie untied his feet and we both helped him up. When he was seated in the wing chair, we released his hands. Coleman was only a hundred feet away. Allan wouldn't get far if he tried to run for it. And I didn't think he would.

"Thanks," he said. "You promise you'll look after Katherine and Avery?"

"A solemn oath."

"And she'll take excellent care of them," I said. "Nothing at Tinkie's house lacks for comfort or love."

"Tell us how all of this came about."

Allan pointed to a cut-glass decanter on the one table the dogs hadn't wrecked. "A drink, please."

I poured him a neat whiskey while Tinkie set up her phone to record whatever he said. When he had his drink, he took a long swallow.

"Okay, here's how it happened. About two months ago, Krystal called to tell me about Grace and the Elvis belt. We'd suspected she had some terrific piece of art. I guess we'd all heard rumors that Sippi had created a masterpiece, but we hadn't seen it. Krystal confirmed that it was a real thing and that Grace had insurance on it. She had photos of the belt. That's critical to remember."

This was going to go bad for Krystal. I could see it coming a mile down the road. "Go on," I said. "Tell it all and save yourself."

"Krystal had hatched this plan to take the belt and hold it for a while. It was mean. Really mean. But not criminal. Not really. At least it wasn't supposed to be."

I watched Allan's face closely. He had called the dogs into his lap and he stroked them as he talked. They seemed to give him a lot of comfort.

"Krystal proposed that we take the belt—"

"You mean steal it?" Tinkie asked.

He made a face. "Not really steal. Not with the intent of keeping it. We were going to remove it from the display and keep it just long enough to drive Grace batshit."

"But someone got greedy."

"Exactly." Allan looked relieved that we were following his tale so closely. "That would be Krystal. She tore up the check Grace sent to cover the policy on the belt and took out a policy herself. I didn't know this. I had no idea. Krystal never intended to return the belt to Grace. Not ever. She was going to melt it down and get the money from that, as well as the insurance money."

"And you knew nothing of this? Sounds pretty darn convenient to me." If Tinkie was going to be caring for his dogs, then I had to play the tough guy.

"It may sound convenient, but I assure you it's true. And I've been trying to talk Krystal into giving the belt back, but she now claims someone stole it from her. She swears it's gone and she has no idea where."

"And you believe that?" How gullible was he? The belt was on the way to some person who'd pull out the jewels and melt down the gold.

"No. I don't. I think Krystal, and maybe Kent, have the belt tucked away somewhere. As you suspected, they will break it down and sell the jewels and gold separately. Just as soon as they think they can get away with it. Krystal also has the insurance check. But you have to believe I wasn't part of this."

"But you were," I pointed out. "A big part."

"Well, technically, I helped Krystal, but she physically took the belt. I wasn't around the Arena Center. She got Kent to turn off all the safety systems and she slipped in and took the belt, easy as pie. I supported her in the plan. But only because she was supposed to give it back after we'd had a little fun making Grace go crazy. Or I should say, crazier. That was my only goal. To give Grace some major heartburn. You have no idea how awful she is."

Grace might be awful, but it was Allan who was facing criminal charges. Whatever excuse he wanted to claim, he was in this up to his eyebrows.

The sound of sirens wailed up to the house, and I went to the door to let Yuma and a deputy in. He didn't make eye contact and completely ignored Coleman as he placed Allan under arrest.

"Allan, where is the belt?" Tinkie tried to get that vital information as Yuma helped Allan to his feet.

"Ask Krystal," he said. "She has it."

Then he was out the front door and in the patrol car. When I looked toward the kitchen, Grace was standing in the door, wringing a dish towel with both hands, almost as if it were Allan's neck. "Allan is going to pay for all of this damage," she said. "He gets away with so much, but not this time. Not this time."

"I'd be more worried about getting that belt back than this." I couldn't help it. Grace's priorities were a little skewed.

Her mother came out of the kitchen with a steaming cup of coffee for Coleman. "That's what I told her. Let this little stuff go. Focus on the major crime element."

"Don't you think if I could make them talk I would?" Grace had finally had enough. "If the belt is still intact, I'll get it back. But I promise you, Krystal and Allan will never enjoy the proceeds from the belt. Money doesn't count for much when you're in a state prison."

I looked at Tinkie. "Any suggestions on getting Allan or Krystal to give up the information on the belt?"

"Oh, I can think of a lot of ways to get them to talk. Harold just picked up that little Glock from the pawnshop. I'm ready now to make them dance—and talk! But we'll go to jail, too."

"Not happening. And give that gun to Oscar to keep. You will end up in jail." I wanted to return the belt, but not enough to do a stint in prison. We'd been hired to figure out what happened to the belt and who was responsible. The recovery had been implied, but wasn't a specific part of our contract. From my point of view, we'd figured out who stole the belt and our job was done. "I'm finished with all of this."

"But we haven't found the belt." Tinkie was a little shocked that I was ready to pull the plug.

"Not my problem. We know who stole it, and now it's up to the law to make them return it."

"I can't quit now," Tinkie said. "I can't, Sarah Booth." She checked her watch. "We still have a few hours. Maybe we can find the belt now that we're certain who took it."

She made sense. Krystal had to have the belt hidden somewhere. "Let's search Krystal's office. We can try. Before the clock runs out."

I turned to Coleman. "Would you check on Sweetie Pie and Chablis, and make sure everyone gets to the show tonight? It's the big gala. We'll be there to watch the Elvises. I promise."

"Any leads on where to look?" he asked.

"Would you ask Allan? Remind him that Tinkie is going to take care of his pugs until he gets his legal issues sorted. He might consider making this as easy for us as possible."

"Good leverage," Coleman said. "Will do. I'll text if I find anything."

"Thank you." I gave him a long kiss and then watched him leave.

Grace and Brandi had walked into the parlor. "We'll check back if we find anything." I was ready to go.

"You aren't leaving those dogs here." Grace pointed at the pugs, exhausted from all the mayhem, who'd fallen asleep on the destroyed sofa.

I didn't trust Grace with them, not even for twenty minutes. She might drown them in her koi pond. "Okay. We'll take them."

"I think Harold left the leashes in the car," Tinkie said. "One obstacle down."

I whistled up the dogs and let them out the front door. To my amusement, Lovely Katherine pooped right on the top step. Avery seconded the motion. Both of them had a strong opinion about Grace and her property.

In a matter of minutes, we were parked in front of the insurance office. The dogs were wary. With a little coaxing, they followed us into the office—which was inexplicably left unlocked. It was almost as if Krystal had planned to allow us—or someone else—inside. And if not us, then who? That was the question that gave me hope. And a shiver of concern.

I texted Coleman. "Can you get Yuma to pick up Kent Madison? I don't have any proof, but I think he's involved in this along with Krystal and Allan."

"Yuma is balking at keeping Allan and Krystal behind bars. He says he's questioned Kent and cleared him. I'll text a heads-up when he cuts Krystal loose, because he is determined to do that. He's either part of this, paid off, or hoping for a romance with Krystal. Maybe Budgie or DeWayne would like to be police chief."

"*NO!*" I used the all-caps equivalent of yelling. "We need Budgie and DeWayne in Sunflower County. Find someone else."

His response was a laugh emoji. But he got my point.

I turned my phone off and Tinkie and I slipped into the insurance office. We went through the drawers, files, cabinets, closet, and a half dozen plastic storage bins. Nothing. The belt had to be there. Krystal wouldn't have it at her house, would she? But she'd want it close. I checked my watch. There was only an hour before we had to be at the Elvis show.

Even Katherine and Avery got in on the action. They knocked over trash cans and went through the trash, opened the cabinet doors in the little kitchenette, and destroyed five rolls of toilet tissue in the bathroom. Nada. If the belt was there, it was buried under the flooring.

"What now?" Tinkie asked.

"Let's go to the show." I was defeated.

"We can't just quit." Tinkie was appalled. She might be the child of privilege, but she didn't like leaving a job half finished.

"We'll sneak out at intermission and go through Kent Madison's place. I don't know where it could be." I was at my wit's end.

"Is there anyone Krystal has been friendly with?" Tinkie asked.

It was a genius question. "Sonja Rivera."

"Priscilla?" Tinkie asked. "They're friends?"

"Maybe not friends, but I've seen them talking. It's either her or Kent Madison."

"Or Yuma. What if he has the belt and has had it all along?"

"To get a search warrant of Yuma's place we'd need the district attorney to go to bat for us. I don't even know who that is in Lee County."

"Good point. Few people want to go against the police chief. He has a lot of power. Thank goodness Coleman doesn't abuse his."

"True, but that isn't helping us now. Let's go to the show. Maybe if we act like we're having a great time and leaving in the morning, the culprits will relax and give us some help."

"It's worth a shot."

39

Grace and her band of Christmas helpers had pulled out all the stops for the Elvis finale. The multicolored lights, tinsel, and garland wrapped the Arena Center like a giant, exciting Christmas present. I forced my mind off the Elvis belt and onto the Elvis performers. I was actually delighted to see Wilbur Manning out of jail and performing with the leopard-print Elvises. They did a very entertaining rendition of "Jailhouse Rock." Wilbur didn't have the best voice, but he could work that leg and hip like nobody's business. We gave them a standing ovation.

Brandi had joined Grace as cohost of the festival—a fact that also gave me a bit of pleasure. Whatever bad deeds they'd committed in the past, I hoped they could mend their relationship and enjoy the years they had left. A mother's love was nothing to sneer at.

When Coleman arrived, just a tad late, he told me that Allan and Krystal were in adjoining jail cells in the Lee County lockup. Coleman, bless his devious little heart, had set up a cleverly disguised recording device in the hallway outside their cells. If they blurted out the location of the Elvis belt, we'd have it on tape. None of the information would be usable in a trial, but that didn't matter to me. It wasn't my job to prosecute, only to name the thief and try to recover the belt.

We were doing all we could do. But for the next few hours, I intended to cut loose and have some fun. Tinkie and I had been working too hard, but this case was particularly exhausting because I didn't trust anyone from the sheriff on down to our client.

While plenty of the adult Elvises gave topnotch performances, it was the Elvis Tots—a singing/dancing team of six elementary school boys who'd been awarded a Las Vegas contract—that I instantly knew had won the show. The kids were no older than eight, but in their open-chested white jumpsuits with capes and little chest hairs drawn on with an eyebrow pencil, they tore the house down. "I Believe" was their song, and they sang it with the soul, passion, and emotion that marked all of Elvis's performances.

"They're going to win," I told Tinkie. "Let's go."

"Go where?"

"To the jail."

"Allan and Krystal aren't going to talk to us."

"Krystal, no. Allan, yes. I'm over this. I want the belt and I want to go home. I'm planning on leaving early. Harold said he's going at daybreak because he has to get back to prepare for our party tomorrow night, and I need to take care of some gift wrapping. Either we find the belt tonight or we come back to Tupelo after the holidays."

"The belt will be stripped down and sold by then." Tinkie wasn't trying to guilt-trip me. She was just being factual.

"That's why we need to talk to Allan now. And, to be honest with you, I'm done with Elvis impersonators."

That was a lie, but only a little one. I simply couldn't stay put for any longer. I needed action, some resolution, and the satisfaction that came from closing a case.

We slipped out of the aisle—though Coleman saw us and gave me a nod. In a moment we picked up the pugs from the hotel and were cruising to the jail. The exterior courthouse doors were never locked and, strangely enough, there were no deputies on duty. We just went in with the dogs. It was weird to be in the empty courthouse, our footsteps echoing on the tiles. The hairs on my neck began to tingle—a warning of danger. But as far as I could see, there wasn't anything dangerous around. The bad guys were in the jail. We went through the sheriff's office and through the unlocked door to the holding cells.

The complete emptiness of the building touched Tinkie, too. "There should be a deputy on duty. Or at least a dispatcher," she pointed out.

"You're right about that." The gnawing sense that we were walking into a trap bit a little harder. Something was wrong.

We made it back to the holding cells. Only two were occupied, and, sure enough, the two criminals were in side-by-side cells. I found the recording device—it looked like a book left on a folding chair.

When Allan saw us, he gave me a smug look and a sneer. "I did all the hard work for you. Now let me out." He caught sight of the dogs and gave a squeal of delight. "Avery, Katherine, come give Daddy some loving!"

The dogs were small enough to slip through the bars of the cell and rushed Allan, scrambling over his feet and yapping and licking. He scooped them into his arms and cuddled them for a long moment.

"That's enough, Allan. Either tell us where the belt is or kiss those babies goodbye. Tinkie is taking them to Zinnia when we leave."

"They're my family. You can't just steal them." He was indignant.

"You can't care for them from a jail cell. You can try to stop this, but unless you want them in the dog pound, you would be wise to shut up."

"I will take good care of them," Tinkie said. She had a soft spot for people who loved their pets. "No matter what you hear about how harshly they are being treated, know that I am doing the best I can for them."

And she had a devious streak a mile wide! I wanted to applaud, but I kept my lips zipped.

"You'd better not take my dogs and mistreat them." Allan gripped the bars of the cell. He reached out to grab Tinkie, but she evaded him.

"I will do my very best. Sarah Booth doesn't want them. Who else would even consider taking them? You'd better be grateful. Now, give them to me." She reached her hands out for the dogs.

It was killing Allan. I really thought, as gray as his face had become, that he might have a stroke. I would have felt the same about Sweetie Pie and my critters, and I knew we were practicing horrible emotional blackmail. I'd been here once before, when I first moved home. I'd done a bad thing that had saved Dahlia House, but it was a deed I could never confess to. Watching Allan's face, I could see that the idea of handing them over and not having control of what happened to them was horribly distressing. And Tinkie had played that card like the master of the sting that she was. If Tinkie took Allan's dogs, they would live like royal pups. I knew that. But Allan didn't.

"You can't have them." Allan held the dogs and backed up.

"Where's the belt?" I asked. I was dying to listen to the tape from the book recording device, but I also had a role to play here. Getting Allan to give up the info we needed would be so much easier if he went along willingly.

"I'm not talking to you," he said to me. "Leave us. I'll speak with the short one." He pointed to Tinkie.

"Sure." It was a wish granted! I picked up the book on the chair. "Here you go, Tinkie, have a seat."

"Thanks." She sat and I left.

The recording device Coleman had put in the book was simple. Even I could figure it out. I wound it back and hit play.

"Why didn't you tell me you were really stealing the belt?" Allan's voice was crystal clear on the recording. "I thought this was a prank on Grace. We both dislike her, but a prank and grand larceny are two very different things."

"I don't owe you an explanation." Krystal was equally clear.

"Oh, yes you do. You assured me it was a prank and that you'd return the belt as soon as you made Grace suffer.

Now you've implicated me in a serious crime. You think you're going to walk away from stealing a three-million-dollar belt *and* insurance fraud? You're going to prison, Krystal. Help yourself out and give the belt back."

Krystal laughed. "I'm not going to do a day of time—if I can pin it on you."

I sighed and turned off the recording. We had the confession now. And it appeared Allan had been telling us the truth. He hadn't realized Krystal was stealing the belt for real. He'd assumed it was a prank. I punched the play button and listened more, hoping for a location on where Krystal had hidden the belt. She wasn't the sharpest knife in the drawer, so it was possible she might spill the truth.

"Where is the belt?" Allan asked.

"Someplace you won't ever find it. Or anyone else. I may go to jail but, when I get out, I'm going to have a whole lot of money to live the rest of my life in luxury. What's the worst that can happen? Ten years? It was a nonviolent crime."

"Except it wasn't," Allan pointed out. "You ran Grace off the road. You tried to run over those private investigators. You hired that creepy man to pretend to be Colonel Parker to try to confuse the situation. And everyone is trying to blame my pugs, but he was around the stage lights, too. You put him up to it, and now he's disappeared from Tupelo. You can claim it was all a prank, but you could have killed those Zinnia folks."

Krystal laughed. "Big whoop. This is all going to fall on you and those evil little dogs. All I had to do was put bacon grease on that rope and they were all over it. Everyone will think you put them up to it, though."

"You used my dogs to commit a crime!" Allan was outraged.

I was having a blast listening to this exchange.

"And you will take the blame for all of it."

I clicked off the recorder. Not really. Allan was pretty much in the clear, except for his total lack of judgment in working with Krystal to steal the belt "as a prank."

But we still didn't have the belt.

I listened for a bit longer, but no useful information came out of it. I finally decided to see if Tinkie was having any luck. Just as I was preparing to walk back to the jail, the door opened and a deputy came in. He put his hand on his gun.

"Who are you and what are you doing here?"

I had a sudden bit of inspiration. I gave him my name and why I was in Tupelo. "Yuma sent me to get something out of his office but I was reluctant to do that until someone showed up here. Now I can get what he asked for."

"Which was?"

"Something in his desk with some account numbers on it." I shrugged. "I'm just the errand girl here. I don't really know what this is."

The deputy shook his head. "Me either."

"I was a little concerned when no one was here," I said. "Something going on?"

"False alarm. The sheriff got a call that there was a shooting out in the county. He sent us out to assist the deputies, but when we got there, no one was around. Waste of a good two hours searching for a prank call."

"Where's the dispatcher?"

"Oh, he gave her the evening off to go to the Elvis impersonator event. There wasn't anything going on and I can handle the phones now that I'm here."

I didn't ask, but I wondered if the local law enforcement was so lax all of the time. Maybe this was the job they wanted a law officer to do. Coleman just had a different standard.

I went to the door of Yuma's private office and turned the knob. To my relief, it opened. "I'm going to grab that list Yuma wanted. My friend is back in the jail, talking to the prisoners. She brought Allan his dogs for a visit. I hope that's okay."

"I'm thinking not."

"Could you help her get the dogs and come on? We do need to go." I was eager for him to go into the jail so I could really search Yuma's office without him coming in on me. If there was anything in the office, I had to find it fast.

"Stay right there," he said as he went to the back.

Luckily, Yuma was a neatnik at his desk. No paperwork littered the clean surface, and even when I checked out the drawers, none of the files held anything remotely useful.

I was at another dead end—until Tinkie came out of the cells with both pugs in her arms. "Do you have a leash?" she asked.

I had a couple in my purse that I'd taken from the car for Sweetie Pie and Chablis, though Chablis was so tiny, Tinkie seldom needed a leash on her. "Let's get out of here," Tinkie said.

"Okay." There didn't seem to be a lot of point in hanging around. I had Krystal's confession on the recorder, but she hadn't revealed any clues as to where she'd hidden the Elvis belt.

When I hooked the leashes onto the pugs, they went wild. Instead of going out the door of the sheriff's office, they rushed back to the jail. The pugs were determined to get to Allan. I stumbled behind them as they tugged me. Who would have thought the little dogs would have such strength and determination.

"Shut up about the bathroom!" Krystal was saying when I hurtled into the jail area.

"Or what?" Allan said. "I've called my agent and I'll be out of here in another fifteen minutes. A lawyer has been hired. You won't be taking a bath in that huge, giant tub you had installed any time soon. That tub is all I've heard about for the past four days."

I rounded the corner with the dogs. Tinkie was right behind me, and with her help, I managed to get the pugs into my arms. They wanted their daddy, but I didn't have time. "Tinkie will bring them to you if you get out of jail any time soon," I promised Allan. "Let's go, Tinkie."

"What's up?" she asked when we were outside the courthouse.

"I know where the belt is, I think!"

40

Gaining access to Krystal's house was a piece of cake. I'd been prepared to break a window or employ Tinkie's lock-picking expertise, but it wasn't necessary. Her door wasn't locked.

We left the pugs in the car and slipped inside. I didn't have to turn on the lights to realize that Krystal's house was wrecked. Dirty dishes were everywhere. Discarded clothes were strewn from the front door into the bedroom. Whatever she'd been doing, it wasn't housework. Then again, cleaning wasn't my forte either. But I wasn't half as nasty as she was.

"Why are we here?" Tinkie asked. "Yuma and Coleman searched the house."

"Exactly. Yuma was in charge. And I just got some insight." I led the way back to the master bath. I'd assumed the bath had just been remodeled, and I was correct. It was beautiful. The large tub with massage jets could have come out of a home decorator's magazine. The blue, green, and white color scheme worked perfectly with the mosaic tile. This was going to get ugly fast. "I need a hammer."

"You are not going to break any of this new tile." Tinkie knew me too well.

"Oh, but I am." I left the bath and went to the garage. It didn't take me long to find several hammers. I handed Tinkie one.

"Why are you doing this?"

"I know where the belt is."

Tinkie made a big O with her mouth. "In the walls of the bathroom?"

"The tub surround."

"Are you sure?"

"Sure enough to break it."

"Should we call Yuma?"

I gave her the hairy eyeball. "Not on your life. Now let's do this. It's almost midnight. We've abandoned our friends and lovers and dogs." The Zinnia crowd had made plans for an after–Elvis performance party. We should have joined them half an hour earlier.

"Okay. I trust your judgment." Tinkie wielded her hammer like Thor as she walked into the bathroom and gave the tile surround a mighty whack. The beautiful blue-and-green mosaic shattered, and shards flew onto the floor.

I set to work on the other end. It took a lot more hammering than I'd anticipated, but at last we were clearing out the tile and dust. Pushed into the far corner of the hole behind the tub was a black case. I heaved a sigh of relief. "There."

"Well, I'll be damned," Tinkie said with excitement.

As the petite partner, Tink wiggled into the opening, reached into the hole, and pulled the case out. When we popped it open, the beautiful artistry of the belt made me shake my head. "At last."

I got my phone and dialed Coleman. When I told him what we'd done and what we'd found, he said, "Wait there. Don't leave. Don't do anything else."

I was more than happy to oblige.

Tinkie and I were sitting on the front porch of Krystal's house when Coleman and Yuma pulled up. The belt was in its case in the rubble of the bathroom. Tinkie and I had decided to keep our lips zipped and let Coleman handle this. We'd broken several laws, but we hoped the end would justify the means.

Tinkie led the lawmen to the bathroom. I heard their exclamations of surprise when she showed them the belt. It was done. We'd solved the case and recovered the belt. Our tactics were unorthodox, but not even Yuma could argue with our success.

Yuma collected the belt and headed out. I couldn't stop myself. "Where are you taking that?" I asked.

"To the police chief's office, and then to the jail to charge Krystal."

"What about Allan?" I had the pugs in my car, but if Allan was held in jail, I'd need to make arrangements.

"I'll have to examine the evidence. You know, the tape recordings, the witness testimony. I have to be sure before I press charges or release him."

That sounded reasonable to me. And there were half a

dozen officers and Coleman to witness Yuma taking the belt. He wouldn't get away with trying to do anything illegal if that was his inclination. I was still torn about Yuma. Had he sold out to the criminals or was he just enormously incompetent at his job? I didn't know, and now that my work in Tupelo was done, I didn't need to have an opinion. The people of Tupelo and Lee County could speak at the ballot box when they elected a new mayor and board of aldermen.

Lovely Katherine and Avery sat with me on the courthouse steps as we waited for Allan to be released. When he came out, he hugged the little dogs to him as they licked his face.

"I owe you a thank-you."

"No, you don't. I just did my job."

"Krystal intended for me to go down for all of that. If you and your partner hadn't figured it all out, I'd be headed on the Midnight Special to Parchman."

I was pleased at his nod to the blues and the long history of that unique form of music in the Mississippi State Penitentiary. "We had a lot of help."

"Sheriff Peters, from your county. He was super nice. And all of your friends. Y'all hang together. It's good to see."

"When are you leaving for Hollywood?" It was almost dawn. The paperwork had taken longer than I'd anticipated. Everyone except Coleman had gone back to the hotel to catch some shut-eye so we could leave Tupelo and head home.

"Today. I have a flight out." He hesitated. "I'm going to feature Cece on the show. She's coming out to California in February, along with that harmonica player. They are something else."

I was pleased for Cece. She'd never give up her journalism or her place at the *Zinnia Dispatch,* but she could expand her world—and she would. She might enjoy Hollywood, but she'd always come home.

"I'm thinking about doing a segment on my show, maybe three or four times a year, of a roving reporter finding local Mississippi talent and featuring it."

I grinned. "That would be fabulous. And Cece is perfect for the job."

"Yeah. I know she'll never leave Mississippi. And honestly, I'd like to spend more time here. Grace can have the whole Los Angeles superstar bull crap."

"Taking my name in vain, are you, Allan?" Grace came to sit beside us on the steps. She had the case with the Elvis belt. "You did a great job, Sarah Booth. And Tinkie. And your friends."

The door behind her opened, and Sippi Salem came out with Sonja Rivera. The handsome artist and the Priscilla look-alike appeared to have hooked up. So much for his proposal to Grace. Love was fleeting in the world of an artist. Life marched on in Tupelo. The Elvis festival was over for at least six months, and Sippi had a new model. I could only hope Sonja got a new hairstyle. I was still concerned about the whole roach rumor, though everyone had assured me it was an urban legend. The duo made a cute couple, and Grace seemed to give them her blessing.

"Our work is done here." I stood up and offered Grace my hand. "Good luck with everything." I wouldn't have time to sleep at the hotel, but I could sleep in the car going home with Coleman and Sweetie Pie. I stifled a yawn.

"Thank you and your partner, Sarah Booth. You did everything I asked."

As I was leaving, Wilbur and Sherman Manning came up, along with some of the Arena Center volunteers. It was a happy reunion, with Grace showing off the recovered belt. I slipped away from the courthouse and walked down the empty streets of Tupelo to my hotel. By the time I got there, Coleman had packed the car. Sweetie Pie was in the back. All of my Zinnia friends were also packed and ready to head across the state to Sunflower County. We'd caravan, singing carols or, in my case, catching some sleep. It was almost Christmas Eve.

"Next Christmas, I want a contract signed in blood that you will not work on a case," Oscar said as he pulled Tinkie into the crook of his arm. "Maylin and I missed you."

Tinkie rolled her eyes. "You had a fine time. I don't even think you noticed I wasn't around."

"Don't push your luck, Tinkie," Millie said as we all laughed.

We were gathered in Harold's game room, where a hotly contested match of pool was ongoing between Harold and Jaytee. Dean Martin was singing Christmas carols, and the smell of roasting turkey and all the sides came to us on a mélange of spices. Pumpkin pie, my favorite, cooled in the refrigerator. Harold had outdone himself on the menu.

The huge oak trees that lined Harold's drive sparkled with white twinkle lights. It never failed to remind me of fairies, which always made me think of my parents and how much I missed them. Especially at holidays.

I stepped out on the porch for a moment alone. I'd slept

all the way home from Tupelo and then taken another nap in the bed with Coleman. We had our own unique holiday traditions, and as Aunt Loulane had told me repeatedly, a well-brought-up young woman doesn't tell everything she knows.

From down the driveway, I heard music. Elvis! He stepped onto the gravel between the trees in his signature white jumpsuit. "Love me tender, love me true," he sang. I walked down the steps toward him. I knew he wasn't there. Not really. His ghost had followed me home from Tupelo.

Either that, or Jitty was lurking in Harold's front yard.

I didn't want to interrupt the song. It was special to me. I enjoyed the spectacle until he said, "Thank you. Thank you very much."

"What are you up to, Jitty?"

"My job. Singing the songs people love."

"Merry Christmas, Jitty." That gave her pause. She brushed a lock of black hair from her forehead.

"Any message for me from the Great Beyond?" I had a real hankering to hear from my parents. At holidays and special occasions, sometimes I found myself trapped in a time bubble from the past. There was Christmas when my parents were alive, and then all the Christmases since.

"Your dad is impressed with the resolution of your case."

That made me smile. "Yeah?"

"Yeah. And your mom loves that you are blessed with such good friends. Not to mention Coleman."

Even when I was in grammar school, my mama had liked Coleman Peters. "So, they're happy for me?"

"Yes." Jitty was slowly coming into her own as she shifted out of Elvis and into her own beautiful skin. "They want to know if you'll get pregnant next year."

"They don't want to know that. You want to know it!" I wasn't going to be tricked by a clever ghost. Jitty was all about me having a child to continue the Delaney bloodline. Who would she haunt if I died without an heir?

"You are always so stubborn, Sarah Booth. Fighting against the very thing that could make you the happiest."

A baby might make me happy or it might drive me to drink with worry. "I'm very happy right now, Jitty. Live in the moment. That's my new motto."

"You are cantankerous."

Jitty was the cantankerous one. Right behind her, another figure was taking shape. It was a tall, heavy man in a fedora and smoking a cigar. I recognized him instantly as Elvis's former manager. And so did Jitty. This was not the man I'd seen in Tupelo, sneaking around. This was an incorporeal Colonel. At first I thought it was a Jitty prank, until I realized she was not pleased.

Jitty suddenly had a baseball bat in her hand, and she turned on Parker. "Later, Sarah Booth, I have some business to attend to here. Someone needs a good ass stomping and I'm about to deliver it!" She took off at a run, chasing the ghost of Colonel Parker.

I laughed. Sometimes Jitty's retribution was a very good idea, even if it took decades too long to come around.

I could hear the joyful noises of the party going on in Harold's house. Any minute Coleman would come out to check on me. He knew that melancholy was a pothole for me this time of year.

Just as I was about to go inside, a large black raven perched on the porch railing. It was Poe, a bird that had taken up with me.

"Nevermore," he said.

I laughed. Jitty had disappeared, but I still talked to her. "See, Jitty. Even Poe thinks a baby is a bad idea."

I heard the front door creak open and the firm footsteps of my man. Coleman put his arm around my shoulders. "What are you doing out here?"

"I thought I saw Elvis down the driveway."

He laughed and kissed me. "No more eggnog for you!"

"Merry Christmas, Coleman." Eggnog was at the bottom of my list. What I wanted was a Christmas kiss, and luckily he was eager to give me one.

"Merry Christmas, Sarah Booth. You're the only present I'll ever want."

Acknowledgments

With each book in the Sarah Booth Delaney mystery series, I have come to understand more deeply how wonderful it is to have the St. Martin's publishing team working on my books. And this year there are *two* Sarah Booth books.

Writing them involves a lot more than me sitting at a computer and thinking up a story. That's part of it, yes, but only the beginning. Once the book is written, it has to be edited several times—developmental edit, line edit, etc. And once it is in production, then the whole PR team comes into play. I am very, very lucky to work with Hannah O'Grady, Maddie Alsup, Lisa Davis, Sara LaCotti, Sara Eslami, and, as always, my agent, Marian Young.

I also want to thank all of the booksellers and librarians who have been especially good to me over the years.

Murder by the Book, the Haunted Book Shop, Alabama Booksmith, and so many more. Many of the wonderful booksellers I worked with for years have closed their doors. Covid, the economy—it's been a struggle. But those who love books will always find a way to write and read them. Thank goodness!

The Tupelo Elvis celebration is held every year in June—not Christmas. This was a fabrication for the purposes of this book. But wouldn't it be a great idea?